Praise for the Captain Alatriste series

'In ...s hard-boiled, mordantly funny, unapologetically enterta...ng Captain Alatriste series, Pérez-Reverte firmly buckles his swash and swaggers into the muddy, bloody streets of 1?...-century Madrid' *Time*

'A worthy successor to Zorro and Scaramouche' *Herald*

'A...turo Pérez-Reverte is the great European storyteller of the ...t century in the tradition of Dumas'
                                        Simon Sebag Montefiore

'... thinking man's adventure novel, where sword fights and ...les of derring-do are interwoven with wonderful passages ... poetry and gems of historical and cultural information'
                                                            The Times

'...tterly unputdownable . . . This is glorious stuff, the kind ... book to remind us how exhilarating old-fashioned adventure ...iting can be' *Daily Express*

'...quipped with a quick-witted, charismatic hero and much to ...voke and goad him, Mr Pérez-Reverte has the makings of ...lamboyantly entertaining series' *New York Times*

Arturo Pérez-Reverte lives near Madrid. Originally a war correspondent, he now writes fiction full-time. His novels have been translated into thirty-four languages and published in more than fifty countries. In 2003 he was elected to the Royal Spanish Academy. His website can be visited at www.perez-reverte.com

By Arturo Pérez-Reverte

The Flanders Panel

The Club Dumas

The Seville Communion

The Fencing Master

The Nautical Chart

The Queen of the South

Captain Alatriste

Purity of Blood

The Sun over Breda

The Painter of Battles

The King's Gold

The Man in the Yellow Doublet

Pirates of the Levant

PIRATES OF THE LEVANT

ARTURO PÉREZ-REVERTE

Translated from the Spanish by
Margaret Jull Costa

PHOENIX

A PHOENIX PAPERBACK

First published in Great Britain in 2010
by Weidenfeld & Nicolson
This paperback edition published in 2011
by Phoenix,
an imprint of Orion Books Ltd,
Orion House, 5 Upper St Martin's Lane
London wc2h 9ea

An Hachette UK company

1 3 5 7 9 10 8 6 4 2

First published in Spain as *Corsarios de Levante*
by Alfaguara

A CIP catalogue record for this book
is available from the British Library

ISBN 978-0-7538-2862-5

Typeset by Input Data Services Ltd, Bridgwater, Somerset

Printed in Great Britain by Clays Ltd, St Ives plc

The Orion Publishing Group's policy is to use papers that
are natural, renewable and recyclable products and
made from wood grown in sustainable forests. The logging
and manufacturing processes are expected to conform to
the environmental regulations of the country of origin.

www.orionbooks.co.uk

To Juan Eslava Galán and Fito Cózar
for the Naples we never knew
and the ships we never plundered

The hurly-burly movement on the galleys,
The falling into flames or into water,
The brave deaths in a hundred thousand ways,
The furies and the terrible disquiet,
The hauling down and hoisting up of flags,
The killings, then the deaths that must be paid.

Cristóbal de Virués

1. THE BARBARY COAST

Chasing after a ship makes for a long pursuit, and I swear to God this one had tested our patience to the limit. Our mood was little improved by having spent an afternoon, a moonlit night and a whole morning following our prey over a buffeting sea, which, every now and then, shook the galley's fragile frame with its blows. With her two taut sails aloft, the oars stowed and galley-slaves, soldiers and sailors all sheltering as best we could from the wind and the spray, the *Mulata*, a twenty-four-bank galley, had travelled nearly thirty leagues after the Berber galliot that we now finally had within range. As long as we didn't break a mast – the older sailors kept glancing up anxiously – she would be ours before the angelus.

'Tickle her arse!' ordered Don Manuel Urdemalas.

Our galley captain was standing in the stern – he had scarcely moved from the spot in the last twenty hours – and from there he watched as our first cannon shot plummeted into the water beside the galliot. When they saw how close the shot had come, the gunners and the men at the prow, standing round the cannon in the central gangway, all let out a cheer. Things would have to go very badly wrong for us to lose our prey now: it was within our grasp and to leeward as well.

'They're shortening their sail!' someone shouted.

The galliot's only sail, a vast canvas triangle, flapped in the wind as the crew rapidly brailed it in, lowering the mast. Rocked by the swell, the galliot showed us first its stern and then its port side, and that was when we got our first proper look at it: it was a long, slender half-galley with thirteen banks and, we reckoned, a hundred or so men on board. It resembled one of those light, swift craft described by Cervantes:

The thief who hopes to strike
And never yet be caught
Should move as fast as lightning—
A hit, then home to port.

The galliot had appeared to be nothing more than a sail to windward, but revealed itself to be a corsair when it brazenly approached the merchant convoy the *Mulata* was escorting, along with three other Spanish galleys, between Cartagena and Oran. Under full sail, we had gone after this fugitive white triangle and its stern which, little by little, and with the help of a south-westerly wind, grew larger as we closed in on her.

'The dogs are finally going to surrender,' said one soldier.

Captain Alatriste was by my side, watching. With the mast lowered and the sail furled, the crew were bringing out the oars.

'No,' he murmured. 'They're going to fight.'

I turned towards him. He was screwing up his eyes against the dazzle of the sun and beneath the broad brim of his old hat, his eyes appeared even paler and greener than usual. He was unshaven and, like everyone else, his skin was grimy and greasy from days spent at sea and the sleepless nights. He was intently following the activities on the galliot: some men were running along the deck towards the prow, the oarsmen were turning the vessel, with those on one side rowing in one direction, and those on the other the opposite.

'It looks as though they want to try their luck,' he added calmly.

He pointed to the pennant fluttering at the top of our mainmast, indicating the direction of the wind. During the chase, this had swung round from north-west to north north-east, and there it was staying – for the moment. Only then did I understand. The corsairs, realising that flight was impossible and having no desire to surrender, were using the oars to position themselves to face into the wind. Galleys and galliots alike had but one large cannon at the prow and short-range *pedreros* – stone-throwers – along the sides. The crew of the galliot were not as well-armed as we were, and there were fewer of them, but if they were prepared to play their last card, one lucky shot could unmast us or injure a good few of our men. And using their oars meant they could manoeuvre the vessel despite the adverse wind.

'Lower both masts! Shirts off! Row!'

It was clear from the orders he gave, sharp as pistol shots, that Captain Urdemalas had also understood. The two masts were quickly lowered, the sails furled, and the galleymaster took up his position in the central gangway, whip in hand.

'Come on! Come on!' he urged, forcing the galley-slaves, bare-chested now, to take their places, four men per bank on either side and forty-eight oars in the water while that son of a whore lashed their backs until they bled.

'Soldiers, to your posts!'

The drum beat loudly while the soldiers, muttering the oaths, complaints and blasphemies typical of the Spanish infantry – but also mumbling prayers, kissing medallions and scapulars and crossing themselves five hundred times – padded the sides of the galley with mattresses and blankets to provide some protection from enemy fire. They then equipped themselves with the tools of the trade – harquebuses, muskets and *pedreros* – and took up their places in the prow and in the corridors that ran along either side of the galley above the oars. The slaves were already maintaining a good rhythm while the galleymaster and under-galleymaster used their whistles to mark time and gaily flailed at their backs. From prow to stern, the match-cords of harquebuses were starting to smoke.

I still lacked the strength needed to use a harquebus or a heavy musket on board ship; we Spaniards took aim by holding the sight to one eye, and if your hands weren't strong enough to cope with the rolling motion of the galley, the recoil could dislocate your shoulder or knock out your teeth. So I took up my pike and my sword – a short, broad one because a long sword was too cumbersome on deck – tied a kerchief tightly round my head and, thus armed, followed Captain Alatriste. As an experienced, trustworthy soldier, my master – well, he wasn't my master any more, but old habits die hard – took up his position in the bulwarks, the very position, ironically enough, that good Don Miguel de Cervantes was given on the *Marquesa* during the Battle of Lepanto. Once we had taken our places, the Captain glanced at me distractedly and, smiling only with his eyes, he smoothed his moustache.

'Your fifth naval battle,' he said, then blew on the lit match-cord of his harquebus. His tone was suitably cool, but I knew that he was as worried about me as he had been on the four previous occasions, even though I had just turned seventeen – or perhaps because of that. When it came to boarding an enemy ship, not even God recognised his own.

'Don't board the galley unless I do, agreed?'

I opened my mouth to protest, but, at that moment, there was a loud report at the prow, and the first cannon shot from the enemy galliot sent splinters as sharp as knives flying across the deck.

It was a long road that had led the Captain and myself to be on board that galley, which, on that noontide at the end of May 1627 – the dates are there among my yellowing service records – was about to join battle with a corsair galliot just a few miles to the south of the island of Alboran, off the Barbary Coast.

Captain Alatriste's head had been only inches away from the executioner's block following a dispute with Philip IV over a shared mistress. However, after the disastrous affair of the man in the yellow doublet, when our young Catholic monarch had only just survived a plot dreamed up by the Inquisitor Fray Emilio Bocanegra, the Captain had managed to preserve both life and reputation thanks to his sword. With more modest thanks to my sword and that of the actor Rafael de Cózar, he had saved the royal skin during a sham hunting party in El Escorial. Kings, however, are both ungrateful and forgetful, and the incident brought us no further reward. Moreover, the Captain had twice crossed swords and words with the Count of Guadalmedina, the royal confidant, over the King's dalliance with the actress María de Castro. The first time left him with a cut to his cheek and the second with some painful bruises; and the Count's affection for my master, which dated from Flanders and from Italy, had eventually turned to rancour. And so the El Escorial affair had brought us only enough to balance our accounts.

In short, having done our work, we had been left without a *maravedí* in our purses, but were relieved not to have ended up in prison or six feet under in an unmarked grave. The catchpoles led by the lieutenant of constables Martín Saldaña – who was recovering from a serious wound inflicted by my master – kept well away from us, and Captain Alatriste was finally able to walk the streets without always having to look over his shoulder. This was not the case for the others involved, upon whom the royal fury fell, albeit with the discretion demanded by such circumstances. Fray Emilio Bocanegra was sent to a hospital for the mentally infirm – as a man of the cloth he merited a certain degree of consideration – while other conspirators of lesser rank were quietly strangled. Of Gualterio Malatesta, the Italian hired killer and personal enemy of the Captain and myself, we had no certain news. There was talk of terrible torture followed by execution in a dark dungeon, but no one would swear to this. As for the royal secretary, Luis de Alquézar, whose complicity could not be proved, his high position at Court and influential friends in the Council of Aragon saved his neck, but not his position, a brusque royal order despatching him to New Spain. And as you, dear reader, will know, the fate of that dubious character was far from being a matter of indifference to me, for with him went the love of my life, his niece, Angélica de Alquézar.

I intend to speak of this in detail later on, so I will say no more for the present, except that this last adventure of ours had convinced Captain Alatriste of the need to assure my future by putting me beyond the reach of Fortune's caprices – if such a thing were possible. Opportunity came by the hand of Don Francisco de Quevedo, who, since my brush with the Inquisition, had become my unofficial godfather. His prestige at Court continued to grow, and he was persuaded that, with help – in the form of the Queen's fondness for him, together with the Count-Duke Olivares' continuing benevolence – and a little good luck, when I reached the age of eighteen, I would be able to enter the corps of the royal couriers, an excellent first step towards a career at Court. The only problem was that if I was ever to be promoted to the rank of officer, I would need either a suitably impressive background or a convincing record of accomplishments, and some military experience would carry the necessary weight.

I certainly had more experience of war than the average tavern braggart − I had, after all, spent two hard years in Flanders, and fought at the siege of Breda − but because of my youth, I had been obliged to enlist not as a soldier, but as a page, which meant that I had no service record. I would, therefore, have to acquire one. The remedy was provided by our friend Captain Alonso de Contreras, who was returning to Naples after some time as a guest of Lope de Vega. The veteran soldier invited us to accompany him, arguing that the Spanish infantry − who were based in Naples, where many of his and my master's old comrades were also stationed − would be a perfect way of acquiring those two years of military experience. It would also provide me with an opportunity to enjoy the delights of the city of Vesuvius itself, as well as giving us the chance to amass some money from the incursions the Spanish galleys made into the Greek islands and along the African coast.

'Follow your calling,' Contreras advised. 'Give to Mars what you gave to Venus, and perform deeds of such derring-do that they will astound the incredulous! To your good health, young sir!'

The truth is that Captain Alatriste did not mind leaving Madrid. He had no money, he had finished with María de Castro, and Caridad la Lebrijana had been mentioning the word 'matrimony' far too often. After giving the matter much thought, as he usually did, quietly downing many pitchers of wine, he came to a decision: in the summer of 1626, we set off for Barcelona, paused briefly in Genoa, then continued south to Naples, where we joined the Spanish infantry. For the rest of that year, until St Demetrius' Day, which signalled the close of the season for galleys, we pursued corsairs and enemy ships off the Barbary Coast, in the Adriatic and the Morea.

During the customary winter truce, we spent part of our booty on the innumerable temptations of Naples and we visited Rome, so that I could admire that astonishing city, Christianity's majestic seat. In May we re-embarked, the galleys now freshly careened and made ready for the new campaign. Our first voyage – escorting a shipment of money from Italy to Spain – had taken us to the Balearics and to Valencia; this most recent one – protecting merchant ships carrying supplies from Cartagena to Oran – would bring us back to Naples. The rest – the galliot, the chase when we left the convoy, the battle off the African coast – I have more or less described. I will add only that I was no longer a callow youth, but a prudent seventeen-year-old, and alongside Captain Alatriste and the other men on board the *Mulata*, I did battle with those Turkish corsairs (we called anyone who sailed the sea 'Turkish', be they Ottoman, Moor, Morisco, or whatever else was served up to us).

Just what this new Íñigo Balboa had become you will find out in this adventure in which I propose to describe how Captain Alatriste and I fought shoulder to shoulder, no longer as master and page, but as equals and comrades. I will tell of skirmishes and pirates, of blithe youth and boarding ships, of killing and of pillaging. I will also explain precisely what it was that made Spain's name respected, feared and hated throughout the Levant. Ah, but how long ago it all seems, now that even my scars are old and my hair grey! I will show that the devil has no colour, no nation and no flag. I will show, too, that all it took back then to create a hell both on sea and on land was a Spaniard and his sword.

*

'Stop the killing!' ordered the captain of the *Mulata*. 'Those people are worth money!'

Don Manuel Urdemalas was a man who liked to keep a tight hold on his purse-strings and abhorred any unnecessary waste. And so we obeyed, slowly and reluctantly. Indeed, Captain Alatriste had to grab my arm just as I was about to slit the throat of a Turk who had jumped into the water during the fighting and was now trying to clamber back on board. The fact is that our blood was up, and we had not yet done enough killing to sate our desires. As the two galleys had closed on each other, the Turks – later, we learned that they had a good gunner with them, a Portuguese renegade – had had time to aim and fire their cannon at us, killing two of our men. That's why we had hurled ourselves on them, prepared to give no quarter – all of us shouting, 'Row, row! Ram them! Ram them!' – with our pikes and half-pikes and harquebuses at the ready. Meanwhile, amid lashes from the galleymaster's whip, blasts from his whistle and the clank of chains, the galley-slaves rowed for all they were worth, and our galley struck the galliot, holing its prow. The helmsman, who evidently knew his job, had steered us into exactly the right position, and, within seconds, our three cannon, loaded with nails and tinplate, had cleared half the deck. Then, after a volley of harquebus fire and stones, the first of the boarding parties, with cries of 'Forward, for Santiago and Spain!', scrambled along the ram and onto the galliot's foredeck, killing everyone in their path. Those Turks who did not fling themselves into the water died right there, among the blood-drenched benches, or else retreated to the stern. To be fair, they fought with great courage until our second boarding party reached the bulkhead where the last of the crew were still fighting.

Captain Alatriste and I were in that second party, he – once he had emptied his harquebus – armed with sword and shield, and I wearing a leather corslet and wielding a pike which, halfway through, I swapped for a sharp spear wrenched from the hands of a dying Turk. And thus, always keeping a watchful eye on each other, advancing prudently from bench to bench, leaving not a soul alive behind us just in case, not even those lying on the deck pleading for clemency, we finally reached our comrades in the stern. We continued to press home our advantage until the badly wounded Turkish captain and those survivors who had not jumped into the sea threw down their weapons and begged for mercy. Such mercy, however, was a long time in coming, for what ensued was nothing less than a bloodbath, and it took a repeated command from our captain before we men ceased our labours, infuriated as we were by the pirates' resistance – for along with those killed by their cannon shot, the battle had cost us nine lives and twelve wounded, not counting galley-slaves. Even the Turks in the water were being shot at like ducks, despite their pleas, or lanced or beaten to death with oars when they tried to climb on board.

'Leave it,' said Diego Alatriste.

I turned, still breathless from my exertions. He had cleaned his sword on a piece of cloth – a Moorish turban – picked up from the deck, and was putting it back in its sheath as he watched the unfortunates drowning or swimming, afraid to come too close. The sea was fairly calm, and many of them managed to stay afloat, although the wounded floundered, groaning and gasping for air, water bubbling from their lungs as they died among the red-tinged waves.

'That blood isn't yours, is it?'

I looked at my arms and felt my corslet and my thighs. Not a scratch, I discovered to my joy.

'Everything in its place,' I said, smiling wearily. 'Just like you.'

We surveyed the landscape post-battle: the two ships still locked together, disembowelled bodies sprawled among the benches, the prisoners and the dying, the men trying to climb on board despite the threat of pike and harquebus, and our comrades brazenly plundering the galliot. The easterly breeze dried the Turkish blood on our hands and faces.

'Right, let's see if there are any spoils to be had,' sighed Alatriste.

'Spoils' was what we called the booty from a ship, but this time there was almost nothing. The galley, chartered in the pirate port of Saleh, had not yet taken any booty itself when we saw it approaching our convoy; and so, even though we lifted every plank on the deck and smashed all the bulkheads, we found nothing of value, only food and weapons, not even a gold coin to pay the King his wretched quint. I had to make do with a fine cloth tunic – and I almost came to blows over that with another soldier who claimed to have seen it first – and Captain Alatriste found a large damascene knife, with a good blade skilfully worked, which he filched from the belt of one of the wounded. He returned to the *Mulata*, while I continued foraging on the Turkish galley and looking over the prisoners.

Once the galleymaster had, as was the custom, taken the sails from the captured vessel, the only items of any value left were the surviving Turks. Fortunately, there were no Christians at the oars – the corsairs themselves rowed or fought, depending on the circumstances – and when Captain Urdemalas, very sensibly, ordered the killing to stop, there were still some sixty men alive: those who had surrendered, the wounded and the remaining survivors in the sea. On a rough calculation, that meant eighty or a hundred *escudos* each, depending on where the slaves were sold. Once you had subtracted the King's quint and what was due to the captain and the other officers, and when that was shared out among the fifty sailors and seventy soldiers on board – the two hundred or so galley-slaves, of course, got nothing – it certainly wouldn't make us rich, but it was better than nothing. That's why the captain had shouted out, reminding us that the more Turks that were left alive, the greater the profit. Each time we killed one of the men trying to scramble back on board, more than a thousand *reales* went to the bottom of the sea.

'We have to hang the galliot captain,' Captain Urdemalas said.

He murmured this in a low voice, so as to be heard by only a few, namely Ensign Muelas, Sergeant Albaladejo, the galleymaster, the pilot and two trusted soldiers, one of whom was Diego Alatriste. They were gathered in the stern of the *Mulata*, next to the lantern, looking down at the galliot still skewered by the ram of our boat, its oars shattered and with water pouring in through its sides. They all agreed that there was no point in trying to tow it, for at any moment it might sink to the bottom like a stone.

'He's a Spanish renegade,' Urdemalas continued, scratching his beard. 'A Mallorquin called Boix or, to give him his infidel name, Yusuf Bocha.'

'He's wounded,' added the galleymaster.

'All the more reason to string him up before he dies of his own accord.'

Urdemalas glanced at the sun, which was now close to the horizon now. There was perhaps another hour of daylight, thought Alatriste. By nightfall, the prisoners should be chained up on board the *Mulata* and the galley heading off to some friendly port where they could be sold. The prisoners were currently being questioned to find out which language they spoke and where they came from, so that they could be divided up into renegades, Moriscos, Turks and Moors. Every pirate galley was a Babel full of surprises. It was not uncommon to find renegades of Christian origin, as was the case here, or even Englishmen and Dutchmen. That is why no one disputed the need to hang the corsairs' leader.

'Prepare the noose now and be quick about it.'

The hanging, as Captain Alatriste knew, was inevitable. A gallows death was obligatory for any renegade in charge of a vessel that had put up resistance and caused deaths on a Spanish galley, especially if that renegade was a Spaniard himself.

'You can't hang just *him*,' Ensign Muelas said. 'There are some Moriscos too: the pilot and at least four others. There were more than that – mostly Morisco rebels – but they're all either dead or dying.'

'What about the other captives?'

'Paid oarsmen, Moors the lot of them, and people from Saleh. There are two light-skinned men – we're checking their foreskins now to see whether they've been clipped or are Christians.'

'Well, you know what to do. If they've been clipped, they go straight to the rowing benches, and then we hand them over to the Inquisition. If not, we'll hang them too. How many of our men did they kill?'

'Nine, not counting the galley-slaves. And there are more who won't make it through till morning.'

Urdemalas made an angry, impatient gesture. 'God's teeth!'

He was a blunt old seadog, and his weather-beaten skin and grey beard bore witness to thirty years spent sailing the Mediterranean. He knew exactly how to treat such men, who set sail from the Barbary Coast at night in order to reach the Spanish coast by dawn, where they frequently sacked and plundered villages before returning home to sleep peacefully in their own beds.

'The rope for all six of them. That'll keep the Devil busy.'

A soldier approached with a message for Ensign Muelas, and the latter turned to Urdemalas.

'Apparently the two light-skinned men have been clipped, Captain. One is a French renegade and the other's from Livorno.'

'Right, set them to the oars.'

This explained why the Turkish galliot had fought so long and so hard: its crew knew what the consequences would be. Most of the Moriscos on board had preferred to die fighting rather than surrender; and that, as Ensign Muelas remarked dispassionately, was sure proof that they had been born in Spain, even if they were now corsair dogs. After all, it was common knowledge that no Spanish soldier would respect the life of a renegade compatriot turned corsair captain, nor the lives of their Morisco crew; unless, that is, the latter gave in without a struggle, in which case, they would later be handed over to the Inquisition. The Moriscos – baptised Moors whose Christian faith was suspect – had been expelled from Spain eighteen years before, after a great deal of trouble and treachery, and many bloody uprisings and false conversions. Cast out upon the road, they were often ill-treated, murdered, stripped of their possessions, and saw their wives and daughters raped, and when they reached the North African coast, even their brother Moors failed to welcome them. When they finally settled in the pirate ports of Tunis, Algiers and, especially, Saleh – the nearest to the Andalusian coast – they became the bitterest and most hated of Spain's enemies, as well as the cruellest in their raids on the Spanish coastal villages, which, with their knowledge of the terrain, they attacked ruthlessly and with the understandable rancour of settling old scores. As Lope de Vega put it in his play *The Good Guard*:

> *And Moors from Algiers – pirates—*
> *Who lurk in coves and bays*
> *From which they later slip*
> *And sail their hidden frigates.*

'But don't make a fuss about hanging them,' Urdemalas advised. 'We don't want any trouble from the captives. Wait until they're all safely chained up.'

'We'll lose money by hanging them, Captain,' protested the galleymaster, envisaging more *reales* going to waste on the yard-arm. The galleymaster was even more avaricious than the captain; he had an evil face and a worse soul, and earned a little extra money, which he shared with the overseer, through taking bribes and secret payments exacted from the galley-slaves.

'I piss on your money, sir, and everything you buy with it,' Urdemalas declared, giving the galleymaster a withering look.

Long accustomed to Captain Urdemalas's odd ways, the galleymaster merely shrugged and stalked off down the gangway, asking the under-galleymaster and the overseer to find some ropes. The bodies of the slaves killed during the battle – four Moors, a Dutchman and three Spaniards who had been condemned to row in the galleys – were being unchained and tossed overboard so that their places could be taken by the captured corsairs. Another half-dozen or so badly wounded galley-slaves were sprawled, still in their chains, on the gore-soaked benches, waiting to be seen by the barber, who served as both blood-letter and surgeon and whose treatment for any wound, however terrible, consisted of applying vinegar and salt to it.

Diego Alatriste's eyes met those of Captain Urdemalas.

'Two of the Moriscos are very young,' he said.

This was true. I had noticed them when the galliot's captain was wounded: two boys crouched among the benches at the stern, trying to keep out of the way of all that whirling steel. The captain himself had placed them there, to prevent them having their throats cut.

Urdemalas pulled a surly face. 'How young?'

'Young enough.'

'Born in Spain?'

'I have no idea.'

'Circumcised?'

'I suppose so.'

Urdemalas muttered a few well-turned oaths and regarded the Alatriste thoughtfully. Then he turned to Sergeant Albaladejo.

'See to it, Sergeant. If they've got hair on their tackle, they've enough neck to be hanged; if not, set them to rowing.'

Albaladejo walked reluctantly down the gangway towards the galliot. Pulling down boys' breeches to see if they were man enough for the rope or fodder for the galleys was not exactly his favourite occupation, but it went with the job.

For his part, Urdemalas was still studying Diego Alatriste. His look was inquisitive, as if wondering whether Alatriste's concern for the boys was based on something more than common sense. Even if they were mere boys, born in Spain or elsewhere – the last Moriscos, from Valle de Ricote in the province of Murcia, had left around 1614 – as far as Urdemalas and the vast majority of Spaniards were concerned, there was no room for compassion. Only two months before, on the

Almería coast, the corsairs had carried off and enslaved seventy-four men, women and children from one village, having first plundered it and crucified the mayor and eleven others whose names they had on a list. A woman who had managed to escape was later able to confirm that several of the attackers were Moriscos and former villagers.

Everyone had an account to settle on that turbulent Mediterranean frontier. It was a melting-pot of races, languages and age-old hatreds. In the case of the Moriscos, who knew every bay, water-hole and path of the country to which they were returning to take their revenge, they enjoyed an advantage that Miguel de Cervantes – who knew a lot about corsairs, as both soldier and captive – described in his play *Life in Algiers*:

Because I've known this land from birth
And all its entrances and exits,
I know how best to fight upon its earth.

'You were there, weren't you?' Urdemalas asked. 'In 1609, when the Moriscos were expelled from Valencia?'

Alatriste nodded. There were few secrets on board a small ship. Urdemalas and he had friends in common, and Alatriste, although not an officer, received extra pay for taking on the duties of corporal. The sailor and the veteran soldier respected each other, but they also kept their distance.

'They say,' Urdemalas went on, 'that you helped to crush the rebels, the ones who took to the hills.'

'I did,' Alatriste replied.

That was one way of putting it, he thought. The searches carried out among the steep, rocky hills, sweating beneath the sun; the ambushes, the sudden attacks, the reprisals, the killings. There had been cruelty on both sides, and the poor people caught in the middle, both Christians and Moriscos, had paid the highest price, with the numerous rapes and murders going unpunished. And then there were those long lines of unfortunates trudging the roads, forced to leave their homes and sell off cheap what they couldn't take with them, harassed and plundered by peasants and soldiers alike – many soldiers even deserted in order to steal from them. The paths they trod led to ships, and to exile. As Gaspar Aguilar wrote:

> *Strip them of their house and all their wealth,*
> *Ye powers that rule the world;*
> *For alms, leave them their lives and petty health.*

'By my life,' said Captain Urdemalas with a cynical smile, 'you don't seem very proud of service done for God and King.'

Alatriste gave him a hard look, then slowly smoothed his moustache.

'Are you referring to the service performed today, Captain, or to that performed in 1609?'

He spoke very clearly and coldly, almost softly. Urdemalas glanced uneasily at Lieutenant Muelas, the pilot and the other corporal.

'I have no criticism of your performance today,' he replied in quite a different tone, studying Alatriste's face as if he were counting the scars. 'With ten men like you, I could take Algiers in a night. It's just that ...'

'It's just what?'

'Well,' Urdemalas said with a shrug. 'There are no secrets here. People say you were unhappy about what happened in Valencia and that you took your sword and your services elsewhere.'

'And do you have an opinion on the matter, Captain?'

Urdemalas' eyes followed the movement made by Alatriste's

left hand, for it was no longer smoothing his moustache but was by his side, just inches away from the scratched and battered hilt of his sword. Urdemalas was a determined man, as everyone knew, but every man has his reputation, and Diego Alatriste's had preceded him onto the *Mulata*. Mere words, one might say, but, having seen how he had fought that day, even the lowliest cabin boy was convinced. Urdemalas knew this better than anyone.

'No, no opinion at all, I assure you,' he said. 'Everyone's different, after all, but you can't stop people talking.'

He maintained the same firm, frank tone, and Alatriste considered the matter carefully. There was not, he concluded, anything to object to in either the captain's voice or his words. He was a wise man. And prudent too.

'Well, if that's what they say,' Alatriste said at last, 'they're quite right.'

Ensign Muelas thought it best to change tack a little.

'I'm from Vejer myself,' he said. 'And I remember how the Turks used to attack us with the help of the Moriscos who lived there – they told them when they could most easily catch us unawares. A neighbour's son went out to herd the goats ... or maybe he went off fishing with his father ... anyway, he woke up in a souk in Barbary. He's probably like one of these renegades here, up to goodness knows what ... Not to mention what they do to the women.'

The pilot and the other corporal nodded grimly. They knew about the villages built high up, away from the shore, as a precaution against the Barbary pirates who scoured the sea and haunted the coast; and they knew how afraid the villagers were of the pirates' boldness and of their embittered Morisco neighbours. They knew, too, about the bloody rebellions led by the Moriscos who refused to accept baptism and the authority of the King, about their complicity with Barbary and the secret petitions made to France, to the Lutherans and to the Great Turk to join them in a general uprising. After the wars of Granada and the Alpujarras, attempts to disperse them had failed, as had Philip III's ineffectual policy of conversion, and three hundred thousand Moriscos – an enormous number in a population of only nine million – had settled on the vulnerable Levant and Andalusian coasts. Almost none of them were true Christians, and they remained rebellious, ungovernable and proud – like the Spaniards they also were – dreaming of their lost liberty and independence, and unwilling to become part of the Catholic nation, forged a century ago, that was intent on waging war on all fronts; against the greed and envy of France and England, against Protestant heresy and against the immense power of the Turks. This was why, until their eventual expulsion, the last Muslims in the Peninsula had been a dagger permanently pointed at the side of a Spain that was, at the time, master of one half the world and at war with the other.

'You could never feel at ease,' Muelas went on. 'From Valencia to Gibraltar, the old Christians were caught between the Moriscos in the mountains and the pirates at sea. These supposed Christian converts, so suspiciously reluctant to eat pork, would send signals at night, then help their friends to disembark and plunder the villages ...'

Diego Alatriste shook his head. He knew that this wasn't the whole story.

'There were honest people too,' he said, 'newly converted Christians who genuinely believed and were faithful subjects of the King. I knew a few in Flanders. They were helpful and hard-working. There wasn't a gentleman, villain, friar or beggar among them. In that respect, it's true, they didn't seem like Spaniards.'

Everyone stared at him in silence. Then, the ensign bit off

a piece of fingernail and spat it over the side of the boat.

'That's beside the point. We had to put a stop to all that worrying, all those terrible acts. With God's help, we did, and it's over now.'

Alatriste thought to himself that it certainly wasn't over yet. The silent civil war between Spaniards was still being waged elsewhere and by other means. A few Moriscos, very few, had managed to return to Spain secretly, helped by their neighbours, as had happened in Campo de Calatrava. As for the others, they took both their anger and their nostalgia for a lost homeland to the corsair towns of Barbary; and the power of the Turks and of North Africa had been strengthened by exiled *mudéjares* – unconverted Muslims – from Granada and Andalusia, and by the *tagarinos* – Muslims who passed as Spaniards – from Aragon, Catalonia and Valencia, who were skilled in many trades, particularly those that then proved useful to the corsair enterprise.

Such men were often to be found as harquebusiers – there were a dozen of them on the captured galliot – and as well as bringing with them their knowledge of the coasts and the villages, they built ships, made firearms and powder arms, and they knew better than anyone how to sell the slaves they captured. They also became skilful captains, pilots and crews of galleys and fustas. Their hatred and their courage, their skill as marksmen and their determination to give no quarter in battle, meant that they were as good as the best Turkish soldiers and better than those crews composed solely of Moors. This is why they were the fiercest of corsairs, the most pitiless of slave-traders and Spain's greatest enemy in the Mediterranean.

'You have to admit they're brave though,' commented the pilot. 'The bastards fought like tigers.'

Alatriste was gazing down at the water surrounding the

galley and the galliot which was strewn with the debris of combat. Almost all the dead had gone under by now. Only a few, due to the air trapped in their clothes or their lungs, floated tranquilly on the surface, just like the old ghosts that floated in his memory. Not even he would have denied the need for that expulsion. Times were harsh and neither Spain nor Europe, nor the world, was in placatory mood. But he had been troubled by the manner of the expulsion: the bureaucratic coldness and the military brutality, crowned, in the end, by an appalling lack of humanity – 'they should be prevented from taking so much money with them, for some are quite happy to leave', wrote Don Pedro de Toledo, chief of the Spanish galleys, to the King.

And so, in 1610, when he was twenty-eight, the soldier Diego Alatriste, a veteran of the old Cartagena regiment – brought from Flanders with the aim of crushing the Morisco rebels – had asked to be released from his unit and had enlisted in Naples to fight the Turks in the eastern Mediterranean. If he was going to have to slit the throats of infidels, he argued, he would prefer infidels who were at least capable of defending themselves. Twenty years on, here he was – one of life's little ironies – doing exactly the same thing.

'In 1610 and 1611, I was in charge of transporting the beasts from Denia to the beaches of Orán,' Captain Urdemalas said. 'The dogs.'

He placed special emphasis on the word 'dogs' and fixed Diego Alatriste with a hard stare.

'Dogs ...' said Alatriste thoughtfully.

He remembered the lines of rebels chained together, being taken to the mercury mines in Almadén. Not one returned. And the old Morisco in a small Valencian village, the only one who had not been expelled because of his great age and infirmity; he had been stoned to death by the village boys, without a single neighbour, not even the parish priest, doing anything to stop them.

'Dogs come in all shapes and sizes,' he concluded. Alatriste was smiling bitterly, his green eyes fixed on those of Urdemalas. And from the expression on the latter's face, he knew that he liked neither the look nor the smile. But he knew, too – for he could weigh up men at a glance – that Urdemalas would be very careful not to give voice to his feelings. After all, no one could be said to have shown a lack of respect here.

Then again, not everything happened on board ship, where military discipline ruled out open dispute. Life was full of moonless nights, ports with dark, silent alleyways, discreet places where a galley-captain, with only his sword to rely on, might easily find himself with a foot of steel between chest and back before he could say 'Amen'. And so, when Diego Alatriste seasoned both look and smile with a pinch of insolence, Captain Urdemalas observed for a moment how Alatriste's hand was again resting, with apparent nonchalance, near the hilt of his sword, and then transferred his gaze to the sea.

2. SEND A HUNDRED LANCERS TO ORAN

When the galliot finally sank, I looked back at the lifeless bodies of its captain, pilot and the three Moriscos silhouetted against the fading light. They hung from the lateen yard, their feet almost touching the sea as if they were about to be swallowed up by its shadow. Among them was one of the young men, on whose private parts, alas, Sergeant Albaladejo had found incriminating hair. The other boy, fortunately still hairless, had been put to row, as had some of the other captives; the rest were in chains in the hold.

The Morisco pilot, who turned out to be Valencian, had sworn in good Castilian, and with the noose already round his neck, that despite being expelled from Spain as a boy, he was a true convert and had always lived a Christian life. He claimed he was as indifferent to the sect of the Prophet as that Christian in Oran who said:

I don't deny our Lord nor yet accept Mohammed,
And if I seem to be a Moor in voice and dress,
I do so simply for the riches I'll possess.

He had only been circumcised, he claimed, to silence wicked tongues when he was living in Algiers and Saleh. Captain Urdemalas replied that he was very pleased to hear this, for since he had clearly been such a good Christian, he would soon die as one too and with no chaplain on board, he would need only a credo and an Our Father to be ready for the next life. For that reason, Captain Urdemalas said he would be perfectly happy to grant the pilot a little time before hanging him by the neck. The Morisco took this very badly and blasphemed against God and the Holy Virgin, less in Castilian this time and more in the lingua franca of Barbary laced with the dialect of the Valencian Muslims. He only paused in these insults to spit a well-aimed gob of saliva on Captain Urdemalas' boot. At this point the Captain halted the ceremony, and said that there would be no bloody credos either.

The pilot, hands tied behind his back, was hoisted straight up onto the yard, kicking furiously and without another chance to consign his soul to God. As for the other wounded corsairs, regardless of whether they were Moriscos or not, they were thrown unceremoniously, hands bound, into the sea. There was only one man left standing, and because he had been stabbed in the neck, he could not be hanged. His wound was half a span long, although no vein had been cut and he wasn't bleeding much – indeed, viewed from one side, the poor devil looked as fresh as a daisy, albeit somewhat pale. But the overseer was of the opinion that if they hanged him, the wound in his neck would tear, which would make for a very ugly scene. The Captain took one look at him and agreed, so the man ended up being tossed into the sea along with his comrades.

I went in search of Diego Alatriste, almost feeling my way in the dark. A gentle north-east wind was blowing, the moon had not yet come up and the sky was thick with stars. The deck was packed with soldiers and sailors resting after the battle, having first eaten some salt fish and drunk a little wine to restore their strength, and I won't say that they stank, although they did, because I myself was part of the stink and was, I'm sure, contributing more than my fair share of odours and emanations.

The galley-men had stowed their oars, leaving the ship to the care of the favourable wind, and had received some hard-tack and a little oil and vinegar, which they ate lying down between their benches, talking quietly, and occasionally singing softly to pass the time or complaining about their cuts and bruises. The lines from a song drifted over to me, accompanied by the clink of chains and the slapping of hands on the leather that covered the benches:

I'll have it known
Through all the lands
That Christian galleys,
Short of feet,
Are always short of hands.

It was a night like many others. The *Mulata* was heading south on a calm sea, gliding slowly through the darkness, with its great sails billowing and swaying above the deck like two pale stains that alternately concealed and revealed the starry sky. I found Captain Alatriste at the prow of the ship, next to where the ropes and cables were kept. He was standing utterly still, leaning against the netting stretched over the side of the ship and gazing at the dark sea and sky. Towards the west, a trace of reddish light was still visible. We talked a little about the events of the day, and I asked him if what the men were saying was true – that we were heading for Melilla and not Oran.

'Our Captain doesn't want to remain at sea too long with so many captives on board,' he replied. 'Melilla is closer, which is why he prefers to sell them there. Then we can continue on our way ... less heavily laden.'

'And richer too,' I added, smiling. I had done my calculations, as had everyone else, and had worked out that the day should bring us at least two hundred *escudos*.

The Captain shifted position slightly. It was growing cool in the darkness and I realised he was fastening his buff coat.

'Don't get your hopes up,' he said at last. 'Slaves don't fetch such a good price in Melilla, but because we're alone, near the coast and forty leagues from Oran, Urdemalas is anxious to avoid any more encounters.'

I was pleased, nonetheless, for I had never visited Melilla. Captain Alatriste was quick to put me straight, though, telling me that the town was little more than a small fortress built on a rock beneath Mount Gurugu: a few fortified houses ready for battle and surrounded, as were all Spanish enclaves on the African coast, by hostile *alarbes*. *Alarbe* or *alárabe* – if I may enlighten the idle reader – was the name we gave to the bellicose, untrustworthy Moors from the countryside, to distinguish them from the city Moors, whom we simply referred to as Moors, in order to differentiate them, in turn – although they were, in fact, Berbers – from the Turks of Turkey, of whom there was never any shortage, for they were always shuttling back and forth from Constantinople. That was where the Great Turk lived, and Moors and Berbers, or whatever you called them, all paid fealty to him in one way or another. And that is why, to simplify matters, we called them all Turks. 'I wonder if the Turks will come this year,' we would say, regardless of whether they actually were from Turkey or not and regardless, too, of whether a Turkish fusta or galliot was from Saleh, Tunis or Anatolia.

And then there was the intense trading that went on between every nation and these populous corsair cities, where, as well as the local Moorish inhabitants, there were innumerable Christian slaves – Cervantes, Jerónimo de Pasamonte and others experienced this at first hand, and I will leave them to describe it in their own words – as well as Moriscos,

Jews, renegades, sailors and traders from every shore. You can imagine, then, what a complicated world it was, that interior sea bordering Spain to the south and east, a sea that belonged to no one and to everyone; an ambiguous, shifting, dangerous place where diverse races mixed and mingled, making alliances or doing battle, depending on how the dice rolled. It must be said, though, that while France, England, Holland and Venice negotiated with the Turk, and even made alliances with him against other Christian nations – especially against Spain when it suited them, which it nearly always did – we, for all our many errors and contradictions, always held firm to the one true religion, never retracting so much as a syllable. And being both arrogant and powerful, we poured swords, money and blood – until there was no more – into a struggle, which, for a century and a half, kept at bay the Lutherans and the Calvinists in Europe, and the Mohammedans in the Mediterranean.

There, where pants the rebel Belgian,
And where the Berber, sweating, stands,
Working, the one, with his bare hands,
The other wielding his bare sword,
To fashion for locks a master key,
Locks that long have had a ward,
Our fleets its shape, its shape our sea.

I hope Don Francisco de Quevedo will forgive me for mentioning his enemy, Luis de Góngora, who wrote these Gongoristic lines in 1610 in praise of the taking of Larache, which was followed, four years later, by the seizure of La Mamora. Both were Barbary towns which, like all such towns, we took from the Moors by dint of great effort, clung on to through great suffering, and, to our great shame and misfortune, finally lost, as we lost everything, due to our own idleness. In this, as in most things, we should have done as others did, and paid more attention to profit than to reputation, opening ourselves up to the horizons we had discovered and broadened instead of becoming entangled in the sinister soutanes of royal confessors, in the privileges of blood, in our dislike of hard work, in matters of the cross and the sword whilst leaving our intelligence, our nation, our soul to rot. But no one gave us the choice.

In the end, much to History's surprise, a handful of Spaniards was able to make the world pay dearly, by fighting until not one of us was left standing. You will say that this is poor consolation, and you may be right, but we were simply doing our job and we paid no heed to governments, philosophies or theology. We were, after all, merely soldiers.

Captain Alatriste and I watched the last red light fade from the horizon. Now the only thing that distinguished sea and sky was the starry vault beneath which our galley sailed, driven by the east wind, and guided only by the knowledge of the pilot who kept one eye on the North Star and the other on the binnacle, in which the ship's compass was lit by the tenuous glow of a candle. Behind us, near the mainmast, we heard someone ask Captain Urdemalas if they could light the poop-deck lantern, to which he replied that if anyone lit anything, however small, he would personally dash their brains out.

'As for rich soldiers,' Captain Alatriste said after a while, as if he had been turning over my words in his mind, 'I've never yet met one who was rich for very long. It all goes on cards, wine, whores, as you very well know.'

There was a significant pause, brief enough for it not to sound like a reproach, but long enough for it to be just that.

And I knew exactly what he was referring to. We had been together for five years, but had spent only some seven months in Naples and on the galleys, during which time he'd had ample opportunity to notice certain changes in my person. Not only physical ones – for I was as tall as he was now, slim but elegant, with good legs, strong arms and not a bad face – but other deeper and more complex changes. I was aware that, ever since I was a child, the Captain had wanted me to have a future away from the army. He had, for this reason, always tried to encourage me – with the help of his friends Don Francisco de Quevedo and Father Pérez – to read good books and translations from the Latin and the Greek. The pen, he used to say, has greater reach than the sword, and someone learned in books and the law and with a good position at Court would always have more of a future than a professional killer. My natural inclination, however, proved impossible to change, and although, thanks to his efforts, I did acquire a taste for literature – after all, here I am, all these years later, writing our history – my destiny was shaped by the character I inherited from my father, who died in Flanders, and by having lived at Captain Alatriste's side since I was thirteen, sharing his dangerous life and adventures. I wanted to be a soldier, and I was; I applied myself to the task with the resolute passion and energy of my youth.

'There are no whores on board, and the wine's scarce and very rough,' I replied, rather wounded by his comment. 'So you have no reason to reprimand me. As for cards, I don't intend giving to a louse the money I risked my life to earn.'

I was not using the word 'louse' lightly either. Captain Urdemalas, sick of the quarrels over cards and dice, had banned both, threatening any transgressor with the shackles. But the horse knows more than its rider, and so the soldiers and sailors had invented a new game. We chalked various circles on a piece of board and placed in the very centre one of the many lice that were eating us alive – 'having visitors' we called it – and then we bet on which direction the creature would go.

'When we go back to Naples,' I said in conclusion, 'then we'll see.'

I kept glancing at him out of the corner of my eye, expecting some riposte, but he remained silent, a dark shape by my side being rocked, as I was, by the motion of the boat. The truth was that, however much he tried to protect me, Captain Alatriste could not keep me from the less savoury aspects of military life, not counting the usual risks of the profession, just as, in the years since my poor mother had entrusted me to him, I had found myself embroiled in certain of his own murky enterprises, with grave risk to life and liberty. Now I was a grown man, or about to become one, and the Captain's sage advice, when he proffered it – he was, as you know, a man who preferred sword thrusts to words – did not always find the response he expected, for I believed myself to be a man of the world. And so, because he was experienced, discreet and wise, and because he loved me, he avoided sermonising and tried instead to stay close by in case I needed him. He only imposed his authority – and dear God, he could certainly do that when he needed to – in extreme situations.

As for wine, women and gambling, I admit that he had good reason to be angry with me. My wage of four *escudos* a month, along with the money from previous booties – two Turkish *karamuzals* captured in the Mayna channel, a profit-able raid on the coast of Tunis, a ship seized off Cape Passero and a galley off the island of Santa Maura – had been spent, every last penny, in the same soldierly fashion as my comrades had spent theirs, and exactly as the Captain had done in his youth, as he himself would sullenly admit.

In my case, though, my lack of experience and a taste for the new meant that I hurled myself into these pastimes with great gusto. For a spirited Spanish lad such as myself, Naples was paradise: good inns, excellent taverns, beautiful women; in short, everything that could help relieve a soldier of his pay. And, as chance would have it, my fellow page from Flanders, Jaime Correas, was there to assist and encourage me. Having served in Italy for some time, he was no stranger to such vices. I will have occasion to speak of him later, so I will say only that it was in his company, and beneath the frowning gaze of Captain Alatriste, that I had spent a good part of the winter months, when the galleys were out of action, embroiled in various escapades involving gaming houses, taverns and — rather less assiduously on my part — the occasional bawdyhouse.

Not that my former master was the kind of man who could die without confession and stand fearlessly face to face with Christ, far from it, but the truth is that gambling, which has bled many a soldier's purse dry, had never tempted him. On the other hand, if he did occasionally frequent certain ladies practised in the art of love — he didn't need to go to whores, for he always grazed in rich pastures — they were few in number and always reliable. As for Bacchus, the Captain certainly worshipped at his table and had the devil of a thirst. But although he often drank too much, especially when he was angry or melancholy — and that was when he was especially dangerous, because wine dulled neither his senses nor his reactions — he always did so alone and without witnesses. I think that, rather than as a pleasure or a vice, he downed whole tumblers in order to quell the inner torment and demons known only to him and God.

At first light, we cast anchor outside Melilla, the Spanish fortress town captured from the Moors one hundred and thirty years before. And in order to remain safely out of sight of Moorish eyes, we anchored not in the lagoon, but in the narrow inlet of Galapagos cove, sheltered by Melilla's soaring walls and towers. The town's imposing appearance was just that – mere appearance – as I was able to see for myself when I set off to wander through the close-packed, treeless streets and along the city walls. While the galley-captain haggled over a price for the slaves, I saw how neglected it all was. Eight centuries of struggle against Islam had died on that wretched frontier and not a single *maravedí* from the gold and silver brought from the Indies ever reached these shores. What did not end up in the hands of Genoan bankers was stolen by the Dutch and English – Devil take 'em – in the western seas. Flanders and the Indies were the apples of our royal eyes, and our old African enterprise, once so dear to the Catholic kings and to the great Emperor Charles V, was scorned by Philip IV and his favourite, the Count-Duke of Olivares. Indeed, many satirical verses were written on the subject:

It surely matters not a toss
If far Melilla's deemed a loss,
And do not let yourself be vexed
Should it turn out that Ceuta's next.
Bring on the flags of Barbary!
No more for us the rosary,
Once the Gospel city of Oran
Bends the knee to the Koran.
What does it matter – not a jot –
If those brave Arabs take the lot?

It was a miracle that these North African fortress towns survived at all. In truth, they did so more by virtue of their reputation than anything else, for although they deprived the corsairs of a few ports and important bases, the latter still had Algiers, Tunis, Saleh, Tripoli and Bizerta. Our soldiers were housed in cramped quarters within fortifications whose casemates and bulwarks were crumbling for lack of money; many of the soldiers were old and infirm, with no one to relieve them, and they lived there with their families, ill-clothed and ill-fed, without so much as a scrap of land to cultivate, and with barely enough money, and sometimes none at all, to resist the surrounding enemy. Any aid from the Peninsula was at least a day's journey away, and such aid was far from certain, for it depended on what the conditions at sea were like and on how quickly help could be organised in Spain. And so Melilla, like our other African possessions – including Tangiers and Ceuta, which, being Portuguese, were also therefore Spanish – found itself relying on the courage of the garrison and on diplomacy with the neighbouring Moors, from whom the inhabitants obtained, voluntarily or by force, the necessary supplies.

As I said, I gleaned much of this simply from visiting the city and its massive water cisterns, on which life there was totally dependent. I visited the hospital, the church, the Santa Ana tunnel and the square, *intra muros*, where the Moors from the surrounding area came to sell meat, fish and vegetables. During the day this was a lively place, but at nightfall, before the city gates were closed, all the Arabs left – apart, that is, from a trusted few who were allowed to stay as long as they agreed to be locked up in the House of the Moors, outside which a constable stood guard. This, however, I did not see, because that same night, in order to escape the notice of the Arabs along the coast, the *Mulata* weighed anchor and left Melilla secretly, powered only by her oars. Then, taking advantage of the wind blowing from the shore-ward, we set sail in an easterly direction, and dawn found us off the Chafarinas Islands, halfway to Oran, where, on the following afternoon, we spotted the Needle Rock and anchored without incident or mishap.

Oran was quite different from Melilla, but it was still far from being a paradise. The town found itself in the same state of abandonment as Spain's other fortress towns in Africa, with poor lines of supply and even poorer communications, and its defences were neglected and inadequate. In the case of Oran, though, it wasn't just an arid fortified promontory, but a real town with a river, abundant water, and surrounded by gardens and orchards. It also had a proper garrison, which, though far from ideal — at the time Oran was home to about one thousand three hundred soldiers and their families, as well as five hundred inhabitants plying various trades — was nevertheless capable of putting up a reasonable defence and, if necessary, of mounting an attack. So although, in general, these fortress towns had pretty much been abandoned to their fate, Oran was certainly not the worst.

The proof of this was the presence of the supply convoy anchored in the bay of Cap Falcon, the town's harbour, between Mazalquivir's formidable fort and Mona Point beneath the castle of San Gregorio. There we finally rejoined the convoy we had left in order to give chase to the corsairs. We anchored close to land, next to the tower, and were borne to shore in feluccas. We walked the half league to the town which was built on top of a cliff and therefore had no good port of its own, which is where Mazalquivir came in. From that vantage point, looking out over the river that ran between the town and the fort of Rozalcazar, there were splendid views of the surrounding gardens, orchards, woods and windmills.

As I said, we were happy to be back on land and with money in our pockets, and although Oran was no Naples – far from it – there were plenty of distractions. There were taverns run by former soldiers, a recent truce with the Moors meant that the market was well supplied, and everyone was pleased to see the wheat, cloth and gunpowder we had brought from Spain. There were even a few decent brothels. In garrison towns like Oran, even the bishops and theologians of our Holy Mother Church – after much debate and having resigned themselves to the inevitable – had concluded that a few sprightly doxies not only salved a soldier's itch but also safeguarded the virtue of maidens and married ladies, reducing the number of rapes and forays into Moorish territory in search of women. Indeed, as soon as we disembarked, soldiers and sailors alike were planning to do their duty and visit one of these brothels the moment they entered the town. However, no sooner had Captain Alatriste and I passed through the Canastel gate – the closer to the harbour of Oran's two gates – than we had a most pleasant, extraordinary and unexpected encounter, which just goes to show how life, with all its twists and turns, can still surprise us.

'Well, I'll be hanged,' said a familiar voice.

And there, as small and wiry as ever, was Sebastián Copons, hands on hips and sword at his side, standing in the shade, chatting to some soldiers, in his role as corporal in charge of the guard at the gate.

'And so that's what happened,' he said, draining his mug.

The three of us were sitting at a table outside a small, grubby tavern, beneath a much-patched bit of sailcloth that served as an awning. True to his old self, Copons wasted few words in summarising the last two years, which was how long it had been since we said our farewells in an Andalusian inn, after the massacre on board the *Niklaasbergen* and that business with the King's gold, when, with the help of a few comrades, we made short work of Flemings and hired killers alike at Barra de Sanlúcar.

Since then, he told us, a run of bad luck had put paid to his plans to leave the army and set himself up in Huesca with a bit of land, a house and a wife. The first unfortunate episode took place in Seville and the second involved a death in Zaragoza. This latter incident attracted constables, lawyers, judges, scribes and all the other parasites that lie in wait amongst the paperwork like bedbugs in the seams of a sheet. Relieved of all his money and with his belly and pockets empty, he had been forced back to the barracks to earn his living. His attempts to get himself sent to the Indies failed: it wasn't soldiers they needed now, but functionaries, priests and artisans. Then, just as he was about to enlist for Flanders or Italy, a tavern brawl, in which two catchpoles were beaten up and one constable slashed across the face, brought him up against the law once more. This time, he had no money with which to blind Justice, and so the judge – who, like him, was from Huesca – offered him a choice between spending four years behind bars or one year as a soldier in Oran for fifty *reales* a month. So there he was, one year and five months later.

'Why don't you leave?' I asked innocently.

Copons and Captain Alatriste exchanged looks – as if to say he may look like a grown man, but he's still green about the gills – and then refilled their mugs with wine. It was a pretty rough vintage and God knows where it came from, but it was wine after all, we were in Africa and it was as hot as hell. More to the point, it had been a long time since we three had shared a jug, and we had been through a lot together — the Ruyter Mill, Breda, Terheyden, Seville, Sanlúcar ...

'I can't because the Sergeant Major won't let me.'

'Why's that?'

'Because he says the Marquis of Velada, the town's governor, won't let *him*.'

Then between sips of wine, he explained what life was like in Oran: the people, ill-fed and poorly paid, simply rotted away between its walls, with no hope of promotion or any glory other than that of growing old there, alone or with their family if they had one, slogging on until they were deemed too feeble to work. Any complaints or petitions went unanswered. Even a veteran with forty years' service was not allowed to return to Spain because that would leave the post unfilled; new soldiers sent to Barbary simply deserted before they even embarked.

You just had to go for a stroll through the city to see how many ragged, vulnerable people there were; and if you did manage to buy something — food or clothes — this would be followed by weeks of hunger and dearth, because the pay didn't arrive, not even a half or a third of it, even though the troops in Oran were the worst paid in all of Spain. Some secretary in the Treasury had evidently decided — and been backed up in his decision by our master the King — that as long as there was sufficient water, fertile fields and friendly Moors on hand, the troops should have no problem making ends meet. Soldiers were only offered help in dire emergencies. Copons himself, after seventeen months' duty there, had not seen one *maravedí* of the one hundred or so *escudos* that were owed to him. The only thing the soldiers could do to help themselves was to go on the occasional cavalcade.

'Cavalcade?' I asked.

Copons winked but said no more and it fell to Captain Alatriste to explain.

'You know ... raids, incursions, the kind of thing our grandfathers did when they rode out into the countryside and attacked the camps of hostile Moors. They used to call them *almogavarías*.'

'Well, that's what Oran has had to stoop to, as if she was some old procuress,' Copons added.

I looked at him, confused. 'I don't understand.'

'You will.'

He poured more wine. He was as thin, sinewy and strong as ever, but he looked older and wearier and, what was even stranger, he had become talkative. Like Captain Alatriste, he had usually been slow to speak and quick to draw his sword. However, it seemed that in Oran, in his silence, he had accumulated far too many thoughts and feelings, so that the unexpected encounter with us and the warmth of our friendship had suddenly made them flow forth. It was hot and he had unfastened his grimy leather doublet – he wore no undershirt, for he had no money for such things. Above his left ear, he bore the scar earned at the Ruyter Mill, still visible through his short hair, which had grown greyer, and he had some white hairs too on his ill-shaven chin.

'Tell him about the hostile Moors,' said Captain Alatriste.

And he did. The Arabs who lived nearby could be divided into three classes: peaceful Moors, hostile Moors and what were known as *mogataces*. The peaceful Moors made truces with the Spaniards, sold them food, and so on. They paid tax, or *garrama* as it was known here, and that made them 'friends' until they stopped paying. Then they became hostile Moors.

'Sounds dangerous,' I commented.

'It is. They're the ones who'll slit our throats and cut off our privates if they catch us, although we'd do the same to them.'

'And how do you tell them apart?'

The Captain shook his head. 'You can't always.'

'Sometimes that works to our detriment,' said Copons, 'and sometimes to theirs.'

I considered the grim implications of this answer. Then I asked who the *mogataces* were. The Captain explained that they were Arabs who fought on our side as soldiers of Spain, but without changing their religion.

'Can they be trusted?'

Copons pulled a face. 'Some of them can.'

'I don't think I could ever trust a Moor.'

Their looks were mocking. I must have seemed extraordinarily naïve to them.

'You'd be surprised. There are Moors and Moors.'

We ordered another jug of wine, which was brought to us by a man with ugly bare feet and an even uglier face, as black as pitch. I watched thoughtfully as Copons filled my mug.

'How do you know which ones can be trusted?'

'A question of experience,' said Copons, tapping the side of his nose, 'and instinct. But let me tell you, in my time I've seen no end of Christians roaring drunk, but never a Moor. They don't gamble either, even though the deck of cards is as old as Mohammed.'

'Yes, but they don't keep their word,' I objected.

'That depends on who they are and who they give their word to. When the Count of Alcaudete's men were nearly torn to pieces, his *mogataces* stood firm and fought to the bitter end. That's why I say there are Moors and Moors.'

While we were dispatching this latest jug of wine – and the jug had been baptised many times – Copons continued to enlighten us about life in Oran. The lack of men was a grave problem, he went on, because no soldier wanted to come to these African outposts unless he was forced to: once a soldier arrived, he risked being stuck here for ever. That's why the garrisons were never filled. That year alone, they were four hundred men short, and the soldiers who did come were the dregs of Spain, ill-natured and unwilling; the unruly type, fit only for the galleys, or else raw recruits who had been cruelly deceived, like the contingent that had arrived last autumn: forty-two men who had enlisted for Italy, or so they were told. Once embarked in Cartagena, they were taken straight to Oran and there was nothing they could do about it; in fact, three had been hanged for mutiny, and the others had been assigned to the local regiment, with no hope of leaving. It was no coincidence that the Spanish phrase to describe a particularly unpromising enterprise was that it was about as likely to happen as sending a hundred lancers to Oran.

'That's how it is with the people here – they're desperate, ragged and hungry.' Copons lowered his voice. 'It's hardly surprising that the weakest-willed, or those who simply can't take any more, desert as soon as they can. Diego, do you remember Yndurain, the Basque? The one who defended that old hamlet in Fleurus, along with Utrera, Barrena and the others, until the only ones left were himself and a bugler?'

The Captain nodded and asked what had become of the man. Copons stared into his mug, turned aside in order to spit under the table and then looked at him again.

'He was here for five years and hadn't been paid for the last three. About two months ago, he had words with a sergeant. He stabbed him with his knife and jumped over the wall, along with another comrade who was on guard duty. I'm told that, with great difficulty, they finally arrived in

Mostaganem, where they promptly joined the Moors, but who can say ...'

He and the Captain exchanged knowing looks; my former master took another sip of wine and shrugged. It was a resigned shrug – for himself, for his friend and for the others, all of them, for poor, unhappy Spain. At that moment, I recalled some lines from a play I had seen a couple of years before in Madrid. They had shocked me then, but now I understood:

I, a soldier, on bended knee
Surrender my embattled blade;
I can no longer stand to be
Both brave and badly paid.

'Can you imagine,' the Captain suddenly said to Copons, 'Yndurain salaaming to Mecca?' He gave a kind of half-smile.

Copons gave an identical smile, only briefer. They were sceptical, entirely lacking in humour, the smiles of old soldiers with no illusions.

'And yet,' replied Copons, 'when the drum rolls, we never lack for swords.'

This was very true, as the passage of time would continue to prove. However abandoned, neglected and poverty-stricken these North African garrison towns were, there was rarely a shortage of men available to defend them when the need arose. And this was done without payment, without help and without glory, out of desperation, pride and concern for reputation. And so as not to end up as slaves. I know of what I speak, as you, dear reader, will learn from this story. There has always been a certain kind of man for whom, at the final moment, paying dearly for his life has brought some degree of consolation. Among Spaniards, this was a familiar story, and so it went until, one by one, those towns, forgotten by God and by the King, fell into the hands of Turks or Moors.

This had already happened in Algiers in the previous century, when Barbarossa attacked El Peñón. One hundred and fifty Spanish soldiers were blocking the entrance to the harbour there, and what happened? Spain abandoned them to their fate and they waited in vain for help to come. 'The Emperor,' according to his chronicler Father Prudencio de Sandoval, 'had more important matters to deal with at the time.' The soldiers fought like the men they were, and, after sixteen days of artillery fire that demolished the redoubt stone by stone, the Turks took only fifty prisoners who were battered and wounded. Barbarossa, enraged at such fierce resistance, had one of the prisoners, Captain Martín de Vargas, beaten to death with sticks. As for Larache, a few years after the events I am describing, it was attacked by twenty thousand enemy troops, who were repelled by a mere one hundred and fifty Spanish soldiers and fifty ex-soldiers who all fought like demons. The loss and recovery of the so-called Tower of the Jew was particularly fiercely fought – all to defend six thousand feet of city wall.

Oran, too, had honourably withstood various assaults; indeed, one provided the inspiration for Don Miguel de Cervantes' play *The Brave Spaniard*. We also owe to Cervantes – he was not a veteran of the Battle of Lepanto for nothing – two sonnets written in memory of the thousands of soldiers who died fighting, abandoned by their King – a very Spanish custom. The poems, which he included in *Don Quixote*, recall the defenders of the fort of La Goleta, opposite Tunis, who were killed after resisting twenty-two attacks by the Turks and killing twenty-five thousand of the enemy, so that, of the few Spaniards who survived, not one was captured unscathed.

'Life failed before valour did,' says one of those sonnets, and the second begins:

> From this battered, sterile land
> From these clods of earth brought low
> Three thousand soldiers' holy souls
> Rose, still living, to a better home.
> Having first, in vain, spent all
> The strength and effort of their arms,
> Until, at last, so few, so weary,
> To the enemy's blade they gave their life.

As I said, all this sacrifice was futile. After Lepanto, which marked the extreme point of the collision between the two great Mediterranean powers, the Turk had turned his interest more to Persia and Eastern Europe and our Kings had turned theirs to Flanders and the Atlantic. Philip IV showed no interest either, discouraged by his minister, the Count-Duke of Olivares, who disliked ports and galleys (not that he ever visited such places; the stench, he said, would give him a headache). Olivares despised sailors, too, for he considered theirs to be a low and vulgar occupation, fit only for Dutchmen – except, that is, when it brought back from the Indies the gold he needed for his wars. And so, what with Kings, their favourites and one thing and another, once the days of the great corsair fleets and the stalemate of various empires' naval chess games were over, the Mediterranean became a blurred frontier, the realm of low-grade pirates from the countries along its shores; and piracy, while it changed the course of many lives and many fortunes, did nothing to quicken the pulse of History. Also, more than a century had passed since the conclusion of the Christian Reconquest, a period that had lasted nearly eight hundred years during

which we Spaniards had forged our identity; and the subsequent policy of carrying the fight into Islamic territory,
once backed by Cardinal Cisneros and the old Duke of Medina
Sidonia, had now been abandoned. Africa held very little
interest for a Spain that was at daggers drawn with half the
world.

The garrison towns in Barbary were more symbolic than
anything else. They were maintained only in order to keep
the corsairs at bay, as well as France, Holland and England,
who, watching for the arrival of our galleons in Cádiz, did
their utmost to establish themselves there with their pirates,
as they had in the Caribbean. They were always snapping at
our heels, which is why we would not leave the way free for
them, although in the corsair republics they were already
well supplied with consuls and merchants. And although we
will return to this subject, I will only say that, years later,
Tangiers ended up belonging to the King of England for two
decades – thanks to the Portuguese rebellion – and that
during the siege of La Mamora in 1628, a year after the
events I am describing, the men digging the trenches and
directing the siegeworks were English sappers. Well, bastards
of a feather will flock together.

We went out for a stroll. Copons guided us through the
narrow, whitewashed streets with their tightly packed houses,
which, apart from the flat roofs, reminded me a little of
Toledo; the buildings had solid stone quoins and few windows,
the latter being set low and protected by blinds or shutters.
The damp sea air had caused the plaster and rendering to
flake, leaving dark ugly patches. Add to this the swarms of
flies, the clothes strung along washing lines, the ragged
children playing in courtyards, the occasional crippled soldier
sitting on a stone bench or on the steps outside his house,

eyeing us suspiciously, and you have a fairly faithful picture of how Oran appeared to me. Yet there was also something inescapably military about the place, for in essence the town was a vast barracks inhabited by soldiers and their families.

As I discovered, it was spread over quite a large area and was arranged on different levels, with no shortage of ordinary shops, as well as bakers, butchers and taverns. The grand, well-proportioned kasbah, which housed the governor and was the military headquarters, dated from the days of the Moors — some said from Roman times — and it contained a magnificent parade ground. The town also had a prison, a military hospital, a Jewish quarter — to my surprise, there were still Jews living there — and various monasteries: Franciscan, Mercedarian and Dominican; and in the eastern section of the medina, there were several ancient mosques that had been converted into churches, the main one having been transformed by Cardinal Cisneros, at the time of the Conquest, into the Church of Our Lady Victorious. And everywhere, in the streets, in the cramped squares, beneath canvas awnings and in doorways, people stood absolutely still — women glimpsed behind shutters; men, many of them veteran soldiers maimed and scarred and clothed in rags, their crutches leaning against the wall beside them — all of them staring into space. I thought of that former comrade, Yndurain, whom I had never met, leaping over the wall at dead of night, prepared to go over to the Moors rather than stay here, and a shudder ran through me.

'So what do you make of Oran?' Copons asked me.

'It's as if the town were sleeping,' I replied. 'All these people ... standing so still, staring.'

Copons nodded and wiped the sweat from his face.

'People only wake up when the Moors attack or when we organise a cavalcade,' he said. 'Having a scimitar at your throat or pelf in your pocket works wonders.' At this point, he turned to Captain Alatriste. 'And speaking of pelf, you've arrived at just the right time. Something's afoot.'

There was a flicker of interest in the Captain's pale eyes, beneath the broad brim of his hat. We had just reached the arched Tlemcen gate, on the opposite side of the town to the harbour, where a few reluctant stonemasons – Moorish slaves and Spanish convicts, I noticed – were trying to patch up the crumbling wall. Copons greeted the sentinels sitting in the shade and then we strolled outside the town. From there we could see the village of Ifre – inhabited by friendly Moors – situated about two harquebus shots from the town wall. That whole section was in a parlous state, with bushy plants growing in between the stones, many of which had fallen to the ground. The sentry box was dilapidated and roofless, and the wooden drawbridge over the narrow moat – almost entirely clogged with rubble and filth – was so rotten that it creaked beneath our feet. It was a miracle, I thought, that the town could resist any attack at all.

'A cavalcade?' asked Captain Alatriste.

Copons gave him a knowing look. 'Possibly.'

'Where?'

'No one's saying, but I suspect it will be over there.' He indicated the Tlemcen road that ran south through the nearby fields. 'There are a few Arabs in that direction who are none too happy about paying their taxes. There are livestock and people – so there'll be some decent booty to be had.'

'Hostile Moors?'

'They can be, if it serves our purpose.'

I was watching Copons and listening intently. This business of cavalcades intrigued me, and so I asked for more details.

'Remember those raids we used to go on in Flanders?' he said. 'Well, it's the same here: you leave at night, march quickly and in silence, and then you strike. We never go further than eight leagues from Oran, just in case.'

'And you take harquebuses?'

Copons shook his head. 'As few as possible. The whole thing is very much hand-to-hand so as not to waste gunpowder. If the village is near, we take people and livestock. If it's further away, we just take people and jewellery. Then we march back as fast as we can, see what we've got, sell it and share out the booty.'

'And there's plenty of it?'

'That depends. With slaves we can earn maybe forty *escudos* or more. A healthy female of child-bearing age, a strong Black man or a young Moor means thirty *reales* in the pot. If they're suckling babes and in good health, ten ... We did well out of the last cavalcade. I made eighty *escudos*, and that's double my year's wages.'

'Which is why the King doesn't pay you.'

'As if he damn well would ...'

We were nearing the fertile, leafy banks of the river, along which there were mills and a few waterwheels. I admired the view – the green terraced fields dotted with trees, the town with its kasbah perched halfway up the hill and, downriver, the sea, spreading out like a blue fan into the distance. An old Moor and a little boy passed us on their way into town. They were both wearing threadbare djellabas and carrying baskets full of vegetables on their backs.

'Without the cavalcades and what these fields produce,' added Copons, 'we wouldn't survive. Until you arrived, we'd spent four months with just a bushel of wheat per month and sixteen *reales* for any soldier with a family. You've seen the state of the people here, almost naked because their clothes are literally falling off their backs. It's the old Flanders trick, eh, Diego? You want your pay? Well, see that castle full of Dutchmen over there? Go and attack it and then we'll pay you. Moors or heretics, it's all the same to the King.'

'Do they take the royal quint from you here as well?' I asked.

'Of course,' said Copons. There was the King's quint, and the governor's 'jewel', as it was known. The latter got the pick of the bunch: the best slaves, even a village chief's entire family. Then it was the turn of the officers, with the normal soldiers last in line, according to how much they earned. Even people who hadn't gone on the cavalcade had a right to a share. Not forgetting the Church.

'You mean the monks dip their fingers in too?'

'You bet they do, to supplement their alms. The cavalcades benefit everyone, including the tradesmen and merchants, because later the Arabs come into town to buy back their loved ones, with money or produce, and the whole city becomes one great bazaar.'

We stopped beside a lean-to made of planks and roofed with palm leaves. At night it provided shelter for the guards at the bridge that connected the town and the fields with the castle of Rozalcazar on the other side of the Ouahran River, and with the castle of San Felipe further inland. The former, Copons told us, had almost completely collapsed and the latter had not yet been fully fortified. For although Oran was famous for its fortresses, it was all show, the town itself having only an old wall with hardly any moat to speak of, no ditches, no stockade, no covered entrance, no parapets and no redoubts. Indeed the town's only real fortifications were the living, breathing bodies of those who had to protect it. As some poet or other had said: our only gunpowder our swords, and our only walls the balls of Spain.

'Could *we* go?' I asked.

Copons glanced at me, then at Captain Alatriste, before

looking back at me. 'And where exactly do you want to go?' he asked with an indifferent air. I adopted a bold, soldierly demeanour and held his gaze without a flicker.

'Where else?' I replied coolly. 'With you, on the cavalcade.'

The two veterans again exchanged glances, and Copons rubbed his chin. 'What do you think, Diego?'

My former master studied me thoughtfully, then shrugged. 'A bit of extra money always comes in handy, I suppose.'

Copons agreed. The problem, he said, was that the whole garrison usually wanted to take part in these outings, in order to get a bigger share of the profits.

'Although sometimes,' he added, 'when there are galley crews in town, they do take reinforcements. In fact, you may be in luck, because there's a lot of fever about at the moment – brought on by drinking bad water, because there's no shortage of water here, but it's brackish – and a number of people are either ill or in hospital. I'll speak to Sergeant Major Biscarrués. He's a Flanders veteran, too, and a countryman of mine. But don't say a word. Not a word to anyone.'

He wasn't addressing the Captain when he said this. I returned his gaze – knowingly at first, then reproachfully. Copons stood thinking for a while, then turned to Captain Alatriste.

'The little lad's grown up,' he murmured, 'damn him.'

He looked me up and down, and his eyes lingered on my thumbs looped through my belt, next to my dagger and sword.

I heard the Captain sigh. He did so with a touch of irony, I think, and perhaps some weariness too.

'You don't know the half of it, Sebastián.'

3. THE CAVALCADE TO UAD BERRUCH

In the distance, a dog howled. Lying face down among the undergrowth, Diego Alatriste jerked awake. He had been resting his head on his arms, but with the instinct of an old soldier, he suddenly opened his eyes and looked up. He had not slept for long, only a matter of moments, but, like any experienced soldier, he took advantage of every opportunity to rest. In his line of work, you never knew when you might have another chance to sleep or eat or drink. Or empty your bladder. All around him, the slope was dotted with silent, motionless shapes, soldiers making the most of their last opportunity to do just that, rather than have their guts sliced open with their bladder still full. Alatriste unfastened his breeches and did likewise. A man fights best on an empty bladder and an empty belly, that's what his first sergeant in Flanders used to tell them. His name was Don Francisco del Arco, and he had died at Alatriste's side in the dunes of Nieuwpoort, by which time he'd been promoted to Captain. Alatriste had served under him towards the end of the last century, when he was only fifteen, in the war against the Estates General and France, when Amiens was attacked under cover of night and the city was sacked. Now that had been a profitable cavalcade, although the worst came later, when they spent nearly six months besieged by the French.

While he relieved himself, Captain Alatriste gazed up at the sky. He could see the occasional laggardly star, but the grey light of dawn was growing in the east. The bare hills still cast their shadow over the tents and walnut trees, and it wasn't bright enough yet to tell a white thread from a black in the large dried-up riverbed that the guides called Uad Berruch, five leagues from Oran. When he had finished, Alatriste lay down again, having first checked his belt and his weapons, and fastened his buff coat. The latter would weigh on him later, in the heat of the day, when the African sun was at its highest, but in the dawn chill, he was glad of it. And as soon as the attack began, he would be gladder still of that old buffalo hide, for a knife-thrust was a knife-thrust whether it came from a Moor, a Turk or a Lutheran. He recalled the various places where he had received such blows – eyebrow, forehead, hand, legs, hip, back ... He counted as far as nine if he included the harquebus shot and ten if he counted the burn to his arm. He didn't have room on his body for many more such wounds.

'Damned dog,' someone whispered nearby.

The dog howled again and, shortly afterwards, was joined by another. It would be bad news, thought Alatriste, if they had scented the presence of the marauders and were alerting the people sleeping in the encampment. He reckoned the group on the opposite side of the riverbed would be in position by now, keeping their horses well back, in case their whinnying spoiled the surprise. Two hundred men on that side and the same number on this, including fifty *mogataces* – more than enough to take on the three hundred or so Arabs, including women, children and the old, who were camped there with their animals, asleep and unaware of what awaited them.

He had been given the background the previous evening in Oran, when the order had come to get ready. He had found out more details during the six-hour march through the night, guided by *mogataz* scouts. They had marched hard, first in ranks and then in single file, down the Tlemcen road, along the riverbank, and then on past the lake, the house of the local marabout, the well and the fields, after which they headed west, skirting the hills before dividing into two groups to wait in silent ambush for dawn to break.

According to what he had been told, the people in the encampment belonged to the Beni Gurriaran tribe, who were considered by the Spanish garrison to be peaceful Moors. The agreement was that the garrison would protect them against other hostile Berber tribes in exchange for agreed quantities of wheat, barley and livestock to be handed over every year on predetermined dates. However, last year, the wheat and barley harvest had been late and the contribution rather sparse – a third of it was still owing to the garrison – and now the Moors were trying to avoid handing over the livestock that had been due in the spring. They still had not done so, and rumour had it that the people of Beni Gurriaran were preparing to move somewhere far from Uad Berruch, beyond the reach of the Spanish.

'So we're going to catch them napping,' Sergeant Major Biscarrués had said, 'before they can even say knife.'

Sergeant Major Biscarrués was from Aragon; he had seen long service as a soldier and had the confidence of the governor of Oran. He was a typical denizen of those North African towns: as hard as nails, his tanned skin parched and lined by the sun, the dust and by a life spent fighting, first in Flanders and latterly in Africa – with the sea at his back, the King in far-off Spain, God preoccupied with other matters, and the Moors only a sword's length away. He commanded a troop of soldiers whose one hope was to win some booty, and he carried out his job with due rigour, for these men of his were dangerous, potential deserters, fodder for the gallows and the galleys, and as ready to mutiny as they were to kill each other. He was, in short, a cruel but approachable bastard, and no more venal than most. That, at least, was how Sebastián Copons had described Biscarrués before we met him on that first evening.

The meeting had taken place in a small barracks in the kasbah, where we found him bent over a map spread out on the table, each of the map's four corners weighted down, respectively, by a jug of wine, a candlestick, a dagger and a small pistol. With him were two other men: a tall Moor with a white cloak over his shoulders, and a thin, dark individual dressed in Spanish fashion, clean-shaven and with a prominent nose.

'With your permission, Sergeant Major, may I introduce my friend Diego Alatriste, a fellow veteran of Flanders now deployed on the galleys in Naples. Diego, this is Don Lorenzo Biscarrués. These two men are Mustafa Chauni, the chief of our *mogataces*, and Aron Cansino, our interpreter.'

'Flanders, eh?' The sergeant major eyed Alatriste curiously. 'Amiens? Ostend?'

'Both.'

'A lot of rain has fallen since then. At least in Flanders, on those damned heretics. There hasn't been a drop here for months.'

They chatted for a while, discussing comrades they had in common, both alive and dead. Finally, Copons explained the present situation and obtained the sergeant major's permission for us to join the cavalcade, while Alatriste studied both him and the other two men. The *mogataz* was an Ulad-Galeb whose tribe had served Spain for three generations. In appearance he was typical of such men: grey-bearded and swarthy-complexioned; he wore slippers, a curved dagger at his waist, and his head was entirely shaved apart from the small tuft that some Moors left so that, if their head was cut off in battle, an enemy would not have to stick his fingers in the decapitated head's mouth or eyes in order to carry it off as a trophy. He led the harka of one hundred and fifty warriors chosen from among his tribe or family – which, in those parts, amounted to the same thing. They lived with their wives and children in the village of Ifre and nearby encampments. As long as those men were assured of pay and booty, they were prepared to fight under the St Andrew's cross with a courage and loyalty one would like to have seen in many subjects of the Catholic King.

As for the other man, it came as no surprise to Alatriste that a Jew should act as interpreter in the town, for although the Jews had been expelled from Spain, their presence was tolerated in the Spanish enclaves in North Africa for reasons to do with commerce, money and their mastery of the Arabic language. As he found out later, among the twenty or so families living in the Jewish quarter, the Cansinos had been trusted interpreters since the middle of the last century, and even though they observed Mosaic law – Oran was alone in having a synagogue – they had always shown absolute competence as well as loyalty to the King. This was why the various governors of the town had honoured and rewarded them, allowing the profession to pass from father to son. The translators combined their linguistic skills with a little espionage, for all the Israelite communities in Barbary were in regular communication.

The other reason why the Oran Jews were tolerated was their vital importance as merchants and traders, despite the heavy taxes imposed on them because of their religion. When times were hard, they were the ones who lent the governor money or wheat or whatever he might need. In addition, there was the role they played in the slave trade: on the one hand, they mediated in the ransoming of captives and, on the other, they owned most of the Turks and Moors sold in

Oran. After all, regardless of whether they worshipped Mary, Mohammed or Moses, as far as everyone – Jew, Moor or Spaniard – was concerned, a silver coin was a silver coin. As Don Francisco de Quevedo would have said, Sir Money was a powerful gentleman. And the man was a fool who would bother going to light a candle at anyone else's altar.

The dog barked again in the distance, and Alatriste touched the well-primed pistol at his waist. In a way, he thought, he wouldn't mind if the dog kept on barking so that the Moors in the encampment, or at least some of them, were awake, with scimitar in hand, when Sergeant Major Biscarrués gave the order to attack. Slitting the throats of sleeping men in order to steal their livestock, women and children was easier than slitting their throats while they were awake, but it would take a vast amount of wine to wash the blood from his memory.

'At the ready.'

In a whisper that gradually grew louder, the order was passed down the line. When it reached me, I, too, passed it on, and heard the words move off into the crouching shadows until it vanished like the fading of an echo. I ran my tongue over my cracked lips and then clenched my teeth to stop them chattering in the cold. I tied on my espadrilles, removing the rags in which I had wrapped both my sword and the blade of my half-pike to avoid making any inopportune noise. I looked around. I couldn't see Captain Alatriste among the various silhouettes in the dawn light, but I knew he was lying with the others close by. I could see Sebastián Copons, a dark, motionless figure, smelling of sweat, greased leather and steel burnished with oil. There were similar figures among the lentiscus bushes, the prickly pears and the thistles that in Barbary are called *arracafes*.

'We attack in two credos' time,' came the new order.

Some, either out of devotion or simply to calculate the time, started mumbling the creed out loud. I heard them all around me, in the half-darkness, in different accents and intonations: Basque, Valencian, Asturian, Andalusian, Castilian; Spaniards who only came together to pray or to kill. *Credo in unum Deum, patrem omnipotentem, factorem caeli et terrae* ... Such pious murmurings as a prelude to bloody battle always struck me as odd; all those male voices whispering holy words, asking God to let them survive the fight, to capture gold and slaves aplenty, to be granted a safe return to Oran and to Spain, laden with booty and with no enemies nigh, for as they all knew – Copons and the Captain had both emphasised this point – the most dangerous thing in the world was fighting Moors on their own territory and then withdrawing and finding oneself pursued down those dried-up riverbeds and through that arid landscape, beneath the implacable sun, with no water, or else paying in blood for each drop, or being wounded and falling into the hands of Arabs, who had all the time in the world to kill you. Perhaps that was why the murmur was spreading among the crouching shadows: *Deum de Deo, lumen de lumine, Deum verum de Deo vero* ...

After a while, I found myself mechanically murmuring the same words, without thinking, like someone singing along to a particularly catchy ballad. Then, when I realised what I was doing, I prayed with real devotion: *Et exspecto resurrectionem mortuorum et vitam venturi saeculi, amen.* At the time, I was still young enough to believe in such things, and a few other things besides.

'Forward for Santiago ... for Santiago and Spain!'

The words were spoken in a howl, punctuated by a few sharp blasts on the bugle, while the men scrambled to their feet and ran through the undergrowth, holding high the King's standard and flag. I stood up too and ran forwards, aware of shots being fired on the far side of the encampment, where the darkness was dotted with flashes of harquebus fire.

'Forward for Spain! Attack! Attack!'

It was awkward running along the sandy bed of the river, and my legs felt like lead when I reached the other side, where a hawthorn hedge protected the livestock. I tripped over a motionless body on the ground, ran a few steps further, only to scratch myself on the spiny branches. God's teeth! There was now the sound of harquebus fire on our side too, while the silhouettes of my comrades rushed like a torrent through the tents. I caught sudden glimpses of lit fires, of terrified figures who either fought or fled. To the shouting of Spaniards and *mogataces*, reinforced by the thundering hooves of our horsemen charging in from the other side, was added the cries of dozens of women and children, wrenched from sleep, who were now emerging from their tents, clinging to each other or running to their menfolk, also barely awake, but who, in trying to protect them, fought desperately and died. I saw Sebastián Copons and others hurl themselves among these people, cutting and slashing, and I followed suit, wielding my half-pike and losing it at my first encounter, when I plunged it into the half-naked body of a bearded Arab who emerged from a tent bearing a scimitar. He fell at my feet without uttering a sound, but I didn't have time to recover my pike, because just as I was trying to, another young Moor, even younger than me, came out of the same tent, in his nightshirt, and started lashing out at me with a dagger, so fiercely that if he had hit home, Christ and the Devil would have been well served, and the people of Oñate would have had one fellow countryman less. I staggered backwards, drawing my sword – an excellent galley sword, broad and short and bearing the mark of Toledo on its blade. Fighting back with more aplomb now, I managed to slice off half his nose with my first blow and the fingers of his hand with my second. He was already on the ground when I delivered a third and final blow, slitting his throat with a backward slash. I peered cautiously inside the tent and saw a huddle of women and children in one corner, screaming and shouting in their own language. I let the curtain fall, turned and went about my business.

It was nearly over. Diego Alatriste kicked away the Moor he had just killed, removed his sword from the man's body and looked around. The Arabs were barely resisting now, and most of the attackers were more concerned with plundering whatever they could find – almost as if they were Englishmen. He could still hear harquebus fire in the encampment, but the screams of rage, despair and death had given way to the groans of the wounded, the moans of prisoners, and the buzz of flies swarming above the pools of blood.

The soldiers and *mogataces* were rounding up, as if they were mere livestock, women, children, the old, and any men who had thrown down their arms. Others were collecting any objects of value and herding together the real livestock. The women – their children clinging to their skirts or clutched to their bosom – were screaming and striking their faces at the sight of the corpses of fathers, husbands, brothers and children; and some, overwhelmed by pain and rage, were trying to scratch the soldiers, who were obliged to beat them off. The men were clustered together in a separate group; bewildered, bruised, and terrified, they squatted in the dust, guarded by swords, pikes and harquebuses. Some – adults and older men who were trying somehow to preserve their dignity – were shoved around or slapped in the face by the victorious soldiers.

The order, as usual, was not to kill anyone who could bring in some money, but this was the soldiers' way of avenging the half-dozen or so comrades who had lost their lives in the assault.

This displeased Alatriste, who was of the view that while one could kill a man, one should not humiliate him, still less in front of his friends and family. That century, however, like most centuries, was not particularly abundant in scruples. Embarrassed, he looked across at the outskirts of the encampment. Among the hills, the soldiers on horseback were pursuing any Moors who had managed to escape and were hiding among the reedbeds and fig trees. The captives were led back, their hands tied to the tails of the horses.

Some of the plundered tents were on fire now, with all the furniture, pots, silver, carpets and clothes piled up outside. Sergeant Major Biscarrués, who was keeping an eye on everything, shouted to his men to look lively and get the booty together so that they could leave. Diego Alatriste saw him squint at the newly risen sun and then glance anxiously about him. It wasn't hard for Alatriste, a fellow soldier, to guess his thoughts. A column of tired Spaniards, taking with them a hundred or so livestock and more than two hundred captives, would be extremely vulnerable to attack by hostile Moors if they were not safe inside the walls of Oran by sunset.

Alatriste's throat was as dry as the sand and stone he walked upon. God's teeth, he thought, I can't even spit out the dust and blood that are making my tongue stick to my palate. He looked about him and met the friendly but fierce gaze of a red-bearded *mogataz* who was earnestly beheading a dead Arab. Closer to him, an old Moorish woman was kneeling down tending a badly wounded man, whose head rested in her lap. She had a wrinkled face, with blue tattoos on forehead and hands, and when Alatriste stopped in front of her, sword still in his hand, she looked up at him with blank eyes.

'*Ma*. Water. *Ma*,' he said.

She didn't respond until he touched her shoulder with the point of his sword. Then she gestured indifferently towards a large tent and, ignoring everything else, continued to tend the wounded Moor who lay moaning on the ground. Alatriste headed for the tent, drew back the curtain and stepped inside.

As soon as he did so, he realised that he was going to have problems.

I spotted Captain Alatriste in the distance, among all the plundering and the comings and goings of soldiers and prisoners, and I was glad to see that he was safe. I tried to call out to him, but he didn't hear me, so I headed in his direction, avoiding the burning tents, the heaps of clothing, the wounded and the dead. I saw him go inside a large, black tent, and I saw, too, that someone went in after him. I couldn't quite see who it was, but he looked like one of our Moors, a *mogataz*. Then a corporal stopped me and ordered me to keep watch over a group of Arabs while they were being tied up. This delayed me briefly, but, when I had finished, I continued towards the tent. I lifted the curtain, crouched down to go inside and was astonished by what I saw: in one corner, on an untidy pile of mats and rugs, lay a young Moorish woman, half-naked, whom the Captain was helping to get dressed. She had a bruise on her tear-stained face and was wailing like an animal in torment. At her feet lay a child of only a few months, waving its arms, and next to her was one of our soldiers, a Spaniard, his belt unbuckled, his breeches round his knees and his head blown apart. Another Spaniard, fully clothed but with his throat slit from ear to ear, lay face-up near the entrance, blood gushing from his wound. In the few moments in which I was still able to think clearly, it occurred to me that the very same blood was staining the blade of the curved dagger that a surly, bearded *mogataz* had pressed to my throat as soon as I entered. All of these things – well, put yourself in my place, dear reader – drew from me an exclamation of surprise that made the Captain turn round.

'It's all right. He's like a son to me,' he said quickly. 'He won't talk.'

The *mogataz*'s breath, which I could feel on my face, stopped for a moment as he studied me closely with bright, dark eyes edged with such thick eyelashes they could have been those of a woman. That, however, was the only delicate thing about his tanned, weather-beaten face; and his pointed reddish beard accentuated the fierce expression that froze my blood. He must have been about thirty or so, and he was of average build, but with powerful shoulders and arms. Apart from the usual lock of hair at the back, his head was shaven, and he wore a long scarf looped about his neck, silver earrings in each ear and, on his left cheekbone, a strange blue tattoo in the form of a cross. He duly removed the dagger from my throat and wiped it on his grey-striped burnous before putting it back in the leather scabbard at his waist.

What happened?' I asked the Captain.

He slowly got to his feet. The woman, filled with fear and shame, covered herself with a grey-brown veil. The *mogataz* said a few words to her in her own language – something like *barra barra* – and she, picking up her crying child and wrapping it in the same veil, walked lightly past us, head bowed, and left the tent.

'What happened,' said the Captain calmly, 'is that these two valiants and I had a disagreement over the meaning of the word "booty".'

He crouched down to pick up the pistol he had fired and stuck it in his belt. Then he looked at the *mogataz*, who was still standing in the entrance to the tent, and something like a smile appeared on his lips.

'Things weren't going too well for me when this Moor appeared and took my part.'

He was studying the *mogataz* intently, from top to toe, and he seemed to like what he saw.

'Speak Spanish?' he asked.

'I do,' the Moor replied in good Castilian.

The Captain looked at the dagger in the man's belt.

'That's a good knife you have there.'

'I think so.'

'And an even better hand.'

'*Uah.* So they say.'

They regarded each other for a few moments in silence.

'What's your name?'

'Aixa Ben Gurriat.'

If I was expecting more words, more explanations, I was disappointed. A half-smile similar to the Captain's appeared on the Moor's bearded face.

'Let's go,' the Captain said, taking one last look at the corpses. 'But first, we'd better set fire to the tent. That way we can avoid any awkward questions.'

This proved to be an unnecessary precaution. No one missed the two ruffians – we learned later that they were a pair of friendless, low-life, good-for-nothings – and their names were simply added to the list of men lost. As for the return journey, it proved hard and dangerous, but triumphant too. The road from Tlemcen to Oran, beneath a vertical sun that reduced our shadows to a dark line at our feet, was filled by a long column of soldiers, captives, plunder and livestock, with the beasts – sheep, goats, cows and the occasional camel – in the vanguard, in the care of *mogataces* and Moors from Ifre. Before leaving Uad Berruch, however, we experienced a moment of great tension, when the interpreter, Cansino, after interrogating the prisoners, fell silent, turning this way and that. He reluctantly informed Sergeant Major Biscarrués that we had attacked the wrong place, that the *mogataz* guides had made a mistake – or had deliberately misled us – and directed us to an encampment inhabited by peaceful Moors who always paid their dues promptly. We had killed thirty-six of them, and I assure you I have never seen anyone as angry as the sergeant major became then. He turned bright scarlet, the veins in his neck and forehead bulged as if they were about to burst, and he swore that he would have every guide hanged, along with their forefathers, their whorish mothers and their porcine progenitors.

The fit of rage was quickly over, though. After all, there was nothing to be done, and so, ever practical and prepared for whatever life might throw at him, Biscarrués finally calmed down. Regardless of whether they were peaceful or hostile, he concluded, the Moors would still fetch a good price in Oran. They were certainly hostile now, and there was no more to be said.

'What's done is done,' he said, settling the matter. 'We'll be more careful next time. So not a word, eh, and if anyone's tongue runs away with him, by Christ, I'll tear it out myself.'

And so, after tending the wounded and having something to eat – bread baked in the ashes, a few dates and some curdled milk we'd found at the encampment – we marched with a lighter step, harquebuses at the ready and keeping a watchful eye open, hoping to find ourselves safely back in town before nightfall. And on we went, with the livestock in the vanguard, followed by most of the troops and the baggage, and then, in the middle, the captives, of whom there were two hundred and forty-eight, men and women and those children of an age to walk. A select squad of soldiers, armed with pikes and harquebuses, brought up the rear, while the cavalry either rode on ahead or protected our flanks, just in case any hostile Moors should try to block our retreat or deprive us of water. There were, in fact, a few minor fights and skirmishes, and before we reached a place known as the hermit's well, where there were plenty of palm trees and carobs, the Arabs, a good number of whom were on the lookout for stragglers or some other opportunity, made a serious attempt to keep us from the water: a hundred or so bold horsemen, shouting and hurling the usual obscenities, attacked our rearguard. However, when our harquebusiers prepared their weapons and then sprayed them with lead, the horsemen turned tail, leaving some of their men dying on the field.

We were in high spirits over our victory and the booty, and were eager to reach Oran and claim our share. The lines from a well-known song came spontaneously to my young lips:

Such was the custom of the age,
That a fiercely gallant knife or sword,
Which put to death a slew of Moors
Would also glorify Our Lord.

Nevertheless, two incidents overshadowed any pleasure I felt during the retreat from Uad Berruch. One involved a newborn baby who, though dying in his mother's arms, was still not spared the rigours of the march. When he saw this, the chaplain, Father Tomás Rebollo, who had accompanied the cavalcade as part of his duties, summoned the sergeant

major and said that since the child was dying, the mother
had therefore lost all her maternal rights, which meant that
he could legitimately baptise the child against her will. Given
that there was no council of theologians on hand to pronounce
on the matter, Biscarrués, who had other things on his mind,
told the priest to do as he thought best; the priest, ignoring
the mother's protests, snatched the child from her and baptised
it there and then, with a few drops of water, oil and salt. The
child died shortly afterwards, and the chaplain congratulated
himself, saying that, on such a day – when so many enemies
of God, members of the pernicious sect of Mohammed, had
been condemned to Hell – an angel had been sent up to
Heaven to learn more of its secrets and to confound its
enemies, etcetera, etcetera. Later, we learned that the Mar-
chioness of Velada, the governor's wife – a very pious woman
who gave alms, said her rosary and took communion daily –
had praised Father Tomás's decision and ordered that the
mother be sent for so that she could console her and convince
her that she would one day be reunited with her son, thereby
attempting to convert her to the one true faith. This proved
impossible. On the same night that we arrived back in Oran,
the woman hanged herself out of despair and shame.

The other lingering memory is that of a little Moorish boy
of about six or seven who kept pace with the mules on which
were tied the heads of the dead Arabs. At the time, the
governor of Oran offered a reward – or, rather, said he
would – for every Moor killed in an act of war, and, as I said,
the raid on Uad Berruch was deemed to be just that. And so,
to provide the necessary proof, we were carrying the heads of
thirty-six adult Moors, who would add a few *maravedíes* to
our share of the booty. Anyway, this boy was walking alongside
a mule on which a dozen heads were slung in two bunches
on either side of the saddle. Well, if the life of any clear-

thinking man is full of ghosts that come to him in the dark and keep him from sleeping – and by God, my life has more than its share – what stays with me is the image of that grubby, barefoot, runny-nosed child, his tears carving dirty trails down his dusty cheeks, walking next to the mule, and returning again and again, however often the guards drove him off, to brush away the flies from his father's severed head.

The House of La Salka was both a brothel and a smoke-room, and that is where we set up our quarters the following day, as soon as the sale of booty was over. The whole of Oran had been celebrating since the previous night when, with the last light of day, once we had left the livestock in the pens at Las Piletas, near the river, we had made our triumphal entry through the Tlemcen gate, marching in squadrons with the captives before us, flanked by soldiers bearing arms. We marched along the road which was lit up with torches, heading straight for the main church. There, the slaves, hands bound, were paraded past the Holy Sacrament that the priest had brought to the door, accompanied by clergy, cross and holy water. And once the *Te Deum* had been sung in recognition of our victory, every owl went off to his own olive tree until the following day, when the real celebrations began, for the sale of slaves proved highly lucrative, bringing in the goodly sum of forty-nine thousand six hundred ducats. Once the governor's share had been deducted as well as the King's quint, which, in Oran, was used to buy supplies and munitions, and once what was owed to the officers, the Church, the veterans' hospital and the *mogataces* had been paid out, the Captain and I found ourselves richer by five hundred and sixty *reales* each, which meant that we had the agreeable weight of seventy fine pieces of eight in our respective purses. Sebastián Copons, given his rank and position, earned somewhat more.

As soon as we had collected our money from the house of a relative of the interpreter Aron Cansino – we almost had to get our knives out at one point because he wanted to fob us off with coins that had not been weighed or that were worn too smooth at the edges – we decided, naturally enough, to spend a little of it. And there the three of us were, in the house of La Salka, enjoying ourselves to the hilt.

The owner of the brothel was a middle-aged Moorish woman, baptised a Christian, the widow of a soldier, and an old acquaintance of Sebastián Copons, who assured us that, within reasonable limits, she was thoroughly trustworthy. The whorehouse was near the Marina gate, sitting among the terraced houses behind the old tower. From the roof there was a pleasant view over the countryside, with the castle of San Gregorio to the left, dominating the bay full of galleys and other ships below; and in the background, like a greyish wedge between the port and the blue immensity of the Mediterranean, stood the fort of Mazalquivir, its gigantic cross standing before it.

The sun was already setting over the sea, and its warm rays fell on Captain Alatriste, Copons and myself as we sat on soft leather cushions in one corner of the roof terrace, our every wish granted, well supplied with drink and food and the other things one finds in such places. We were accompanied by three of La Salka's girls with whom, shortly before, we had shared rather more than words, although we had stopped short of the final trench; for the Captain and Copons, very sensibly, had managed to persuade me that it was one thing to take pleasure in female company and quite another to loose one's bow, so to speak, and risk catching the French disease or any of the many other illnesses with which such public women – extremely public in the case of Oran – could ruin the health and life of the unwary. They were decent enough doxies. Two of them, not unattractive Christians from Andalusia, had come to earn their living in Oran having suffered far worse vicissitudes in the bordellos of the Sahara, which, in their profession, were the deadest of dead ends; the third was a renegade Moor, too dark for Spanish tastes, but a handsome creature, and skilled in the type of art not written about in books. At the clink of our new silver coins, La Salka had brought them to us, telling us how clean and sensual they were, these graduates in the art of the beast with two backs, although, as I say, we ourselves did not indulge in the latter. Even so, I would give my oath as a good Basque that La Salka was not exaggerating in terms of the woman who fell to me – the Moor, because I was the youngest.

But we did not only eat and drink, for as well as encountering some unusual spices, rather too strong for my taste, it was also the first time I had smoked the Moorish weed, prepared with great dexterity by one of the women, who mixed it with tobacco in long wooden pipes with metal bowls. I had never been keen on the stuff, not even in the form of the snuff that Don Francisco de Quevedo so enjoyed, but I was a novice in Barbary and eager to try anything new. And so, although the Captain declined the experience and Copons took only a couple of puffs, I smoked a whole pipeful and sat there, flaccid and smiling, my head spinning and my words slurred, feeling as if my body were floating above the town and the sea.

This did not prevent me from taking part in the conversation, which, despite the pleasant situation and the money we had on us, was not, at that particular moment, a cheerful one. We knew by then that our galley was due to weigh anchor in two days' time, and Copons, who would have liked to come with us to Naples or, indeed, anywhere, would have to stay in Oran, because the powers that be would still not grant him licence to leave.

'So,' he said sombrely, 'it looks as if I'll be left to rot here until Kingdom come.' With that, he downed a whole pitcher of Málaga wine – which, although a little sour, was strong and flavourful.

I was gazing distractedly at the three doxies, who were standing at the far end of the terrace, chatting and waving to passing soldiers. La Salka knew how freely money flowed after a cavalcade and her own corsairs were trained not to miss any opportunity to drum up trade.

'Perhaps there is a way ...' Captain Alatriste said.

We both looked at him with interest, especially the usually impassive Copons, who had an expectant gleam in his eye. He knew his former comrade never spoke lightly.

'Do you mean a way of getting Sebastián out of Oran?' I asked.

'Yes.'

Copons placed one hand on the Captain's arm, exactly on the spot where the Captain had inflicted a burn on himself years before in Seville, when he was interrogating that Genoan Garaffa.

'God's teeth, Diego, I'm not going to desert. I never have before, and I'm not going to start now.'

The Captain smoothed his moustache and smiled at his friend. It was a rare smile in him, both affectionate and frank.

'No, I'm talking about you leaving here honourably, with your licence neatly rolled up inside a tin tube. As is proper.'

Copons seemed bewildered. 'But I've told you already that Sergeant Major Biscarrués won't grant me a licence to leave. No one gets out of Oran, you know that. Only those who are passing through.'

Alatriste glanced over at the three women and lowered his voice. 'How much money have you got?'

Copons frowned, wondering what on earth that had to do with anything. Then he understood and shook his head.

'Out of the question,' he said. 'Even with the money I earned from the cavalcade, I wouldn't have enough.'

'How much?' insisted the Captain.

'Not counting what I'm going to spend here, about eighty *escudos*, perhaps a few *maravedíes* more. But as I said—'

'Just suppose you struck lucky, what's the first thing you would do in Naples?'

Copons laughed. 'What a question! In Italy and without a penny in my pocket? I'd enlist again, of course. With the two of you, if I could.'

They sat looking at each other for a while. I was gradually descending from the clouds and was watching them closely. The mere idea that Copons might come with us to Naples made me want to shout for joy.

'Diego ...'

Despite the doubtful tone in which Copons uttered the Captain's name, the hopeful gleam was still there in his eyes. The Captain took another sip of wine, thought for a moment longer and nodded.

'Your eighty *escudos*, plus my sixty or so from the cavalcade, that makes ...'

He was tapping his fingers against the brass tray that served as a table, counting it out, then he turned to look at me. The Captain may have been fast with a sword, but his speed did not extend to arithmetic. I forced the last vaporous clouds from my mind, rubbing my forehead.

'One hundred and forty,' I said.

'That's nothing,' Copons replied. 'Biscarrués would demand five times that amount for me to buy myself out.'

'We have five times that amount, at least I think we do. Let's see ... One hundred and forty, plus my two hundred from the galliot we sold in Melilla.'

'You have that much money?' asked an astonished Copons.

'Yes, the strokesman – a gipsy from Perchel, condemned to ten years on the galley and more feared than the galleymaster himself – keeps it safe for me at half a *real*'s interest per week. What does that come to, Íñigo?'

'Three hundred and forty,' I said.

'Right, add in your sixty *escudos*.'

'What?'

'Add them in,' he said, his pale eyes piercing me like daggers. 'What does that make?'

'Four hundred.'

'That's not enough. Add in your two hundred from the galliot.'

I opened my mouth to protest, but from the look the Captain gave me, I realised it was pointless. The last threads of cottony cloud vanished at once. Farewell, savings, I said to myself, my head suddenly clear. It had been wonderful to feel rich – while it lasted.

'Six hundred *escudos* exactly,' I said, resigned now.

Captain Alatriste turned to Copons, his face radiant.

'With the back pay that's owed to you – which, when it arrives, will go straight into your sergeant major's pocket – that's more than enough.'

Copons swallowed hard, looking from me to the Captain and back again, as if the words had got stuck in his throat. I couldn't help, once again, remembering him in different situations: on the front line at the battle of the Ruyter Mill, deep in the mud of the Breda trenches, smeared with gunpowder and blood at the Terheyden redoubt, sword in hand in a Sevillean garden, or scrambling aboard the *Niklaasbergen* at Barra de Sanlúcar. Always the same: small, silent, wiry, hard.

'God's teeth,' he said.

4. THE *MOGATAZ*

Having donned hats and buckled on swords, we left the whorehouse just as evening came on and the first shadows began to fill the most secluded corners of Oran's steep streets. It was a very pleasant temperature at that hour, perfect for a stroll. The town's inhabitants were sitting on chairs or stools at the doorways of their houses and a few shops were still open, lit by oil lamps and tallow candles.

The streets were full of soldiers from the galleys, as well as from the barracks, all celebrating their good fortune on the cavalcade. We stopped again to wet our whistles – the wine this time was a decent claret – and stood leaning against a wall, opposite a small makeshift tavern installed in the porch of a house and attended by an old cripple. While we were there, a party of five captives, led by a constable, came down the street. They were all chained together, three men and two women, and had obviously been among those who were sold that morning. They were being led home under guard by their new master, who was dressed all in black and wearing a ruff and a sword. He had the look of a functionary grown rich by stealing the wages of the men who had risked their lives capturing these people. All five, including the two women, had been branded on the face with an S that identified them as slaves, and they walked along, heads bowed, resigned to their fate. Branding them was quite unnecessary, and some considered it old-fashioned and cruel, but the Law still allowed slave-owners to mark captives so that they could be identified should they attempt to run away. I saw that the Captain had looked away in disgust, and I imagined the mark – made not with red-hot iron, but with cold steel – that I would make on the master of those poor unfortunates if ever I had the chance. I hoped that when this man travelled back to Spain, he would be captured by some Berber pirates, end up in the prisons of Algiers and be soundly beaten. Although, I thought bitterly, people like him had more than enough money to buy their freedom. Only poor soldiers and humble folk – and thousands were captured at sea or on the Spanish coast – would rot there in Tunis, Bizerta, Tripoli or Constantinople, with no one to pay their ransom.

It was while I was absorbed in these thoughts that I noticed someone walk past and then stop a little further on to observe us. I realised that it was the *mogataz* who had helped Captain Alatriste in Uad Berruch. He was wearing the same clothes: grey-striped burnous and the classic Arab *rexa* draped loosely about his neck, so that his shaven head – apart from the warrior's lock of hair at the back – was bare. The long dagger that had, for a moment, been pressed against my throat – it still made my skin prickle to think of its blade – was tucked in his sash, inside its leather sheath. I turned to point him out to Captain Alatriste, but realised that he had already spotted him.

They observed each other in silence at a distance of six or seven paces, the *mogataz* standing quite still among the passing crowds, calmly holding the Captain's gaze, as if he were waiting for something. Finally, the Captain touched the brim of his hat and bowed slightly. This, in a soldier and a man like him, was more than mere courtesy, especially when directed at a Moor, even if he was a *mogataz* and, therefore, a friend of Spain. Nevertheless, the Moor accepted this greeting as his natural due and responded with an affirmative nod. Then, with equal aplomb, he seemed to continue on his way, although I thought I saw him stop again further on, at the far end of the street, in the shadow of a low archway.

'Let's go and see Fermín Malacalza,' Copons said to the Captain. 'He'll be pleased to see you.'

This Malacalza fellow, whom I did not know, was a former comrade of the Captain and Copons, and was now based in the Oran barracks. He had shared dangers and miseries with them in Flanders when he was a corporal, and risen from the ranks, in the squadron in which Alatriste, Copons and my father, Lope Balboa, had all fought. Copons explained that Malacalza, old before his time, in ill health and invalided out of the army, had stayed on in Oran as he had family there. As poor as everyone else, he survived thanks to the help of a few fellow soldiers – among them Copons – who, whenever they happened to have a little money, would visit him with a few *maravedíes*. And now there was the added satisfaction that Malacalza, as a former soldier, albeit retired, was eligible to receive a small portion of the booty won in Uad Berruch. Copons had been charged with delivering it to him, and I suspect he had added a few coins from his own pocket.

'The Moor is following us,' I said to the Captain.

We were near Malacalza's house, walking down a wretched, narrow street in the upper part of the city, with men sitting at the doors of their houses and children playing among the grime and rubble. And it was true; the *mogataz*, who had stayed close by after he had passed us outside the tavern, was some twenty paces behind, never coming too near, but making no attempt to hide either.

The Captain glanced over his shoulder and observed the Moor for a moment. 'The street's a free place.'

It was odd, I thought, that a Moor should be out after sunset. In Oran, as in Melilla, they were strict about that, wanting to avoid any nasty surprises; and when the town gates were closed, all Moors, apart from a privileged few, usually left, with those who had come in during the day to sell vegetables, meat and fruit going back to Ifre or to their respective encampments. As I have said, any remaining Moors usually stayed in the guarded area known as the *morería*, near the kasbah, until the following day. This man appeared to move about freely, however, which made me think that he was known and in possession of the necessary safe-conducts. This only aroused my curiosity more, but I stopped thinking about him as soon as we reached the house of Fermín Malacalza, who, I could not forget, had been a comrade of my father's.

Had my father survived the harquebus shot that killed him beneath the walls of Jülich, he would perhaps have met the same sad fate as the man who now faced me: a scrawny, grey-haired remnant, consumed by poverty; fifty years old, but looking more like seventy − seventeen of those years spent in Oran − lame in one leg and with his scarred skin the colour of grubby parchment. His eyes were the only part of his face that had retained their vigour − for even his moustache was the matt grey of ashes − and those eyes glittered with pleasure when he looked up from his chair at the door of his house and saw before him the smile of Captain Alatriste.

'By Beelzebub, the whore that bore him, and all the Lutheran devils in Hell!'

He insisted that we come in and tell him what brought us there and so that we could meet his family. The small, dark house was lit by a guttering oil lamp and smelled of mould and rancid stew. A soldier's sword, with a broad guard and large quillons, hung on the wall. Two chickens were pecking at the crumbs of bread on the floor, and beside the water-jug, a cat was greedily devouring a mouse. After many years in Barbary, and having lost all hope of ever leaving there as a soldier, Malacalza had ended up marrying a Moorish woman he bought after a cavalcade. He had forced her to be baptised a Christian, and she had since given him five children who, barefoot and ragged, were making a tremendous racket, running in and out of the house.

'Hey!' he called to his wife. 'Bring us some wine!'

We protested, because we were already a little tipsy after our sojourn at La Salka's and at the tavern in the street, but Malacalza would not take 'No' for an answer.

'We may lack for everything here,' he said, hobbling about the one room, unrolling a rough mat and bringing more stools to the table, 'but we never lack for a glass of wine for two old comrades to moisten their gullets.

'Or, rather, three,' he added, when he learned that I was the son of Lope Balboa.

His wife came in shortly afterwards, a dark, stocky woman, still young, but worn out by childbirth and hard work. Her hair was caught back in a plait, and she was dressed like a Spanish woman apart from her slippers, her silver bangles and the blue tattoos on the backs of her hands. We doffed our hats and sat down at the rickety pine table, while she poured wine into a motley selection of chipped mugs before withdrawing to one corner without saying a word.

'A fine woman,' said the Captain politely.

Malacalza nodded brusquely. 'She's clean and she's honest. A bit quick-tempered, but obedient. Moorish women make good wives, as long as you keep your eye on them. A lot of Spanish women could learn a thing or two from them, instead of putting on airs.'

'Indeed,' said the Captain gravely.

A skinny child of three or four with dark, curly hair approached shyly and clung to his father, who kissed him tenderly and sat the boy on his lap. The other four, the oldest of whom could not have been more than twelve, watched us from the door. They were barefoot and had dirty knees. Copons put some coins on the table and Malacalza looked at them, without touching them. Then he glanced up at Captain Alatriste and winked.

'As you see, Diego,' he said, raising his mug of wine to his lips and indicating the room with a sweeping gesture of his other hand, 'a veteran of the King's army. Thirty-five years of service, four wounds, rheumatism in my bones,' he slapped his injured thigh, 'and one lame leg. Not a bad record really, given that I started in Flanders before either you or I, or Sebastián here, or poor Lope, may he rest in peace,' he raised his glass to me in homage, 'were even of shaving age.'

He spoke without great bitterness and in the resigned tones of the profession, like someone merely stating what every mother's son knows. The Captain leaned towards him across the table.

'Why don't you go back to Spain? You're free to do so.'

'Go back? To what?' Malacalza was stroking his son's curly black locks. 'To show off my bad leg at the door of a church and beg for alms along with the others?'

'You could go back to your village. You're from Navarra, aren't you? From the Baztán valley?'

'Yes, Alzate. But what would I do there? If anyone still remembers me, which I doubt, can't you just imagine the neighbours pointing and saying: there's another one who swore he'd come back rich and a gentleman, but look at him now, a poor cripple, living off the charity of nuns. At least here, there's always the odd cavalcade, and there's always help, however little, for a veteran with a family. Besides, there's my wife.' He stroked his son's face and indicated the other children standing in the doorway. 'Not to mention these little rascals. I couldn't take my family there, with the Holy Office's informers whispering behind my back and the Inquisitors after me. I prefer to stay here, where things are clearer. Do you understand?'

'I do.'

'Then there are my comrades, people like you, Sebastián, people I can talk to. I can always walk down to the harbour and see the galleys, or to the gates and watch the soldiers coming and going. Sometimes I visit the barracks, and the men – the ones who still know me – buy me a drink. I attend the parades and the campaign masses and the salutes to the flag, just as I did when I was on active service. All of that helps to soothe any nostalgia I might feel.'

He looked at Copons, urging him to agree. Copons, however, gave only a curt nod and said nothing. Malacalza poured him some more wine and smiled, one of those smiles that require a certain degree of courage.

'Besides,' he went on, 'you never really retire here, not like in Spain. We're a kind of reserve, you see. Sometimes the Moors attack and besiege the town, and help doesn't always arrive. Then they call on every man available to defend the walls and the bulwarks, even us invalids.'

He paused for a moment and smoothed his grey moustache, half-closing his eyes as if evoking a pleasant memory. Then he looked up sadly at the sword hanging on the wall.

'For a few days,' he said, 'everything is like it was before. There's even the possibility that the Moors will press home their victory and that a fellow might die like the man he is ... or was.'

His voice had changed. Had it not been for the child in his arms and those standing in the doorway, it seemed he would not have minded meeting such a death that very night.

'Not a bad way to go,' agreed the Captain.

Malacalza slowly turned to look at him, as if returning from somewhere far away.

'I'm an old man now, Diego. I know exactly what to expect from Spain and her people. Here, at least, they know who I am. Having been a soldier still means something in Oran. Over there, they don't give a fig for our service records, full of names they've forgotten, if, indeed, they ever knew them: the del Caballo redoubt, the Durango fort ... What does it matter to a scribe, a judge, a royal functionary, a shopkeeper or a friar, whether, in the dunes at Nieuwpoort, we withdrew calmly, flags held high, without breaking ranks, or ran away like rabbits?'

He stopped speaking for a moment and poured out the little wine that remained in the jug.

'Look at Sebastián. He's sitting there as silent as ever, but he agrees with me. See, he's nodding.'

He placed his right hand on the table, next to the jug, and seemed to study it. It was thin and bony, with the same scars on knuckles and wrist that Copons and the Captain bore.

'Reputation ... .' he murmured.

There was a long silence. Then Malacalza raised his mug to his lips and chuckled.

'Anyway, here I am, a veteran soldier in the King of Spain's army.'

He looked again at the coins on the table.

'The wine's finished,' he said, suddenly sombre. 'And I'm sure you have other things to do.'

We got to our feet and picked up our hats, not knowing what to say. Malacalza remained seated.

'Before you go,' he added, 'I'd just like to list those places on our service records that no one else cares about: Calais ... Amiens ... Bomel ... Nieuwpoort ... Ostend ... Oldensel ... Linghen ... Jülich ... Oran. Amen.'

As he said each name, he picked up the coins one by one, his eyes vacant. Then he seemed to recover somewhat, weighing the coins in his hand before putting them in his purse. Kissing the child on his lap and depositing him on the floor, he got to his feet, holding his mug of wine in one hand and resting his weight on his bad leg.

'To the King, may God keep him safe.'

I thought it odd that there was not a hint of irony in his words.

'To the King,' echoed Captain Alatriste. 'And despite the King, or whoever else is in charge.'

Then all four of us turned towards the old sword hanging on the wall and drank a toast.

It was dark by the time we left Malacalza's house. We walked down the street, which was lit only by the light from the open doors of the houses – we could just make out the dark shapes of the people sitting inside – and by the candles burning in the wall niches devoted to various saints. Just then, a silhouette emerged from the shadows, getting up from the ground on which it had been crouched, waiting.

This time, the Captain did not simply give the figure a backward glance; he removed the buff coat he had draped over his shoulders so as to leave sword and dagger unencumbered. And thus, with me and Copons following behind, he went straight up to the dark silhouette and asked, 'What do you want?'

The other man moved a little into the light. He did so deliberately, as if he wanted us to be able to see him more clearly, thereby dissipating any fears we might have.

'I don't know,' he said.

He delivered this disconcerting answer in a Castilian as good as the Captain's, Sebastián's or mine.

PIRATES OF THE LEVANT

'Well, you're taking a chance, following us like that.'

'I don't think so.' He said this confidently, looking at the Captain without even blinking.

'Why is that?'

'I saved your life, my friend.'

I shot a sideways glance at the Captain, to see if such familiarity had angered him. I knew he was perfectly capable of killing someone who addressed him in what he judged to be an inappropriate fashion. To my surprise, though, I saw that he held the *mogataz*'s gaze and did not seem angered in the least. He put his hand in his pocket, but the Moor took a step back as if he had received an insult.

'Is that what your life is worth? *Zienaashin*? Money?'

He was obviously an educated Moor, someone with a story to tell. We could see his face clearly now, his silver earrings glittering in the light of a candle. His skin was not particularly dark and his beard had a reddish tint to it. On his left cheek was that tattooed cross with diamond-shaped points. He was wearing a bracelet, also in silver, and was holding one hand open, palm uppermost, as if to show that he was concealing nothing and was keeping his fingers well away from the dagger at his waist.

'Then go on your way, and we'll go on ours.'

We continued downhill until we reached the corner. I turned at that point to see if the man was still following us. I tugged at Captain Alatriste's buff coat and he looked back too. Copons made as if to unsheathe his dagger, but the Captain grabbed his arm. Then he went over to the Moor again, taking his time, as if pondering what to say to him.

'Listen, Moor—'

'My name is Aixa Ben Gurriat.'

'I know what your name is. You told me at Uad Berruch.'

They stood motionless, studying each other in the gloom, while Copons and I remained a short distance away. The Moor was still making a point of keeping his hands well away from his dagger. I had one hand resting on the hilt of my sword, ready, at the slightest suspicious move on the Moor's part, to pin him against the wall. The Captain did not seem to share my unease. Instead, he stuck his thumbs in his belt, looked to either side, glanced briefly back at us, then leaned against the wall, next to the Moor.

'Why did you go into that tent?' he asked at last.

The other man took a while to respond.

'I heard a shot. I had seen you fighting earlier on, and you seemed to be a good *imyahad* – a good fighter, a very good fighter.'

'I don't usually get involved in other people's business.'

'Nor do I, but I went into the tent and I saw that you were defending a Moorish woman.'

'Whether she was a Moor or not makes no difference to me. The men were an unsavoury pair, and arrogant and insolent to boot. The woman was the least of it.'

The *mogataz* clicked his tongue. '*Tidt.* True, but you could have looked the other way, or even joined in the fun.'

'So could you. Killing a Spaniard is a sure way of getting a noose around your neck – if anyone ever found out.'

'They didn't … fate.'

They fell silent again, but continued to look at each other, as if they were privately calculating which of them had incurred the greater debt: the Moor because the Captain had defended a woman of his race, or the Captain because the Moor had saved his life. Meanwhile, Copons and I were exchanging glances too, astonished by both the situation and the conversation.

'*Saad,*' murmured the Captain in the dog-Arabic spoken in

ports. He said the word thoughtfully, as if repeating the last thing the *mogataz* had said.

The latter smiled faintly and nodded. 'In my language we say *elkhadar*. Fate and destiny are the same thing.'

'Where are you from?'

The *mogataz* made a vague gesture. 'From around ... from the mountains.'

'Far away?'

'*Uah*. Far away indeed, and very high up.'

'Is there something I can do for you?' asked the Captain.

The other man shrugged. He appeared to be considering the question.

'I'm an *azuago*,' he said at last, as if that explained everything. 'From the tribe of the Beni Barrani.'

'Well, you speak excellent Castilian.'

'My mother was born a *zarumia*, a Christian. She was from Cádiz. She was captured as a child and they sold her on the beach of Arzeo, an abandoned town by the sea, seven leagues to the east, on the road to Mostaganem. My grandfather bought her for my father.'

'That's an odd tattoo you have on your face – odd for a Moor, I mean.'

'It's an old story. We *azuagos* are descended from Christians, from the time when the Goths were still here, and for us it's a matter of *isbah*, of honour. That's why my grandfather wanted a Spanish wife for my father.'

'And is that why you fight with us against other Moors?'

The *mogataz* shrugged stoically. '*Elkhadar*. Fate.'

Having said that, he fell silent for a moment and stroked his beard. Then I thought I saw him smile again, his gaze abstracted.

'Beni Barrani means son of a foreigner, you see. We're a tribe of men who have no homeland.'

*

And that is how, after the cavalcade of Uad Berruch in the year 1627, Captain Alatriste and I met the mercenary Aixa Ben Gurriat, known among the Spaniards in Oran as the Moor Gurriato, a remarkable individual, and this is not the last time his name will be mentioned. For, hard though it is to believe, that night was the start of a seven-year friendship, the seven years that separated that day in Oran and a bloody day in September 1634, when the Moor Gurriato, the Captain and myself, along with many other comrades, fought shoulder to shoulder on a wretched hill at Nördlingen. After sharing many journeys, dangers and adventures, and while the Idiáquez regiment withstood fifteen charges by the Swedes in six hours without giving an inch, the Moor Gurriato would die before our eyes, like a good Spanish infantryman, defending a religion and a country that were not his own, assuming he ever had either. He fell, at last, like so many; for an ungrateful, miserly Spain that gave him nothing in return, but which, for reasons known only to himself, Aixa Ben Gurriat, from the tribe of the *azuagos* Beni Barrani, had resolved to serve to the death with the unshakeable loyalty of a faithful murderous wolf. And he did so in a most unusual way – by choosing Captain Alatriste as his comrade.

Two days later, when the *Mulata* left the Barbary Coast and set off north north-west, in the direction of Cartagena, Diego Alatriste had plenty of opportunity to observe the Moor Gurriato, because the latter was rowing in the fifth bench on the starboard side, next to the stroke. He did not have to wear chains, being what was called a *buena boya*, an expression taken from the Italian *buonavoglia* and applied to volunteer crew members. They were usually either the dregs of the ports or desperate men on the run willing to serve for a wage – the Turks called them *morlacos* or jackals. They sought refuge on a galley much as, on land, others might in a church. This was how they had managed to get the Moor on board, since he was determined to accompany Diego Alatriste and try his fortune with him. Once the Captain had sorted out the problem of Sebastián Copons' licence – Sergeant Major Biscarrués had been satisfied with five hundred ducats plus Copons' back pay – he still had some *escudos* in his pocket, and it would not have been hard to grease a few palms to simplify matters. This, however, proved unnecessary. The Moor had his own money – although where he had got it from he did not say. Unrolling a kerchief that he wore beneath his sash, he took out a few silver coins which, despite being minted in Algiers, Fez and Tlemcen, convinced the galleymaster and the overseer to take him on board, once the usual formalities had been gone through, namely a swift act of baptism, to which no one objected even though it was as false as a Judas kiss. That was enough for his name – Gurriato de Orán, they called him – to be written in the galleymaster's book, along with a wage of eleven *reales* a month. It was thus established that, from then on, the *mogataz*, despite being a new convert and a galleyman, was a good Catholic and a faithful volunteer in the King of Spain's army, a situation to which Gurriato accommodated himself as best he could. Ever shrewd and prudent, he immediately adapted his appearance to suit his new circumstances by shaving off his warrior lock – leaving his head as smooth as that of any galley-slave – and replacing *rexa*, sandals, kaftan and baggy trousers with breeches, shirt, cap and red doublet. All that remained of his former outfit was his dagger, stuck in his sash, and the grey-striped burnous, in which he slept or wrapped about himself in bad weather or when, like now, a favourable wind meant that he did not have to row. As for the tattoo on his face and his silver earrings, he was not the only one to wear such adornments.

'He's a strange one,' commented Sebastián Copons.

He was sitting in the shade of the trinquet-sail, overjoyed to have left Oran behind him. At his back, the mast supporting the lateen yard and its vast canvas sail creaked in the easterly wind with the movement of the ship.

'No stranger than you or me,' replied Alatriste.

He had spent all day observing the *mogataz*, trying to get the measure of the man. From where we sat, he seemed barely different from the forced men, slaves and convicts, who had no choice but to row with shackles on ankles or manacles on wrists. There were few who rowed out of necessity or choice, barely half a dozen among the two hundred rowers on the *Mulata*. To these one had to add the forced volunteers; this contradiction in terms could be explained by the very Spanish fact that – as with the soldiers in Oran and Melilla – the lack of manpower on the King's galleys meant that some galley-slaves who had completed their sentences were not allowed to leave, but were kept on and paid the same wage as a free man. In theory, they would only continue to do so until others came to take their place but, since this rarely happened quickly, there were cases of former galley-slaves completing sentences of two, five and even eight years on the galley – ten years was virtually a death sentence and few survived – only to find themselves obliged to stay on for a few more months or even years.

'Look,' said Copons. 'He doesn't budge when the other Muslims pray, as if he really isn't one of them.'

Given the favourable wind, the oars were stowed and there was no need to row, so both forced men and volunteers were idle. The former were lying down on their benches, or else doing their business over the side of the boat or in the latrines in the prow, or de-lousing each other, darning their clothes or performing various tasks for sailors or soldiers. Certain trusted slaves, freed from their shackles, were allowed to come and go on the galley, washing clothes in sea-water or helping the cook prepare the beans for the stew that was steaming on the stove to port of the central gangway, between the mainmast and the supports for the awning. Two dozen or so of the slaves – Turks and Moors – were reciting one of their five daily prayers at their benches, facing east, kneeling, standing up and then prostrating themselves. *La, ilah-la ua Muhamad rasul Ala* they chorused: there is no God but Allah, and Mohammed is His prophet. The soldiers and sailors did nothing to prevent this. Equally, the Muslim galley-slaves took no offence when a sail appeared on the horizon or the wind changed and orders were given to take up their oars, the galleymaster's whip interrupting their prayers and returning them to their rowing and the rhythmic clink of chains. Everyone on the galley knew the rules of the game.

'He isn't one of them,' said Alatriste. 'I think, as he says, he doesn't belong anywhere.'

'And what about that story he told us about how his tribe used to be Christians?'

'It's possible. You've seen the cross on his face. And last night he was telling me about a bronze bell that they kept hidden in a cave. The Moors don't have bells. It's true that in the time of the Goths, when the Saracens arrived, there were people who refused to convert and took refuge in the mountains. It may be that the religion was lost over the centuries, but other things remained. Traditions, memories. ... And he does have a gingerish beard.'

'That could be from his Christian mother.'

'It could. But look at him; he obviously doesn't feel that he's a Moor.'

'Nor a Christian, damn it.'

'Oh, come now, Sebastián. How often have you been to mass in the last twenty years?'

'As little as possible,' Copons admitted.

'And how many of the Church's commandments have you broken since you've been a soldier?'

Copons gravely counted them off on his fingers.

'All of them,' he concluded sombrely.

'And does that stop you being a good soldier to your King?'

'Of course not.'

'Well, then.'

Diego Alatriste continued studying the Moor Gurriato, who was sitting with his feet dangling over the side of the galley, contemplating the sea. This, apparently, was the first time the Moor had been on a ship, and yet despite the swell that had been buffeting them ever since they left behind the cross of Mazalquivir, his stomach had remained steady, which could not be said of some of the other men. The trick, it seemed, was to place some saffron paper over the heart.

'He's certainly not one to complain,' said Alatriste. 'And he adapts well too.'

Copons grunted. 'You're telling me. I just vomited up some bile myself.' He gave a crooked smile. 'I obviously didn't want to take *that* with me from Oran.'

Alatriste nodded. Years before, he had found it difficult to adjust to the harsh galley life: the lack of space and privacy, the worm- and mouse-eaten, hard-as-iron ship's biscuits, the muddy, brackish water, the cries of the sailors and the smell of the galley-men, the itch and discomfort of clothes washed in salt water, the restless sleep on a hard board with a shield as pillow, one's body always exposed to the sun, the heat, the rain and the damp, cold nights at sea, which could leave you with either congestion or deafness. Not to mention the sickness when there was bad weather, the wild storms and the dangers of battle, fighting on fragile boards that shifted beneath your feet and threatened to throw you into the sea at any moment. And all of this in the company of galley-men, hardly the noblest of brotherhoods: slaves, heretics, forgers, criminals condemned to the lash, bearers of false witness, renegades, tricksters, perjurers, ruffians, highwaymen, swordsmen, adulterers, blasphemers, murderers and thieves, who would never pass up the chance to throw dice or shuffle a greasy pack of cards. Not that the soldiers and sailors were any better, for whenever they went on land – in Oran, they'd had to hang a man to teach the others a lesson – there wasn't a chicken run they didn't plunder, an orchard they didn't pick clean, wine they didn't filch, food or clothes they didn't steal, a woman they didn't enjoy, nor a peasant they didn't abuse or kill. For, as the saying goes: Please God, leave the galley to some other poor sod.

'Do you really think he'll make a soldier?'

Copons was still looking at the Moor, as was Alatriste. The latter shrugged.

'That's up to him. For the moment, he's seeing a bit of the world, which is what he wanted.'

Copons gestured scornfully in the direction of the rowing chamber and then tapped his nose. Given the stench from all that humanity crammed together, among coils of rope and bundles of clothes, not to mention the stink from the bilge, it would have been hard to breathe were it not for the wind filling the sails.

'I think "seeing the world" might be a slight exaggeration, Diego.'

'Time will tell.'

Copons was leaning on the gunwale, clearly suspicious.

'Why have we brought him with us?' he asked at last.

Alatriste shrugged. 'No one brought him. He's free to go wherever he likes.'

'But don't you find it odd that he should have chosen us as his comrades, for no apparent reason.'

'Hardly for no reason. And you don't choose your comrades, they choose you.'

He continued looking at the *mogataz* for a while longer, then pulled a face.

'Besides,' he added thoughtfully, 'it's still a little early to be calling him our comrade.'

Copons considered these words, then grunted again.

'Do you know what I think, Sebastián?' said Alatriste after a pause.

'No, damn it, I don't. I never know what you're thinking.'

'I think something in you has changed. You talk more than you used to.'

'Really?'

'Yes, really.'

'It must be Oran. I spent too long there.'

'Possibly.'

Copons frowned, then removed the kerchief he wore round his head and wiped the sweat from his neck and face.

'And is that good or bad?' he asked.

'I'm not sure. It's different.'

'Ah.'

Copons was scrutinising his kerchief as if it held the answer to some complicated question.

'I must be getting old, I suppose,' he muttered at last. 'It's age, Diego. You saw Fermín Malacalza. Remember what he used to be like – before?'

'Yes, of course. I suppose his pack grew too heavy for him. That's what it must be.'

'Yes.'

*

I was at the other end of the ship, near the awning, watching the pilot comparing quadrant and compass. At seventeen, I was a bright, curious youth, interested in acquiring all kinds of knowledge. I retained that curiosity for most of my life and later it helped me make the most of certain strokes of good fortune. As well as the art of navigation, of which I gained a useful if rudimentary grasp while on board ship, I learned a lot of other things in that closed world: everything from finding out how the barber tended wounds – they didn't heal as quickly at sea, what with the damp air and the salt – to a study of the dangerous varieties of humankind created by God or the Devil. I began these studies in Madrid as a mere child, continued them in Flanders as a schoolboy, and completed them on the King's galleys as a graduate, where I encountered the kind of men who might well say, like the galley-slave in these lines written by Don Francisco de Quevedo:

I'm a scholar in a sardine school,
And good for nothing but to row;
From prison did I graduate,
that university most low.

From a distance, I contemplated the Moor Gurriato sitting impassively on the side of the ship, staring at the sea, and Captain Alatriste and Copons, who were still talking beneath the trinquet-sail at the far end of the gangway. I should say that I was still very shocked by our visit to Fermín Malacalza. He was not, of course, the first veteran I had encountered, but it had given me much to think about, seeing his wretched existence in Oran, poor and invalided out of the army after a lifetime of service, with a family to bring up and no hope that his luck would change. For Fermín, the only future would be to rot like meat in the sun or be taken captive along with his family if the Moors ever seized the town. And, depending upon one's profession, thinking is not always the most comfortable of pastimes. When I was younger, I had often recited these lines by Juan Bautista de Vivar, which pleased me greatly:

A soldier's time, so full of strife,
Of war and weapons, fire and blood,
May yet still teach us – by all that's good —
To make the best we can of life.

Sometimes, when I would recite them to the Captain, I would catch an ironic smirk on his face; not that he ever said anything, for he was of the view that no one learns from being told. You must remember that when I was in Oudkerk and Breda, I was still very green, a young lad eager for novelty. What, for others, symbolised tragedy and life at its cruellest was to me a fascinating experience, part game and part adventure. Like so many Spaniards, I was accustomed to enduring miseries from the cradle up. At seventeen, however, more developed and better educated, and with my wits sharper, certain disquieting questions would slip into my head like a good dagger through the gaps in a corslet. The Captain's ironic smirk was beginning to make sense, the proof being that, after visiting Malacalza, I never again recited those verses. I was old enough and intelligent enough to recognise the ghost of my own father in that shadow of a man, and, sooner or later, in Captain Alatriste, Copons and myself. None of this changed my intentions. I still wanted to be a soldier, but the fact is that, after Oran, I wondered if it would not be wiser to think of the military life as a means rather than an end; as a useful way of confronting – sustained by the rigour of discipline, a set of rules – a hostile world I did not know well, but which I sensed would require everything that the exercise of arms could teach me. And by Christ's blood, I was right. When it came to facing the hard times that came later, both for poor, unfortunate Spain and for myself, as regards loves, absences, losses and grief, I was glad to be able to draw on all that experience.

Even now, on this side of time and life, having been certain things and ceased to be many others, I am proud to sum up my existence, and those of some of the loyal and valiant men I knew, in the word 'soldier'. In time I came to command a company and made my fortune and was appointed lieutenant and later captain of the King's guard – not a bad career, by God, for a Basque orphan from Oñate – nevertheless I always signed papers with the words Ensign Balboa – my humble rank on the nineteenth of May 1643, when, on the plains of Rocroi, along with Captain Alatriste and what remained of the last company of Spanish infantry, I held aloft our old and tattered flag.

5. THE ENGLISH SAETTA

We were sailing eastwards, day after day, across the sea known to those on the other shore as *bahar el-Mutauàssit*, in the opposite direction from that taken by the Phoenicians, the Greeks, the gods of Antiquity and the Roman legions when they set sail for our old Spain. Each morning, the rising sun lit up our faces from the prow of the galley and each night, it sank behind us, in our wake. This filled me with pleasure, and not just because at the end of the voyage lay Naples – that soldier's paradise and bounteous treasure chest housing all of Italy's delights. No, when the galley, propelled by the rhythmic strokes of the rowers, slid across waters smooth as a blade of burnished steel, it seemed to me that the blue sea with its red sunsets and calm, windless mornings was weaving a secret connection with something that crouched in my mind like a sensation or a dormant memory.

'This is where we came from,' I once heard Captain Alatriste murmur as we passed one of the bare, rocky islands so typical of the Mediterranean. Perched on top of it, we could see the ancient columns of some pagan temple. It was a very different landscape from the León mountains of the Captain's childhood, or the green fields of my Guipúzcoa, or the rugged peaks of Aragon where Sebastián Copons' soldierly ancestors had been born and bred. Copons stared at the Captain in bewilderment when he heard him speak these enigmatic words. But I understood that he was referring to the ancient, beneficent impulse, which – via language, olive trees, vines, white sails, marble and memory – had arrived at far-off shores of other seas and other lands, like the ripples set in motion by a precious stone dropped into a pool of still water.

We had travelled from Oran to Cartagena with the other ships in the convoy and, having taken on fresh supplies in that city praised by Cervantes in his *Journey to Parnassus* – 'We finally reached the port/ to which the men of Carthage gave their name' – we weighed anchor, along with two galleys from Sicily. Once past Cabo de Palos, we set sail east northeast and in two days we reached Formentera. From there, passing Mallorca and Menorca on our left, we headed for Cagliari, in the south of Sardinia, where we arrived, eight days after leaving the Spanish coast, safe and sound, anchoring near the salt marshes. Then, sails hoisted and with fresh supplies of water and dried meat, we passed Capo Carbonara and, taking a south-easterly direction, sailed for two days to Trapani in Sicily.

This time we kept a sharp eye open, with lookouts posted on the tops of the trinquet- and mainmast, because – this being the Mediterranean's slender waist and therefore a natural funnel through which all nations passed – these waters were full of ships travelling between Barbary, Europe and the Levant. We were on the watch both for enemy ships and for any Turkish, Berber, English or Dutch ships that we might capture. On this occasion neither Christ nor our purses was in luck, for we encountered neither foe nor easy prey.

Trapani, built right on the coast, is spread along a narrow cape and has a reasonable harbour, although its many reefs and sandbanks meant that our pilot was never without a curse on his lips or the sounding-lead in his hands. There, we parted from our convoy and continued on alone, rowing against the wind, until we reached Malta, where we were to deliver despatches from the Viceroy of Sicily and four passengers – Knights of the Order of St John who were returning to that island.

I was still intrigued by the Moor Gurriato, who, by then, appeared to be as accustomed to galley life as if he had been working on one since he was born. He seemed so patient and resigned, with his shaven head and muscular back, that if it hadn't been for the absence of shackles on his ankles – Biscay boots we called them – one might have taken him for just another slave. He ate, like the others, from a wooden bowl and drank the same murky water or watered-down wine from the wooden goblet – the *chipichape* – attached to his bench. He was also respectful and disciplined. He applied himself vigorously to the task of rowing, urged on by the galleymaster's loud whistles and hard lashes – for the galleymaster did not distinguish between voluntary backs and forced ones – never protesting or looking for an excuse not to carry out his duties. Whether standing up – when the order came to row till they dropped – or seated and leaning back when the rowing was easier, he would chant the same songs they all did to maintain the rhythm. And although he did not become close friends with anyone – he was the only free man on his bench, which he shared with a Spanish convict and two Turkish slaves – he was nonetheless a good comrade, well-liked by his companions. The fact that he got on well with both the Christians and the Turks was significant, because if, one day, we were to fall into the hands of the Berbers or the subjects of the Ottoman Empire, the testimony of the Turks, pointing him out as a volunteer who had renounced his religion – or whatever other accusation they chose to make – would be more than enough to get him skewered without the benefit of fat or lard to ease his passing. However, the Moor Gurriato seemed unperturbed by this possibility. He slept between the benches just as his colleagues did, happily engaged in mutual delousing sessions, and when, in rough weather, so as not to get drenched at the prow, a soldier or sailor would inconsiderately do as the galley-slaves did and relieve himself next to the rower nearest the sea – always the worst place to sit – the Moor, having more freedom of movement, would throw a bucket attached to a rope into the sea, fill it with water and wash the deck clean. He treated his companions as considerately as he did everyone else, chatting to them if it fell to him to do so, although he was not, on the whole, a great talker. We thus discovered that he spoke not only Spanish and Moorish Arabic, but also Turkish – picked up, we later learned, from Turkish janizaries in Algiers – as well as the lingua franca that was spoken from end to end of the Mediterranean, a mishmash of all the languages.

I would go over to him occasionally, driven by curiosity, and we would talk, and so I learned more about his life and his desire to see the world and to stay by Captain Alatriste's side. I never got to the bottom of that strange loyalty, and he never explained, as if constrained by a strange modesty. Yet in the events that followed, his deeds never gave the lie to his intention; rather the reverse. As I said, I was astonished at how easily he adapted to this life and, as I discovered, to the many other lives that fell to him while in our company; for, although I prided myself on being a brave lad, I would have found life as a galley-man very hard to take.

At first, I trembled, wanting to withdraw,
But time and custom taught me:
All's within their cure.

What I couldn't stand was the boredom. I had grown used to the promiscuous nature of our existence, to the stench, the discomfort and the noise, but I could not get used to the hours of idleness, which, in the cramped space of a floating piece of timber, were entirely wasted. I would even greet with excitement any sail we spotted, welcoming a chance for a hunt or a fight, or would feel pleased when the sky grew dark, the wind began to howl in the rigging and the sea turned grey. With the prow bucking and the storm harrying us, everyone else on board would be praying and crossing themselves, commending themselves to God and making pious promises that, once back on dry land, they would be most unlikely to keep.

To fill the tedium, I continued to apply myself to reading, a habit greatly encouraged by the Captain, who often led by example; unless he was talking to me or Sebastián Copons or another comrade, he could usually be found sitting snugly in one of the ship's embrasures with one of the two or three books he always carried in his pack. One, which I remember with particular gratitude, for I read and re-read it on that voyage, was Miguel de Cervantes' *Exemplary Novels*. The colloquy between the dogs Ciprión and Berganza and the characters in 'Rinconete and Cortadillo' made me laugh out loud. Another book that I read with great pleasure, even though I found it sourer in style and rather short on ideas, was a very old and dog-eared tome, printed in Venice in the previous century, entitled *Portrait of the Lively Andaluza*. Since it was a work of a somewhat scabrous nature, the Captain was reluctant at first to place it in my hands, and only did so when he discovered that, unbeknown to him, I was reading it anyway.

'After all,' he concluded, 'if you're old enough to kill and be killed, you're old enough to read whatever you choose.'

'Amen to that,' said Copons, who hadn't read a single book in his life and had no intention of doing so.

*

Six or seven leagues before we reached Cape Passero, with the rowers taking it in turns, our galley changed direction. We had come across a Dalmatian tartana carrying dates, wax and leather from the Kerkennah Islands to Ragusa. Its crew, once they were near enough to talk, told us that a three-masted pirate saetta and a smaller ship had called in at the island of Lampedusa to be careened. They had spotted them at dawn the previous day when they approached to take on water, and the saetta looked very much like the one which, for a month now, had been patrolling the sea between Capo Bono and Capo Bianco, the English pirates on board stealing everything they could lay their hands on. So far the ship had eluded both the galleys of Malta and of Sicily.

As the tartana sailed on, a council of war took place under the awning of our ship and, given that the wind was now a fair easterly one, perfect for the *Mulata* to unfurl her two lateen sails and do a good league an hour, we headed south south-west, in the direction of Lampedusa, ready to knock seven bells out of those bastards – that is, if they were still there.

As I have mentioned before, there was nothing unusual about Englishmen or Dutchmen venturing further into Mediterranean waters and frequenting the ports of Barbary and even of the Turk, because what they were interested in was persecuting Spain and the other Catholic nations. The men of fair Albion had been applying themselves to this task with zeal, smuggling and pirating with few interruptions since the days of the Virgin Queen Elizabeth – and I use the word 'virgin' purely as an epithet, not a proven fact. I am referring to that red-haired witch whom our poets, among them the Cordoban Góngora, viewed as the very worst of our enemies:

More she-wolf than lascivious queen,
Wife and daughter-in-law to many,
Vile, libidinous and mean.

And to whom Cristóbal de Virués dedicated these eloquent
lines:

Ungrateful queen, unworthy of the name,
Cast out from God – a Jezebel —
O why disturb this holy armèd peace?
And make a Christian peace a hell?

And whose death – for, thank Heaven, that hour comes
round for everyone – was greeted by Lope, our Phoenix, with
this fitting epitaph:

Here lies Jezebel,
The new Athalia;
Harpy of th'Atlantic gold,
Of oceans, the cruel fire.

While we're on the subject of the English, I should point
out that the people who behaved most shamelessly and
outrageously in the Mediterranean were not the Turks or the
Berbers, who tended to keep punctiliously to any agreements
made between nations, but those pitiless, drunken dogs voy-
aging from their cold seas on the hypocritical pretext of
making war on the papists. They did not behave like corsairs,
but like pirates, buying complicity in ports such as Algiers
and Saleh. So bad were they that even the Turks viewed them
unkindly, for they blithely plundered everyone, regardless of
cargo or flag, under the protection of their sovereigns and
their traders, who, while they dissembled in public, in private

encouraged the raids and pocketed the profits. I said 'pirates', for that is the word that befits them. In the old usage, 'corsair' was a traditional and respectable occupation, a group of private individuals who, granted a patent – royal permission to plunder the enemies of the crown – would set sail on a quest for private profit, on the understanding that they would pay their quint to the king and be ruled by certain laws agreed among the nations. In this respect, we Spaniards, apart from a few corsairs from Mallorca, the Cantabrian coast and from Flanders, played an almost exclusively military role: cruel and ruthless, yes, but always acting under the flag of the Catholic King and in keeping with all ordinances. We would rigorously punish any treaty violations and any excesses or abuses practised against neutral nations.

For reasons of reputation and conduct – and because, centuries before, we had experienced corsairs on our own shores in Spain – the corsair subsequently acquired a very bad name indeed; this was, after all, war by other means, and war waged by soldiers or sailors was one thing; it seemed murky and ungentlemanly when carried out by privateers. There was the added misfortune that, while our enemies would resort to anything to sap our strength both on sea and land, our Spanish corsairs – apart from our intrepid Catholics from Dunkirk, the scourge of the English and the Dutch – gradually dwindled away for lack of crew, the difficulty or inconvenience of obtaining royal permission, or because, if it was granted, the profits were minimal, siphoned off by a bureaucratic tangle of taxes, corrupt functionaries and other parasites. One must not forget the sad end of the Duke of Osuna, Viceroy of Sicily and later of Naples – a close friend of Don Francisco de Quevedo, and to whom we will return later. He was the terror of both Turks and Venetians, the father of our Spanish corsairs, and the implacable bane of our enemies, a man whose triumphs and good fortune aroused such envy that, ultimately, they brought him only discredit, prison and death. And naturally, with such antecedents, when for reasons of politics and war, Philip IV and the Count-Duke of Olivares wanted to arm a fleet of corsairs once more – even promising that the booty would be shared out among the Basque regiment, and that the King would renounce his quint – many privateers, wary, sceptical or already ruined, preferred not to be drawn in.

Lampedusa is a bare, scrubby, sparsely populated island some fifteen or sixteen leagues south-west of Malta. Our lookouts, who could see for about fifteen miles from their vantage points, spotted it late in the afternoon. To ensure that the corsairs, if they were still there, did not in turn spot us – the pilot, who knew those waters, warned that there was a watchtower to the south of the island – Captain Urdemalas ordered the two masts to be struck, and we continued on our way, sail-less and rowing gently, so that we could approach unseen and not before nightfall. While we were thus engaged, making the necessary arrangements to seize the corsair ship before it slipped from our grasp, the pilot told us that the island was used by both Muslims and Christians as a port, and that fugitive slaves from both sides took refuge there. He said there was a small cave containing an ancient image of Our Lady with the Child in her arms, painted on canvas with a wooden backing, where visitors left offerings of dry biscuits, cheese, bacon, oil and the odd coin. The strange thing was that near the cave lay the tomb of an anchorite whom the Turks venerated as a great saint, and where they also left offerings (although not, of course, of bacon). This was so that when any runaway slaves reached the island, they would have something to eat, for there was water to be had from a nearby well, which, although brackish and unpleasant, served its purpose. And whatever the religion of the slave, he would never touch the offerings left by those of the other faith, but would respect both the faith and the needs of his counterparts. For in the Mediterranean, where it was a case of 'I'll do the same for you one day', these lines by Lope fitted like a glove:

When it comes to fathers
No one can be sure.
But when we say 'Our Father',
We're sons of Adam pure.

With sails struck and rowing slowly, we reached Lampedusa from the north-east as the sun was setting on the starboard side. The darkness aided our enterprise and the last thing we saw before the light went was a column of smoke, indicating that, whether or not it was the saetta, someone was on the island. Now that night was almost upon us and any brightness reduced to a fine red line on the horizon, we could see the occasional fire burning. This encouraged us greatly, and we began to prepare for action, feeling our way in the gloom, for Captain Urdemalas had ordered that no lights should be lit on board, nor was anyone to raise his voice; even the galleymaster was ordered not to use his whistle. And so we proceeded in near silence across the dark sea before the moon had risen. The only sound was the hoarse, guttural breathing – a kind of drawn-out uuuh, uuuh, uuuh – of our oarsmen keeping a steady rhythm and the splash of forty-eight oars striking the water.

'Landing party, to your posts! Unload your weapons and woe betide anyone who fires a shot!'

When this murmured order reached them, the twenty men

crouching on either side of the galley began to move towards the ladders at the stern. The skiff and the rowing-boat that would take them to land had been lowered. We had made our final approach with great stealth, masts and lateen yards lowered so that we would not be spotted against the night sky. The pilot was lying face down on the ram at the front of the galley, with a sailor next to him reciting the depth of the water according to the knots on the sounding-lead. Spanish galleys had a very shallow draught and were as subtle and light as the wind; they could sometimes get close enough in for sailors to land without even getting their breeches wet, although not in this case. As a precaution, our men would travel the final stretch in the skiff and the rowing-boat. The disembarkation point was very narrow, and we didn't want to get the harquebus fuses or the gunpowder wet.

'Take care, Íñigo,' whispered Captain Alatriste, 'and good luck.'

He placed his hand briefly on my shoulder, and Copons squeezed the back of my neck. Then they moved off and went down the ladder to the skiff on the starboard side. As I was busy donning my steel corslet, I only muttered a belated 'good luck' when they were out of earshot.

The squad of harquebusiers was split into two groups, one under the command of Ensign Muelas and the other under Captain Alatriste, leaving Sergeant Albaladejo to watch over the sixty soldiers left on board. We could hear the men as they settled into the boats, talking in low voices, muttering oaths whenever anyone pushed or stepped on someone else. Otherwise, the only sound was the oars being fitted into the rowlocks and the metallic clink of weapons, muffled by the rags in which they were wrapped.

The plan was for the harquebusiers to disembark on the sands of a tiny bay which, according to the pilot, lay directly ahead, on the eastern side of the island. The mouth of the bay was only one hundred and fifty paces wide, but it was free of any reefs or rocks that might hamper our passage. The squad would land there, then cross the island in a south-westerly direction, spreading themselves out around the area where the corsairs were encamped, in order to fire on them and prevent them escaping into the countryside or gaining access to the tower and the one well of water. Meanwhile, at first light, the *Mulata*, having rowed silently around the island, would close off their exit via the sea and, after bombarding them with cannon shot, would set about boarding the vessels.

Towards midnight, taking advantage of the thin crescent moon, two sailors, who were excellent swimmers – one of them was a certain Ramiro Feijoo, a remarkable diver, who later became famous for holing a Turkish vessel during the siege of La Mamora – had set off in the smaller of the boats to reconnoitre the large bay to the south of the island. They were able to confirm that there were indeed two ships – one a saetta and the other perhaps a tartana or a felucca – and they said that the saetta did not appear to be ready to set sail, for she was heeled over, as if beached or in the process of being careened by her crew.

'To your oars, men,' said Captain Urdemalas, once the skiff and the rowing-boat had disappeared into the night. 'Set to without a noise or a word. Prepare and arm the pavisades.'

The oars moved into the water while we arranged mat-tresses, shields and *pedreros* along the ship's edge, and the master gunner and his assistants positioned the three cannon at the prow. Then, as soon as the small boats had returned and been secured with a towing line, Captain Urdemalas issued new orders, the helmsman held the rudder firm and, still in silence, the oarsmen turned the ship around. Thus we turned until the pole star was behind us and our prow was pointing towards a low rocky point that rose up nearby. Then, with the pilot keeping a close eye on both the sounding-lead and the shore – in case we should hit a sandbank or an unexpected rock – we followed the coast of Lampedusa south.

About six or seven paces away, a rabbit, its ears erect, poked its head out of a burrow and had a look around. In the hesitant light of dawn, Diego Alatriste watched the creature, resting his chin on the butt of his harquebus, which was loaded with gunpowder and had a bullet in the barrel. The harquebus was wet, as were the scrub, stones and earth on which Alatriste had been lying for more than an hour now, his clothes damp from the night dew. The only dry things were the harquebus pan and the key – wrapped in a waxed cloth – and the slow match, which was rolled up in his pack. He shifted slightly to ease the numbness in his legs and grimaced in pain. The old wound in his hip, acquired four years before – from Gualterio Malatesta during an encounter near the Plaza Mayor in Madrid – ached whenever he remained still for too long in damp conditions. For a moment, he considered the idea that he was no longer up to night dews and dawns spent in the open air, although, lately, he'd had plenty of experience of both. He was tempted to think that his was a roguish profession, but then he dismissed the idea. He might have entertained the thought if he'd had another profession to turn to, but he hadn't.

He looked at his comrades, lying as still as he was. All he could see of Sebastián Copons, crouched behind some bushes, were his espadrilles. Then he glanced up at the stone tower silhouetted against the overcast sky. They had walked a mile to get there, taking the utmost care not to be heard, and had encountered two sentinels at the tower, one asleep and one dozing. The Captain didn't get a chance to find out whether they were English or not because Copons and Ensign Muelas had silently slit their throats, *ris*, *ras*, before they could say a single word, in English or any other language. Then, forbidden to speak or light their fuses until the time was right – the wind might carry the smell down to the beach – the twenty men had spread out around the bay, which they could now see in the early light.

The bay was large enough to hold eight or ten galleys; about half a mile wide at its mouth, it formed a kind of clover leaf with three smaller coves leading off it. In the middle of the largest – and sandiest – of these coves lay a saetta, half-heeled over and kept in place by three anchors as well as by cables that held it fast to the beach and to the rocks to the east. It had a large open deck with no rowing benches and a high stern; the kind of ship that depended entirely on sail power, leaving more space for artillery along the sides. It had three sails, one square mainsail and two lateens, and the lateen yards were lowered and tied down on deck. It also had four cannon on either side, although, at that moment, they were all on the side of the ship that was tilted over. The crew were clearly engaged in careening the hull, either to repair damaged strakes, because of faulty caulking or because they were rotten, or to scrape off the barnacles, a crucial task on a pirate ship, which needed speed and clean lines if it was to attack and flee unimpeded.

The saetta was not alone. To the west of the same cove, a felucca was anchored, its prow facing into the gentle breeze blowing off the land. It was smaller than the saetta, lateen-rigged, with the trinquet sail raked forward to the prow. It didn't look like a corsair ship and had no artillery; perhaps it had been seized by the crew of the saetta. The decks of both ships appeared to be deserted, but a few men were milling around a small fire on the beach. A clumsy error, thought Alatriste: all that smoke and flames were clearly visible at night. Typical of the arrogant English, if that's what they were; for, despite their proximity, with the breeze blowing in the opposite direction, he could barely hear their voices. He had a clear view of them, though, and of the four men posted at the far end of the bay on a rocky promontory, next to one of the saetta's cannon, ready to defend the entrance to the port against inopportune visitors. However, the sea was empty as far as the horizon, and there was no sign as yet of the *Mulata*, which, Alatriste hoped, for his sake and for that of his nineteen companions, would soon be approaching.

The rabbit came out of its burrow, froze when it saw a tortoise hauling itself phlegmatically along, then hopped away and disappeared into the bushes. Diego Alatriste changed position again, rubbing his sore leg. It was a shame to see that rabbit running around, he thought, rather than roasting on a spit. Watching the corsairs enjoy their breakfast, he suddenly felt very cold and devilishly hungry. He looked across to his right, where Ensign Muelas was lying next to the well, and they exchanged a glance. The ensign shrugged and gazed out at the empty sea.

For a moment, Alatriste wondered what would happen if the galley did not appear and they were left to their fate. It wouldn't be the first time. He counted the corsairs on the beach: fifteen in all, although there might be others out of sight, not including the four standing by the cannon and others who might be on board the ships. Too many to keep at bay for very long with their harquebuses – they had six rounds per man, only enough for the initial attack. Once those were spent, it would be a question of swords and daggers, so Captain Urdemalas had better keep his promise.

He noticed that two men had left the group around the

fire and were climbing the slope that led up to the tower and the well. Not good, he thought. They must be coming to relieve the two dead sentinels or to fetch water; it didn't matter which, because they were heading straight towards him. This complicated the situation or would perhaps simply precipitate it. And still no sign of the galley. 'Od's blood. He looked to Ensign Muelas for instructions. Muelas had spotted the two men as well. Alatriste saw him rub one fist against the back of the other and then bend one finger over his harquebus: the signal to light their matches. Alatriste put his hand into his pack, took out flint, steel and slow match and lit the latter. While he was removing the waxed cloth, he blew on the match and attached it to the serpentine, screwing it into place. He noticed that his companions were doing the same, and that the breeze was carrying threads of acrid smoke towards the men coming up the hill. By this point, however, it made no difference. He placed a little gunpowder in the pan and calmly raised the harquebus, resting it on a large, flat stone, and aiming at a point between the two men. Out of the corner of his eye, he saw that Muelas was doing the same; it was up to Muelas, as commander of the squad, to decide who should begin the dance. And so Alatriste waited, his finger off the guard, breathing slowly to keep himself from shaking, until the two corsairs were so close he could see their faces. One had long hair and a bushy beard; the other, a burlier figure, was wearing a leather-lined helmet. The bearded man looked English and was dressed in the ankle-length breeches favoured by that race. They were armed with a musket and two scimitars, and were chatting, unaware of the danger. A few foreign words reached Alatriste's ears, but then the talking stopped, because the bearded man had pulled up short, about fifteen paces away. He was sniffing the air and looking around, an expression of alarm on his

face. Then Ensign Muelas fired a shot that blasted off half
the man's head, and Alatriste, taking that as a signal, shifted
the barrel of his harquebus to the left, aimed at the burlier
of the two, who had turned to run away, and felled him with
a single shot.

The other eighteen Spaniards were a select group, experts
in their field, which is why they had been chosen. The ensign
didn't have to give any order or signal while he and Alatriste
recharged their harquebuses. (This took the time needed to
say two hail Marys or two Our Fathers, which some men
actually did.) Copons and the others were already making the
whole area around the bay echo with a volley of well-directed
shots aimed both at the men on the beach and at those
guarding the cannon. Of those four, three were killed outright,
and one had dived into the water. As for those on the beach,
Alatriste saw only two fall, while the others ran for cover.
They – along with some men who appeared on the deck of
the saetta – were quick to react and began returning fire with
harquebuses and muskets. Fortunately, their shots fell short,
and since the cannon were all on the wrong side of the ship,
they couldn't be used to fend off any attack, from land or
sea.

A boat containing reinforcements was approaching from
the saetta. Like his comrades, who only put the match to the
powder when they were sure of a hit, Alatriste tried to make
good use of his five remaining bullets, firing them off as the
corsairs on the beach advanced up the slope, doubtless having
first calculated the likely number of their ambushers and
taking shelter behind rocks and shrubs as they came nearer.
Alatriste counted more than thirty of them, which was not
many if the galley arrived in time, but a considerable number
if he and his comrades ran out of ammunition and had to
fight with swords. For this reason, he rationed his bullets as

best he could; he hit another corsair, who dropped to the ground somewhere out of sight, and finally, when he came to his last bullet, he aimed it at a man who was only eight or so paces away, shattering his leg. It made a noise like a branch breaking. Then he laid down his harquebus, unsheathed his sword and waited for them to come to him. A glance told him that Ensign Muelas was lying dead by the well; and he was not the only one. He could see, too, that the bushes in which Copons was hiding were waving about wildly, while the butt of a gun rose and fell amidst the sound of blows and curses. Copons was perhaps now regretting having left Oran, for he was fighting for his life.

Alatriste heard voices shouting something in English. He could expect little mercy from them, and so he looked up at the grey sky, took a few deep breaths and gritted his teeth. 'Bloody galley,' he muttered, as he stood, sword in one hand and dagger in the other. Then, at the east end of the bay, the *Mulata* hove into view.

The galley was travelling swiftly through the calm waters of the bay towards the saetta. The galleymaster's whistle set the rhythm for the oarsmen who, chests gleaming with sweat, were putting their all into their work, giving heart and soul to their rowing, the tempo punctuated by the metallic clank of manacles and shackles and the lash of the whip, cracking through the air and making no distinction between the backs of Moors, Turks, heretics or Christians. Their gasps and moans produced a harsh noise like the stertorous breathing of a dying man. Meanwhile, sixty soldiers and fifty sailors, armed to the teeth and spoiling for a fight, were crowded together on the *arrumbada*s – the raised fighting platforms round the edge of the boat and at the prow – impatient to begin. For although they knew that the day would bring more honour than profit, not even the most arrant idler wanted to be left behind. The four Knights from Malta who were travelling as passengers – one French, one Italian and two from Castile – had also asked Captain Urdemalas' permission to join the troops, and there they were, like knights of old, in their elegant red surcoats bearing the white cross, which they wore to go into combat. They would merely have cut a ridiculously fine figure were they not known throughout Christendom as fearsome warriors.

'Row! Row! Row!' we shouted, along with the whistle and the lash. 'Board them! Board them!'

There were good reasons for this ardour of ours, given that our enemies were probably cruel and insolent Englishmen, who, not content with plundering us in the Indies, were now trying to bully and threaten their way into making a space for themselves in our back yard. We could hear firing from the land and knew that any one of those shots might take the life of a comrade. That is why we were so loud in our encouragement of the rowers, and I myself – may God forgive me, if he pays heed to such trifling matters – would have gladly picked up a whip myself and lashed the rowers' backs to make them row faster still.

'Board them! Board!'

From the moment we rounded the point, we headed straight for the saetta, with Captain Urdemalas screaming orders and curses into the ear of the helmsman. From the mouth of the bay, we saw that the saetta, because of the way it was anchored, was sideways on to the wind, while, at its stern and some distance off, the felucca's prow pointed towards the beach. If the saetta had had her cannon ready on the seaward side, she could – given our angle of approach – have done us considerable damage. However, in her current state – slightly listing and held fast by anchors and cables – she was fortunately unable to make use of her artillery. We watched the defenceless vessel gradually grow in size before us through the thin smoke given off by the linstocks held in readiness by the master gunner and his assistants as they crouched behind the cannon and culverins on the prow. The sailors in charge of the *pedreros* had meanwhile taken up positions above the cordage room and along the sides of the galley.

There were barely any harquebusiers on board, for almost all were on land, but we nonetheless bristled with pistols, pikes, half-pikes and swords, and were more than ready to use them. I had got into the habit, like so many soldiers, of tying a kerchief about my head so that my hair didn't get in the way when I was fighting or so that I could pull on a helmet, and on this occasion I was also wearing a corslet attached at the sides with chains so that I could easily pull it off if I fell into the sea, as well as carrying a small wooden shield covered in leather. With my dagger tucked in my belt and my short, wide sword in its sheath, I needed nothing more. Squeezed among my fellows in the gangway on the starboard side near the prow – for no one crossed the ram until the cannon and the other weapons had been fired – I thought about Angélica de Alquézar as I always did before going into battle, and then I crossed myself as did nearly everyone else, in readiness to board the saetta.

'There they are, the dogs!'

Yes, a dozen or so men had appeared at the rail and, in a trice, had raked us with musket-fire. The bullets, fired in haste, whistled over our heads, into the sides of the galley or into the sea, but before our enemies could seek shelter to reload, our gunner and his assistants dealt them a direct blow with a shot from the cannon, loaded with a sack of nails, bits of old chain and bullets. The saetta's rail splintered and there was a terrible sound of breaking shrouds and the creak of broken wood.

Now the English may have been good tacticians and even better artillerymen, but there was one thing they feared like the Devil, and that was what happened next, before they could recover from the shock: the Spanish infantry boarded the ship. For we Spaniards could fight on the deck of a ship as fiercely as if we were on land. Once our galleymaster and our helmsman had manoeuvred the ram of the galley so delicately that it rested against the side of the saetta without damaging so much as a strake, we fell upon the enemy. Half of us, fifty or so men, just managed to hurry across the ram's two feet of narrow planks before the *Mulata* drew back a little and, going round the stern of the saetta, passed between it and the felucca, so that the *pedreros* on our port side could rake that deck with stones, just in case. Then it turned adroitly as it approached the beach, enabling the *pedreros* on the other side to pelt the corsairs there, before landing the rest of our men, who waded through the waist-high water, yelling: 'Forward for Spain! Attack! Attack!' As the saying goes:

With sword or cutlass, dagger or knife,
I'll kill the first who threatens my life.

The truth is that I could not really pay much attention to that part of the manouevre, for by then I had jumped down from the ram on to the listing hull of the saetta. Slipping awkwardly on the grease and covering my clothes with pitch, I managed to get on to the deck. There, I took out my sword and, together with my comrades, fought as best I could. The enemy were, indeed, Englishmen, or so it seemed. We made short work of a few of the fair-haired fellows and finished off the occasional wounded sailor whose blood streamed towards the other side of the deck.

One group tried to take refuge behind the mizzen mast and the piles of canvas and rolls of cable there. They fired on us with their pistols, killing some of our men, but we hurled ourselves upon them, ignoring their shouts and boasting, for they wielded their weapons arrogantly, challenging us to come near. Oh, we came near, all right, enraged by their impudence, capturing their refuge and mercilessly putting them to the sword on the poop deck, from which some, seeing that no quarter would be given, threw themselves into the sea.

We were so athirst for blood that there was not enough meat to sink our teeth into, and so I did not fight with any man in particular, apart from a blue-eyed fellow with long sideburns, armed with a carpenter's axe, with which he cut through my shield as if it were wax, and, for good measure, left me with a dent in my corslet and a bruise on my ribs. I threw down my shield, recovered as best I could, and assumed a crouching position, intending to go for his guts, but it was difficult fighting on that tilted deck. Then one of the Knights of Malta happened by and sliced off the fellow's head just above the eyebrows, leaving me with no opponent and my opponent with his brains hanging out, his soul in hell and his body on its way to the sea.

I searched for someone else to stick my sword into, but there was no one. And so I went down with a few other men to take a look below decks, pilfering what we could while we hunted for anyone who might be hiding there.

I had the grim satisfaction of finding one such sea dog, a big freckled Englishman with a long nose, whom I discovered huddled behind some barrels of water. He crept out, ashen-faced, and fell to his knees, as if his legs would not support him, saying 'No, no' and crying 'Quarter, quarter'. Once deprived of the strength that sheer numbers give them and when they are not in that gregarious frame of mind bestowed by wine or beer, many inhabitants of that 'brave' nation swallow their arrogance with true Franciscan humility as soon as things turn sour. By contrast, when a Spaniard finds himself alone, cornered and sober, he is at his most dangerous, for like a furious beast he will hit out madly, blindly, with neither reason nor hope, with ne'er a thought for St Anthony or the Holy Virgin. But to return to the Englishman in the hold, I was not, as you can imagine, in the sweetest of moods, and so I went over to stick my sword in his throat and finish him off. Indeed I was just raising my weapon, determined to send the rascal off to Satan along with the Anglosaxon whore who bore him, when I remembered something that Captain Alatriste had once said to me: 'Never plead for your life with the man who has vanquished you, and never deny life to someone who pleads for it.' And so, restraining myself like a good Christian, I simply kicked him in the face and broke his nose. *Croc*, it went. Then I bundled him upstairs onto the deck.

I found Captain Alatriste on the beach, along with the other survivors of the attack, Copons among them. They were dirty, exhausted and battered, but alive. And that was some achievement, for as well as Ensign Muelas and the four other men who had been killed, there had been seven wounded, two of whom died later, on board the galley – proof of just how fierce the fighting had been on land. In addition to those losses there were three dead and four wounded during the boarding, including our master gunner, who died when a harquebus blew away half his jaw, and Sergeant Albaladejo, who was blinded when a musket was fired at him at point-blank range. It was no small price to pay for a saetta that was worth at most three thousand *escudos*, but this was tempered by the thought that we had slit the throats of twenty-eight pirates – almost all of them Englishmen, along with a few Turks and some Moors from Tunis – and had taken nineteen prisoners. We had also seized the felucca, and, according to the royal ordinances, we soldiers and sailors would receive a third of the value of its cargo.

The felucca was a Sicilian ship that the English had captured four days earlier. We freed eight crew members from the hold and were able to reconstruct events from what they told us. The captain of the saetta, a certain Robert Scruton, had sailed through the strait of Gibraltar in a square-rigged ship and with an English crew, resolved to make his fortune by smuggling and pirating out of the ports of Saleh, Tunis and Algiers. But their ship had proved too heavy for the light Mediterranean winds, and so they had captured a large saetta, which was faster and more suited to the job, and with that they had spent eight weeks scouring the seas, although they had not succeeded in seizing any vessel that brought them the wealth they coveted. The felucca, which was taking wheat from Marsala to Malta, had realised that the saetta was a pirate ship, but, unable to escape it, had been forced to shorten sail. The pirates, however, had drawn alongside so clumsily – a combination of heavy swell and poor helmsmanship – that the saetta itself came off worst and its starboard side was holed. That is why, being so close to the island, the English had decided to carry out repairs. Indeed, they had already completed them when we attacked, and were considering setting sail again that very day to sell the eight Sicilians, the felucca and its cargo in Tunis.

Having heard the witnesses and verified the information,

the trial was deemed to be over. The sentence was clear. The saetta had not been issued with a corsairs' patent, or with any other document recognised among honest nations. For example, the Dutch, although they were our enemies because of the war in Flanders, were treated by us as prisoners of war when we captured them in the Indies or in the Mediterranean, and our policy was to allow those who surrendered to return home, to relegate to the galley those who fought on once they had struck their flag, and to hang any captains who attempted to blow up their own ship rather than hand it over. These were the polite customs practised by civilised nations, which even the Turks were happy to follow. However, at the time, we were not at war with England – the felucca was from Syracuse in Sicily, which was as much ours as Naples and Milan were – and so these sailors had no right to proclaim themselves corsairs and to plunder the subjects of the King of Spain: they were mere pirates. Captain Scruton's avowals that he had been issued patents in Algiers and had signed agreements authorising him to sail these waters made no impression whatsoever on the stern tribunal watching him, mentally measuring up his neck, while our galleymaster – bearing in mind that this Englishman came from, of all places, Plymouth – prepared his very finest noose. And when the felucca and the saetta – the latter crewed by some of our men – set sail the following morning thanks to a north-west wind that threatened rain, Captain Robert Scruton, a subject of His Royal Highness the King of England, was left hanging by a rope from the watchtower of Lampedusa, a notice at his feet – written in Castilian and in Turkish – which read: *An Englishman, a thief and a pirate.*

The other captives – eleven Englishmen, five Moors and two Turks – were put to the oars and there they stayed, rowing their hearts out for the King of Spain, until the vicissitudes of both sea and war put paid to them. As far as I know, a few were alive when, eleven years later, the *Mulata* sank during the naval battle of Genoa against the French, with the galley-slaves still chained to their benches, because no one had bothered to free them. By then, none of us remained on board, not even the Moor Gurriato who now, with the new influx of rowers from the saetta, had more time on his hands, thus providing me with more opportunities to talk to him, as I will recount in the following chapter.

6. THE ISLAND OF THE KNIGHTS

I was impressed by both the appearance and the recent history of Malta, the island of the corsair Knights of St John of Jerusalem. The fearsome galleys of the Religion, as we called them, were the scourge of the entire Levant, for they patrolled the seas, pursuing Turkish vessels and seizing valuable merchandise and slaves. Hated by all Muslims, the Knights of St John were the last of the great military orders of the Crusades, and their members owed obedience only to the Pope. After the fall of the Holy Land, they settled in Rhodes, but when they were expelled by the Turks, our Emperor Charles V gave them Malta in exchange for a symbolic annual payment of one Maltese falcon. That gift, the fact that we were the most powerful Catholic nation in the world and their proximity to the Viceroyalties of Naples and Sicily – the latter sent aid during the great siege of 1565 – forged strong bonds between the Order and Spain, and our galleys often sailed together. Besides, many of the Knights of Malta were Spanish.

The Knights had taken a vow to fight Muslims wherever they might be. They were hard, spartan men who knew they would receive no mercy if taken prisoner and they so scorned their enemy that their galleys were under orders to attack even if they were one ship against four. Given these circumstances, it is easy to understand why the Order of Malta looked to Spain as its main defender and support, for we were the only power that gave no quarter to Turks and Berbers, whereas other Catholic nations made pacts with them or brazenly sought alliances. The most shameless of these were ever ambivalent Venice and, of course, France. Indeed, France, in her struggle with Spain, had gone so far as to allow her galleys to travel in convoy with the Turks and had permitted Barbarossa's corsair fleet to over-winter in French ports while it plundered the Spanish and Italian coasts, capturing thousands of Christians.

You may consider my state of mind when, having passed the Dragut Point and the formidable fortress of St Elmo, the *Mulata* cast anchor in the great harbour, between Fort St Angelo and the Sanglea peninsula. From there we could view the site of the dreadful siege that had taken place sixty-two years before, an episode that made the name of the island as immortal as that of the six hundred Knights of various nations and the nine thousand Spanish and Italian soldiers and citizens of Malta who, for four years, fought off forty thousand Turks, of whom they killed thirty thousand; battling for every inch of land and losing fort after fort in bloody hand-to-hand combat, until all that remained were the redoubts of Birgu and Sanglea, where the last survivors fought to the end.

As old soldiers, both Captain Alatriste and Sebastián Copons regarded these places with respect, for they could all too easily imagine the tragedy that had played out there. Perhaps that is why they were so silent, from the moment we got into a felucca to cross the large harbour to reach the Del Monte Gate until we passed under its two small towers and entered the new city of Valetta, named in memory of the Grand Master Jean Parisot de la Valette, who had led the defence of Malta during the siege. I remember walking through the city's dusty streets flanked by houses with shuttered balconies and roof gardens, with a Maltese boatman as our guide.

We viewed everything with almost religious awe, first following the city wall straight to the cathedral, then turning to the right towards the sumptuous palace of the Grand

Master of the Order and the lovely square in front of it, with its fountain and column. Then we reached the moat surrounding Fort St Elmo whose impressive star-shaped bulk loomed above. Next to the drawbridge, where the red flag bearing the eight-pointed cross of the Order was flying, our guide told us in a mixture of Italian, Spanish and lingua franca how his father, who had fought in the siege, had helped sailors from Birgu to take volunteer Knights – Spanish, French, Italian and German – from St Angelo to the besieged St Elmo; how every night they broke the Turkish blockade – by boat or swimming – to replace the terrible losses of the day, although the Knights knew full well that this was a one-way journey and that they were going to certain death. He also described how on the last night, they had been unable to cross the Turkish lines, and the volunteers had had to turn back, and how, at dawn, those who were besieged with Grand Master La Valette watched from the forts of Sanglea and St Michael, as a tide of five thousand Turks overwhelmed St Elmo in a final assault on the two hundred knights and soldiers, almost all of them Spaniards and Italians. Worn down, beaten and wounded after five weeks of fighting day and night, battered by cannon shot, the Knights continued to resist among the rubble. He concluded his tale by describing how, injured and unable to go on, the last of the Knights had withdrawn, without once turning their backs on the enemy, to the final redoubt of the church, killing and dying like cornered lions. However, when the remaining Knights saw that the Turks, enraged by the price they had been forced to pay for victory, were showing no mercy to the wounded they came upon, they strode out into the square again, prepared to die like the men they were. So it was that six of them – one Aragonese, one Catalan, one Castilian and three Italians – fought their way through the enemy to the sea, where they hoped to be able to swim to Birgu. Alas, they were taken prisoner in the water. And so angry was Mustafa Pacha – he had, after all, lost six thousand men in St Elmo alone, including the famous corsair Dragut – that he ordered the Knights' corpses to be crucified and personally cut a cross on each chest with his scimitar. Then he set the bodies on the water and let the current carry them across to the other side of the harbour, where Sanglea and St Michael continued to resist. Finally, he brought out all the other captives, stood them on the city walls and ordered their throats to be cut. The Grand Master responded to this barbarous act by killing all his Turkish prisoners and firing their decapitated heads into the enemy camp.

When our guide had finished his story, we stood for a moment in silence, thinking about what we had just heard. Then Sebastián Copons, who was leaning on the sandstone balustrade and frowning down into the moat surrounding the fort, suddenly said to Captain Alatriste, 'We'll probably end up the same way one day, Diego ... Crucified.'

'Possibly, but we won't be taken alive.'

'Not a chance.'

These words shocked me, but not because the idea, however unpleasant, frightened me exactly. I understood what Copons and the Captain were saying, for I had good reason to know by then that almost all men are capable of both the very best and the very worst. The truth is that on the blurred frontier of those Levantine waters, human cruelty – and nothing is more human than cruelty – opened up so many disquieting possibilities, and not only on the part of the Turks. There were nebulous resentments buried deep in the memory: old hatreds and family feuds, which the Mediterranean light, its sun and blue waters kept alive. For Spaniards – born of ancient races, with a centuries-long history of killing Moors or killing each other – slitting the throats of Englishmen was not the same as dealing with Turks, Berbers or the other people who lived on the shores of that sea. Captain Robert Scruton and his crew were mere intruders, and killing them in Lampedusa had been a formality, an act of family cleansing, a delousing before getting back to our proper business: Turks, Spaniards, Berbers, Frenchmen, Moriscos, Jews, Moors, Venetians, Genoans, Florentines, Greeks, Dalmatians, Albanians, renegades and corsairs. We were all neighbours, living round the same courtyard; we were people of the same caste. There was no reason why we shouldn't share a glass of wine, a laugh, a colourful insult, a macabre joke, before – viciously and imaginatively – crucifying each other or exchanging heads instead of cannonballs, with good old-fashioned Mediterranean loathing. For one always slits a person's throat better and with more pleasure when one knows the person in question.

We returned to Birgu that evening, as the dusty air and the last rays of sun tinged the walls of Fort St Angelo with red, making them look as if they were made of molten iron. Before returning to the ship, we had walked for a long time through the steep, narrow streets of the new city, visiting the harbour of Marsamucetto on the west side of the island, and the famous auberges or barracks of Aragon and Castile, the latter with its beautiful staircase. There is an auberge for each of the seven languages, as the Knights of the Order called them: the auberges of Aragon and Castile mentioned above – which, of course, belonged to the Spanish nation – those of Auvergne, Provence and France – belonging to the French nation – and those of Italy and Germany. On our way back, we ended up next to the moat of Birgu in the old part of the city, where the taverns for soldiers and sailors were to be found. And since there was still more than half an hour before the Angelus, when we would have to return to the galley, we decided to forgo yet another bowl of ship's gruel and instead wet our whistles at our own expense, eating a meal fit for Christians.

We duly installed ourselves in a small inn, around a barrel that served as a table, with a leg of mutton, some pork chops, a large round loaf of bread, and a pitcher of strong red wine from Mytilene, which reminded us of Bull's Blood. We were watching people come and go: the swarthy men who looked and behaved like Sicilians and spoke a language that still contained words used by the Carthaginians; and the women, who were very beautiful but, out of modesty, avoided male company and swathed themselves in black or grey shawls because of strictures imposed by their relatives and husbands. Indeed, the men were as jealous as Spaniards, or more so − a legacy, no doubt, of the Moors and the Saracens. And there the three of us were, sitting with our belts loosened, when some Venetian soldiers and sailors who were drinking nearby happened to buy from a passing peddlar some St Peter's stones, which were held in high regard in Malta − legend has it that the saint was shipwrecked there − because they were said to cure the bites of scorpions and snakes.

At this point I did something unwise. I was not a sceptical youth but I did question certain aspects of faith, as I had been taught to do by Captain Alatriste. And with the insolence of youth, I could not repress a smirk when I saw one of the Venetians proudly showing off to his companions the stone he had bought, threaded onto a cord. Unfortunately, he saw that smirk and took umbrage. He was clearly not a very long-suffering fellow, for he strode over to me with a snarl on his lips, one hand resting on the hilt of his sword and backed up by his companions.

'Apologise,' Captain Alatriste muttered to me.

I shot him a sideways glance, taken aback by his abrupt tone and by his order to retract the offence, although, when I thought about it later, I realised he was right. Not because he feared the consequences – although there were six of them and only three of us – but because there really wasn't time to get involved in a dispute, and because quarrelling with Venetians, and in Malta, could prove serious. Relations between Spain and Venice were not good; there were frequent incidents in the Adriatic over matters of pre-eminence and sovereignty, and it took very little to set a match to such quarrels.

And so, swallowing my pride, I gave a forced smile and said, in the lingua franca that we Spaniards used on those seas and in those lands, something like: '*Escusi, signore, no era cuesto con voi.*'

The Venetian, however, remained unappeased. Emboldened by what he believed to be this show of meekness and by the difference in numbers, he flicked back his hair – he wore it long, unlike we Spaniards, who had been wearing our hair short since the days of Emperor Charles – and heaped abuse on me, calling me a thief, which would be enough to enrage anyone, especially a proud lad from Guipúzcoa. I was foolishly about to leap to my feet, when the Captain, still impassive, grabbed my arm.

'He's just a boy and doesn't know the customs here,' he said very calmly and in Castilian, looking the Venetian straight in the eye. 'But he'll gladly buy you a mug of wine.'

Again, the man misinterpreted the situation. Thinking that my two companions were also backing down and made braver still by the presence of his colleagues, he pretended not to have heard the Captain's words and, unwilling to let go of his prey, namely me, he puffed himself up and said very insolently: '*Scende, espagnuolo marrano, ca te volio amasar.*'

Captain Alatriste, without any hint of emotion, removed his hand from my arm and glanced at Copons. Until then, Copons, as usual, had said nothing and had simply been keeping a close eye on our boastful companions. At that point, however, he stood up.

'Lily-livered swab,' he muttered.

'*Che cosa diche?*' asked the Venetian angrily.

'He says,' replied the Captain, also standing up, 'that you can beat your own whorish mother to a pulp, but not us.'

And so began the incident between Spaniards and Venetians that the history of Malta and the records of the time recall as the Birgu riot, a detailed description of which would require more paper than exists in the whole of Genoa. For having spoken those words, the Captain took out his sword, as did Copons and I, with such speed that the 'lily-livered swab' – as Copons had called him – stumbled backwards with a cut to one cheek inflicted by the dagger that had leapt like lightning from its sheath to the Captain's left hand and from there to the Venetian's face. And in less time than it takes to tell it, the man nearest Copons found his upper arm skewered by a sword, while I, light on my feet, took on the third. The latter jumped to one side, but nevertheless felt the blade of my sword against his buff coat, and even though it didn't pierce actual flesh, it was enough to encourage him to keep a respectful distance.

Then matters got out of hand, because, at that moment, the Moor Gurriato appeared from nowhere – later, I learned that he had been waiting for us in the shade ever since we had got into the boat to visit the new part of the city – and, without more ado, he lunged at the Venetian closest to hand and stuck a knife into the small of his back. The tavern was at the bottom of the street that runs from the harbour esplanade up to the church near the moat surrounding Fort St Angelo. It was an extremely crowded place, and at that hour was seething with soldiers and sailors heading back to the ships moored nearby. Attracted by the shouts of the wounded men and their comrades – who, although they had now unsheathed their swords, did not dare to approach – more Venetians came rushing in, putting us in no little danger. And although we formed a defensive semi-circle – in the manner of the old Spanish regiments – using stools and lids for shields, and stabbing and slashing for all we were worth, things would have ended badly had not many of our comrades from the *Mulata* – also awaiting the moment to embark – unsheathed their swords and taken our part without even asking the reason for the quarrel. For although galley-men were not perhaps on the best of terms with Justice, they always helped their comrades, on the understanding that such help would one day be reciprocated. And they would as gladly fight constables and catchpoles as fellow Spaniards or foreigners, it being a point of honour, after any such ruckus, to give refuge on board to any soldier, sailor or galley-slave who sought it, as a church might, only with no higher authority to answer to than the captain of the ship.

Of course, given the kind of people we enlisted – the cream of every house, you might say – in a matter of seconds, Birgu was transformed into Troy. Amid the shouts and screams of the inn-keepers and tradesmen whose furniture and wares were being hurled to the ground, we ended up with fifty or so Venetians doing battle with the same number of Spaniards.

So great was the tumult that men from both sides came to offer reinforcements, for, as soon as news of the affray reached the ships, many disembarked, sword in hand, and from one or two vessels there were even the sound of musket-fire.

Fortunately for us, we Spaniards were popular in Malta, whereas the Venetians – seen as greedy, sly and disrespectful, not to mention being guilty of conniving with the Turk – were hated even by the Italians, and so a number of Maltese men joined in, attacking the Venetians with sticks and stones, throwing some of them into the water and forcing others to dive in voluntarily in order to escape. In the old part of the city, even though no one knew or could remember the original reason for the dispute, there ensued a hunt for anything that so much as smelled of Venice, for a rumour had been put around that several men of that nation had offended the honesty of certain Maltese women – always a good way to start a riot. In the process, several Venetian-owned shops were sacked and various accounts-pending settled. The day was summed up some seventeen years later by Giulio Bragadino, a Venetian and therefore not an entirely disinterested chronicler:

The subjects of the Serenissima suffered much ill-treatment during the night, with damage inflicted to their persons and their goods ... In order to avoid further mayhem, the Grand Master of Malta and the captains of galleys and other ships had to impose their authority, ordering soldiers and sailors to return to their ships and remain there on pain of death. The instigators were sought, but none were found, although it was noted that the Spaniards, who were suspected of having started the quarrel, were very quick to leave the scene.

Nevertheless, the following morning, when the soldiers and sailors on the *Mulata* were being inspected, we got the most almighty telling-off from Captain Urdemalas, who really gave it his all, although some were sure he must have been chuckling inside. All of us were lined up along the corridors on port and starboard, having been ordered to wear full body armour, which weighed about thirty pounds, and a helmet, which weighed another thirty, just to make us suffer – all that metal was scorching in the heat of the harbour. Captain Urdemalas strode up and down from prow to stern, and he kept us standing there for a good long while after the awning had been removed from the galley, even though it was hellishly hot and there wasn't a breath of wind.

It was a spectacle worthy of a painting: those lines of men with tragic, contrite faces, sweating cobs and staring down at their feet – not out of modesty, but prudence – whenever Urdemalas passed, fixing each of us with a gimlet gaze. 'You, gentlemen, are nothing but animals,' he said in a voice loud enough to be heard in Birgu. 'A pack of delinquent braggarts who will be the ruin of me. However, before you succeed in doing so, I will, by my faith and on the souls of my ancestors, hang the lot of you if someone doesn't tell me who started last night's fracas. Gadswoons I will. I swear on myself and on Satan and on the mother who bore me that I'll hang twelve of you today from one yard-arm if someone doesn't own up.'

His voice boomed around the harbour and the city walls. However, as both we and Urdemalas expected, we were all as silent as if we were being stretched on the rack, standing firm beneath the bombardment, but winking at each other in the knowledge that sooner or later it would stop. And we were quite a sight, lined up there, many of us with cuts and bruises, some sporting plasters, bandages and dressings, others with an arm in a sling or a black eye. Far from having had a day's leave to stretch our legs on Malta, it looked as if we had come fresh from boarding a Turkish galley.

When the signal for departure was given a day later – all shore leave having been cancelled – we weighed anchor and headed north-east round the coast of Sicily to Messina. For half of the voyage we had good weather, which pleased the galley-slaves because there was a favourable wind and they barely had to row.

That same night, I had a long conversation with the Moor Gurriato. On the port side, we could see a light in the distance that might as easily have been Cape Passero as the lighthouse at Syracuse. The two sails were creaking, and galley-slaves, soldiers and sailors, apart from those on watch, were all sleeping soundly, emitting the usual snores, groans, belches and other nocturnal noises I will refrain from mentioning. My head ached and I couldn't sleep, so getting up carefully, without disturbing anyone, I walked along the starboard side, crushing cockroaches underfoot as I went and hoping that the night breeze might clear my head a little.

When I reached the bench normally occupied by the strokesman, I saw a familiar silhouette in the faint light of the lantern at the stern. The Moor Gurriato was leaning on the rail, contemplating the dark sea and looking up at the stars, which the sails, by turns, revealed and concealed as the ship rolled. He couldn't sleep either, he told me. He had never been on a ship before embarking with us in Oran, and everything was very new and strange, so that when he wasn't rowing, he spent many nights with his eyes wide open. It seemed a miracle to him that something so large, heavy and complex could move safely over the sea at night. Hoping to discover its secret, he watched the movement of the galley, the occasional faint light on the horizon, and listened to the whisper of the water that glittered phosphorescent along the sides of the ship. He said that the words the sailor on watch sang out in a monotonous voice every half-hour, when he turned over the hourglass, sounded to him like some magical incantation, like a spell or a prayer.

The hour just gone is good,
Better the one to come.
Next man's on watch,
Hourglass is turned.
We'll make good sailing
If God is willing.

It was then that I asked the Moor about the cross tattooed on his cheek, and about the legend according to which his people had once been Christians, and still were, even long after the arrival of the Muslims in North Africa and the fall of Spain in the days of the Visigoths, with Tariq, Muza and the treacherous Count Julian. These names meant nothing to him, he said after a brief silence. But it was true that his father and grandfather had told him that his tribe, the *azuagos* Beni Barrani, were different from other tribes, for they had never converted to the Mohammedan faith. After years of fighting in the mountains, they had lost almost all their Christian customs and become a people without a god or a country. That was why other Moors did not trust them.

'And why do you have that cross on your cheek?'

'I'm not sure. My father used to say it was a mark that dated from the time of the Goths, to distinguish us from the other pagan tribes.'

'The other day, you spoke of a bell hidden in the mountains.'

'*Tidt.* It is true. A large bronze bell in a cave. I've never seen it, although I've been told it has been hidden away for eight or even ten centuries, since the Muslims arrived. It is said that there are books, too, very ancient ones that no one could read, from the days of the Vandals or before.'

'Written in Latin?'

'I don't know what Latin is, but no one could read them.'

A silence fell. I imagined those men, isolated in the

mountains, remaining faithful to a religion that gradually slipped through their fingers with the passing centuries, repeating symbols and gestures whose meaning had long been forgotten. Beni Barrani, I remembered, meant 'without a country'. The children of foreigners.

'Why did you choose to come with us?'

The Moor Gurriato shifted in the dim light. He seemed embarrassed by the question.

'Fate,' he said at last. 'A man should travel while he can, should go to distant places and return wiser. Perhaps that way he will gain more understanding.'

I leaned against the netting on the side of the ship and asked, 'What is it that you need to understand?'

'Where I come from, and by that I don't mean the mountains where I was born.'

'But why?'

'Knowing where you came from will help you to die.'

There was another silence, broken by the routine words exchanged between the man on watch at the prow and the helmsman, the former indicating to the latter that the way ahead was clear. After that we heard only the creak of the yard-arms and the murmur of the water under the galley.

'We spend our life on the edge of death,' the Moor Gurriato added eventually, 'but many people do not know that. Only the *assen*, the wise men, know it.'

'Are you a wise man? Or do you want to be one?'

'No, I am simply a Beni Barrani,' he responded calmly. 'I haven't even seen the bronze bell or the books no one can read. That is why I need other men to show me the way, like that magic needle you have over there.'

He gestured towards the stern, doubtless towards the bin-nacle where, in the gloom, we could see the face of the sailor on watch caught in the glow from the compass light. I nodded.

'I see. So that's why you chose Captain Alatriste to make that journey with.'

'Yes.'

'But he's only a soldier,' I objected. 'A man of war.'

'True, he's an *imyahad*, a warrior. That's why I tell you he is wise. He looks at his sword each morning when he opens his eyes and again each night before he closes them. He knows he will die and he is prepared. Do you understand? That makes him different from other men.'

The word 'die' soon took on an urgent meaning. Until around dawn, the wind had been moderate and favourable, but then it began to blow very hard, becoming a stiff north-easterly that threatened to carry us too near the coast. The galley-slaves were whipped awake, the oars lowered into the water, and with everyone rowing, we gradually pressed ahead into the churning water, the spray drenching the rowers. It was pitiful to see them, half-naked and soaked to the skin, their lungs bursting. Sailors and cabin boys were rushing from side to side, blaspheming and praying in equal measure, while the privileged few took shelter in the stores, the infirmary, or the captain's cabin. We soldiers took our chances, clinging together in the embrasures, some of us vomiting or cursing each time the galley pitched into the heart of a wave and the water flooded the deck. The blankets and bits of canvas we threw over ourselves were of little use because the great swell was joined by a hard, cold rain that ended up sousing us all, and the wind was far too strong for us to put up the awning.

By sheer oar-power – five or six were broken that day – we managed to travel about a league, although it took us all morning. So when the galleymaster mentioned the possibility of a few soldiers lending a hand if things got really bad and there was a risk of us being blown on to the shore, it was curious to hear the chorus of protests, arguing that they were men-at-arms and therefore gentlemen, and that they wouldn't dream of taking up an oar unless, God forbid, the King condemned them to the galleys. Some even said that they would rather be drowned like new-born kittens but with their honour intact; that they would rather be chopped into pieces than see themselves brought down, even for a moment, to the vile condition of galley-slaves. And so, for the time being, there was no further discussion, and everything continued as before, with us soldiers crammed in the embrasures, shivering and soaked, spewing and praying and cursing the universe, and the galley-slaves rowing as hard as they could.

Fortunately, by mid-afternoon the wind had swung round to the south-east, and we were able to pull in the oars. Then, with the mainsail lowered and the wind behind us, a small trinquet-sail was hoist, and that put us back on course. The problem was that a fierce, stormy rain was still falling, enough for a second Great Flood. And thus, alternately lashed by rain and gusts of wind, with lightning playing in the distance and everyone crowded in the stern so as not to weight down the prow, we approached the strait of Messina at a speed, according to the pilot's calculations, of four miles for each turn of the glass. To make matters worse, night had fallen, which made it difficult to verify our position, and somewhere ahead of us lay Scylla and Charybdis, which, in bad weather, was the worst place in the world and had been the terror of sailors since Ulysses' day. However, the heavy seas and the exhaustion of the galley-slaves meant that we could neither beat to windward nor keep our distance.

And that was the situation as we were about to enter the narrow funnel of the strait – unable to turn back even if we wanted to – when some of the men swore that they could see a light on land, and the pilot and Captain Urdemalas, after much consultation, decided to take a chance, uncertain as to whether it was the fire in the Messina tower or the lighthouse about two leagues to the north. And so, leaving the trinquet-sail raised, the oars were brought out again. The galleymaster tried hard to make his whistle heard above the wind howling in the rigging, and the galley-slaves, the Moor Gurriato included, began to row, while the helmsman, battling against the rolling of the ship, struggled to keep the bow pointing towards the distant light. Our hearts in our mouths and clinging on as best we could, we plunged on into darkness, much faster than we wanted, hoping that we wouldn't be wrecked on a sandbank or a rock.

And that is precisely what would have happened if something had not occurred that many claimed was a miracle and others thought was merely the luck of the sea. For the light on the tower suddenly went out, perhaps doused by the sheer quantity of rain, just as we were, according to the pilot, nearing the city of Messina. The wind had rolled round again to the north-east and there we were, in the dark, with the sea a little calmer, looking for the harbour mouth. And had a flash of lightning not lit up the fort of San Salvador a mere pistol shot ahead of us, forcing the helmsman to fling the rudder hard in the other direction, we would have crashed straight into it and been lost just when we had salvation within our grasp.

7 . SEE NAPLES AND DIE

The night sky glowed red, Vesuvius infusing everything as far as the eye could see with a strange, ghostly light. On the other side of the city the moon was rising, and thus the outline of Naples, its buildings, hills and towers, the land and the sea, were eerily lit from two different directions, creating a mass of strange shadows. It was a landscape as unreal as that in the canvases Diego Alatriste had watched burn during the sacking of Flanders – real fire consuming painted fire.

He took a deep, pleasurable breath of the warm, salt air as he put on his belt with sword and dagger. He wasn't wearing a cape. Despite the lateness of the hour – the Angelus bell had rung – the temperature was still very pleasant. That, along with the remarkable nocturnal light, lent the city a certain melancholy enchantment. A poet such as Don Francisco de Quevedo would have written a few good – or bad – lines of verse about it, but Alatriste was no poet; his only poetry lay in his scars and a handful of memories. And so he donned his hat, and after looking both ways – dark nights in remote places were not safe, not even for the Devil – he set off, aware of the sound of his own footsteps, first on the dark stones of the road and then, muffled, on the sandy soil of Chiaia.

As he strolled along, keeping an eye out for any shadows that might be hiding among the fishing boats moored by the sea, he could see at the far end of the beach, the hill of Pizzofalcone and Uovo Castle with its feet in the calm waters. Not a single window was lit, and there were no torches in the streets. Not a breath of wind either. The ancient city of Parthenope was sleeping, wreathed in fire, and Alatriste smiled to himself beneath the broad brim of his hat, remembering. That same light, which only occurred when the old volcano stirred into life, had lit many of his youthful adventures.

That was seventeen years ago now, he thought. He had first come to Italy in 1610, after being caught up in the horror of the Morisco problem in the mountains and on the beaches of Spain. As a soldier on the corsair galleys – *leventes*, the Turks called them – with plenty of booty from the Greek islands and the Ottoman coast within the grasp of any man with enough balls to go after it, the six years of his first term in the Naples regiment had been among the best years of his life. His purse had always been full between voyages, there were the inns and taverns of Mergellina and Chorrillo, Spanish plays put on at the courtyard theatre, good wine, even better food, a healthy climate, and garrison life in the nearby villages, beneath leafy trees and vine trellises, in the company of comrades and beautiful women. He had met a future grandee of Spain there, who was serving on the Neapolitan galleys as a volunteer – which was how young noblemen made a name for themselves. The Count of Guadalmedina was the son of the man who had been Alatriste's general in Flanders at the time of the siege of Ostend.

Yes, Guadalmedina ... While he walked along the shore, Alatriste wondered if, there in his palace in Madrid, Álvaro de la Marca would know that he was back in Naples. Always supposing that the Count, friend and confidant of Philip IV, gave a fig for the fate of the man who, in 1614, in the Kerkennah Islands, had carried him, wounded, on his shoulders and borne him back through the waist-high water to the ships, with the Arabs hot on their trail. But too many things had happened since then, including sword-fights at night outside a certain house in Madrid and a few hard blows to the face by the River Manzanares.

'A pox on him!'

The curse bubbled up inside him, and he turned away with an impatient click of his tongue. The thought of Guadalmedina, whom he hadn't seen since the skirmish at El Escorial, troubled his mind and his pride. To soothe both, he thought of more pleasant matters. For heaven's sake, he was in Naples, surrounded by all the delights of Italy, in reasonable health and with a few coins clinking in his purse. He had good comrades here, too. As well as Sebastián Copons – whom he was very glad to have rescued – there were others who knew how to eat and drink well, comrades with whom a man would happily share his cape. One such was Alonso de Contreras, the oldest of his friends – for with him, when he was barely thirteen, Alatriste had enlisted as a drummer boy in the regiments heading for Flanders. Alatriste and Contreras had met up again ten years later in Italy, then in Madrid and now once again in Naples. Contreras was the same as ever: valiant, talkative and somewhat boastful, although this appearance could prove misleading and dangerous for those who did not know him. He still held the rank of Captain and had become quite famous since Lope de Vega wrote a play about him – *The King with no Kingdom*. He had served on the Maltese galleys during their attacks on the Morea coast and in the Aegean; and while he had never been exactly rich, he had always had more than enough to spend. The Duke of Albuquerque, Viceroy of Sicily, had just given him the command of the Pantelaria garrison, an island halfway to Tunis, as well as a small frigate to go pirating in if he grew bored. As Contreras put it, he was no more a King than when Lope had made him one, but it was a pleasant posting that brought with it regular pay and responsibility.

Alatriste continued along the beach. Just before he reached Pizzofalcone, he walked up the hill to his left. At the top, and after going through a gate that remained open all night near the port of Chiaia, he plunged back into the city streets, taking the usual precautions. On the corner of two streets, the light from a tavern fell across his path. Inside, he could hear the strumming of a guitar, Spanish and Italian voices and the laughter of men and women. He was tempted to go in and drink half a pitcher of wine, but he decided against it. It was late, he was tired, and he still had some way to go before he reached the large area known as the Spanish quarter where he had his lodgings. Besides, he had drunk enough to quench his thirst – and, by God, it wasn't only his thirst he had quenched that night – and he drank to the very dregs only when the demons were dancing in his heart and in his memory, which was not the case that night. His most recent memories were closer to heaven than to hell. The idea made him smile, and when he smoothed his moustache, he could still smell on his fingers the perfume of the woman whose house he had just left. It was very good, he thought, to be alive and back in Naples.

'*Non è vero*,' said the Italian.

Jaime Correas and I looked at each other. Fortunately, neither of us was carrying weapons – in the gaming house, they made you leave them at the door – because otherwise we would have knifed the insolent fellow there and then. His words may not have been offensive to an Italian, but no Spaniard would let them pass without immediately putting hand to sword. And the gambler knew very well where we were from.

'You're the one who's lying through his teeth,' I said.

I stood up, furious at having my word doubted. I grabbed a jug, which I resolved to smash in the man's face at the slightest provocation. Correas did the same, and we stood there, side by side, me facing the gambler and my comrade facing the eight or so surly individuals who were sitting round the table. This wasn't the first time we had found ourselves in such a situation, for as I mentioned elsewhere, Correas was not really one for the quiet life and was accustomed to gambling until the sun came up. He had picked up bad habits in Flanders and become an expert in cheating, gambling and whoring, and was a regular in gaming dens and brothels. He was one of those lost boys who lives his life very close to the edge and who, if he doesn't learn the error of his ways, usually finishes his days on the wrong end of a knife, rowing in the King's galleys or with a rope around his neck. As for me, what can I say? I was the same age, I was his friend, and I was certainly no saint.

So we strode around like two brave fellows, wielding our swords and wearing our hats at a jaunty angle, in that Italy of which we Spaniards had been the masters, more or less, since the old kings of Aragon had conquered Sicily, Corsica and Naples, and since the Great Captain's armies and then Emperor Charles' regiments had kicked out the French. And all this despite the Popes, Venice, Savoy and the Devil.

'You're a lying dog,' said Correas, hammering the final nail into our coffin.

A silence had fallen of the kind that does not bode well, and I cast a soldierly eye about me. Things looked very black indeed. The villain in question was a card-sharper, a Florentine, while the others were Neapolitans, Sicilians or God knows what else, but none of them, as far as I could see, were Spaniards. What's more, we were in a dingy cellar in the Piazza dell'Olmo, opposite the fountain and a long way from the Spanish quarter. The only good thing was that they were all apparently as weaponless as we were, unless they had a knife or sword concealed beneath their clothes. I privately cursed my friend who, once again, with his foolish insistence on playing cards in a disreputable hole was responsible for getting us into this mess. Not that this was the first time, but it looked likely to be the last.

The gamester, for his part, remained perfectly calm. He was a past master, accustomed to such difficulties while plying his worthy trade. His appearance was hardly reassuring: he was extremely thin, had disguised his bald head with a very bad wig, wore thick gold rings on his fingers, and the points of his waxed moustache reached almost to his eyes. He could have passed for a comic actor in a play were it not for the threatening look in his eyes. With a sly air and the falsest of smiles, he glanced at his fellow villains, then indicated the cards spread out on the grimey, wine-stained table.

'*Voacé a fato acua*,' he said coolly. '*A perduto.*'

I looked at the cards placed face-up, more annoyed because they had taken us for fools than because of the trick itself. The kings and the sevens with which he claimed to have won had more marks on them and were more dog-eared than a preacher's Bible. Even a child of two would have noticed, but the reprobate, seeing that we were greenhorns, had thought us more innocent than babes.

'Pick up our money,' I whispered to Correas, 'and let's get out of here.'

My companion didn't wait to be told twice. He quickly put the coins back in his purse. Still with the jug in my hand, I did not take my eyes off the sharper of his consorts for an instant. I was still working out moves in my head, as Captain Alatriste always advised me to do: before you get into a fight, he said, plan your escape route. It was ten paces or a dozen steps to the door where our weapons were located. In our favour was the fact that, to avoid getting the owner of the den into trouble with the law, the regulars did not usually attack there and then, but out in the street. This meant we had a clear run as far as the square. I racked my brains to remember which church to take refuge in should it come to a sword fight. Santa Maria Novella and Montserrate were the nearest.

In the end, we had no difficulty leaving, which surprised me somewhat, although you could have cut the silence with a knife. At the top of the stairs, we collected our knives and swords, gave a coin to the boy in charge, and went out into Piazza dell'Olmo, looking back all the time, because we could hear footsteps behind us.

The rosy-fingered dawn – to use the old cliché – was just appearing behind the mountain crowned by the castle of San Martino, lighting our drawn and sleepy faces, the faces of ne'er-do-wells after a night of too much wine, too much music and too much gaming. Jaime Correas had not grown much taller since Flanders, but he had broadened out in the shoulders and acquired a prematurely thick beard, as well as a sword so long that its point dragged along the ground. He indicated with a jerk of his head that the Florentine, along with three of his consorts, were coming after us. He asked me softly if we should run or unsheathe our swords. I sensed that his preference would be to take to his heels. This cooled my ardour, for I was in no fitter state than he was to be exchanging sword thrusts. Besides, according to the Viceroy's edict, anyone caught fighting in the street and in broad daylight would be sent straight to Santiago prison if he was Spanish and to Vicaria prison if he was Italian.

And so there I was, with the Florentine and his followers at my back, hesitating, like the *Miles Gloriosus* I was, between two tactics. Should I play the hero, shouting 'Forward Spain!' and all that, or imitate that speedy creature, the hare? After all, courage does not necessarily exclude prudence. Then our eyes beheld a miraculous vision: a squad of Spanish soldiers come to relieve the guard at the smaller of the harbours. And so, without further ado, we joined our compatriots and left those Italian rascals stopped in their tracks, although they did take a long hard look at us, so that they would be able to recognise us later on.

I adored Naples. Even now, when I think back to my time as a young man in that city — which was like a world unto itself, as large as Seville and as beautiful as paradise — the mere memory draws from me a nostalgic smile. Imagine me then, a young, handsome Spaniard — fighting beneath the flag of the famous infantry whose nation was the world's greatest power and greatest scourge — living in a delicious place like that: '*Madono, porta mangiare! Bisogno prosciutto e vino! Buongiorno, bella signorina!*' What's more, in Italy, with the exception of Sicily, the women walked the streets during the day without cloaks, showing their ankles, and with their hair caught back in a net or covered only by a mantilla or a light silk scarf. We Spaniards, unlike the mean French, the squalid English or the brutish Germans, still had a certain reputation in that country; for although we were arrogant and boastful, we were also perceived as disciplined, brave and free with our money. And despite our fierce nature — to which the popes of Rome could attest — we got on extraordinarily well with the Italians, especially in Naples and Sicily, where people had no difficulty in speaking Castilian. Many Italian regiments — we had some with us in Breda — spilled their blood beneath our flag, and they were never considered traitors by their compatriots or their historians. It was only later on, when Spain sent along not just the captains and soldiers who kept the French and Turks at bay, but a deluge of tax collectors, judges, scribes and other shameless bloodsuckers, that our great deeds gave way to unscrupulous domination, to the rags, banditry and poverty that would give rise to riots and bloody uprisings, like the one in 1647 led by Masaniello.

But let us go back to the prosperous, fascinating Naples of my youth, and add to this the restless company of my comrade Jaime Correas. We would hang around convents – like would-be suitors to the nuns – although we spent Fridays and Saturdays with the local roughs down by the harbour, bathing in the sea on hot nights or else visiting any balcony or shuttered window likely to conceal the eyes of some woman willing to be courted. And then there were the taverns – whose sign, in Italy, was a sprig of bay – the gaming dens and the brothels. Although, with regard to the latter, I was as restrained as my companion was unbuttoned; because, whereas Jaime would go with any whore who said 'What lovely eyes you have', I, fearful of the diseases that can afflict both health and purse, would keep out of the way, drinking wine and engaging in polite conversation, restricting myself to more peripheral activities, which, while pleasurable, carried little risk. And because – all credit to Captain Alatriste – I had been brought up to be a discreet and generous lad, and because people prefer a clock that tells the time to one that merely shows it, I was always well thought of in the elegant inns near Chiaia beach, in the bawdyhouses in Via Catalana or the Mandraccio or Chorrillo taverns. The ladies there were fond of me and found my youth and my discretion rather touching; some even occasionally ironed – and starched – my cuffs, collars and shirts. The other fellows who grazed in the same pastures all addressed me as 'friend' and 'comrade', for they knew, too, that thanks to my experiences at the Captain's side, I was by profession a swordsman, quick to unsheathe both sword and dagger, and light on my feet. That and having money to spend always gives one a good reputation among ruffians, roughnecks, cutthroats and ne'er-do-wells.

'There's a letter for you,' said Captain Alatriste.

That morning, when he had finished guard duty in Castel Nuovo, he had passed by Don Francisco's sentry post and picked up the sealed letter bearing my name. It was now lying on the table in our room in the inn of Ana de Osorio, in the Spanish quarter. The Captain was looking at me, saying nothing, only half his face and one tip of his moustache lit from behind as he stood by the window. I went over to the letter slowly, as if approaching enemy territory. I recognised the writing at once. And I swear to God that, despite all the time that had passed, despite the distance, my age and everything that had happened since that intense and terrible night at El Escorial, I experienced an almost imperceptible twinge in the scar on my back, as if I had just felt on it the brush of warm lips after the touch of cold steel. My heart stopped for a second, only to begin again, beating wildly. Finally, I reached out my hand to pick up the letter, and then the Captain turned and looked me straight in the eye. He seemed about to say something, but instead, after a moment, he grabbed his hat and belt and walked straight past me, leaving me alone in the room.

Señor Don Íñigo Balboa Aguirre
Company of Captain Don Justino Armenta de Medrano
of the Spanish Infantry in Naples

My dear soldier,

It has not proved easy to find you, although, even far from Spain, I am still kept in touch with what goes on there through relatives and acquaintances. That is how I learned that you had returned to the army in the company of that Captain Batistre or El-Triste, and that, not satisfied with slitting the throats of heretics in Flanders, you have now turned your attentions to the Turk, always, of course, in support of our universal monarchy and of the one true religion, which does you credit as a valiant, hard-working gentleman.

If you think that I am living here in exile, you are quite wrong. New Spain is a novel and exciting place, full of possibilities, and my Uncle Don Luis' name and connections are as useful here as they were at Court; even more so, given that letters take such a long time to come and go. I need say only that his position remains unchanged, indeed he has grown in prestige and fortune, despite the false accusations levelled against him last year, in relation to that incident at El Escorial. I hope to see him fully rehabilitated in the eyes of the King, our lord, for he still has influential friends and family at Court. I have good reason to believe this, too, for we have enough powder for a countermine, as you might say in your soldier's jargon. In Taxco, where I live, we produce the best and most beautiful silver in the world, and a large part of the silver carried on the fleets to Cádiz and Spain passes through my uncle's hands, that is, through mine. As Father Emilio Bocanegra would say – and I'm sure you will remember that saintly man as fondly as I do – the ways of the Lord are unknowable, especially in our Catholic homeland, which is the bulwark of the faith and of so many fine virtues.

As for you and me, a lot of time has passed and many things have happened since our last encounter, of which I remember every moment and every detail, as, I hope, do you. I have grown within and without, and I would like us to compare such changes at closer quarters; and so I very much hope that we will meet face to face on some not too distant day, when this period of difficulties, voyages and distance is a memory. As you well know, I am good at waiting. Meanwhile, if you still harbour the same feelings for me, I demand an immediate response in your own hand, assuring me that time, distance and the women of Italy and the Levant have not erased from you the marks left by my hands, my lips and my dagger. If not, then damn you, and I wish for you the worst evils in the world, imprisonment in Algiers, a spell on the galleys and impalement by a Turk. However, if you are still faithful to she who has not yet killed you, I swear I will reward you with unimaginable torment and joy.

As you see, I think I still love you, but don't rely on that or on anything else. You will find out only when we are once more face to face, looking into each other's eyes. Until then, stay alive and avoid any unpleasant mutilations. I have interesting plans for you.

Good luck, soldier. And when you attack your next Turkish galley, call out my name. It pleases me to think that I, and my name, have been on the lips of a brave man.

Yours,
Angélica de Alquézar

After a moment's hesitation, I went out into the street. I found the Captain – doublet unfastened, hat, sword and dagger on a stool beside him – sitting at the door of the inn, watching the passers-by. I was holding the letter in my hand and generously held it out to him. He didn't even want to look at it and merely shook his head.

'The name "Alquézar" has always brought us bad luck,' he said.

'She's my business,' I replied.

I saw him shake his head again, distracted. He seemed to be thinking about something else. The inn was on Three Kings Hill, and he had his eyes fixed on the junction of our street with that of San Matteo. In between two miserable shops, one selling coal, coke and kindling and the other tallow candles, some mules, tethered to rings on the wall, were liberally sprinkling the ground with their droppings. The sun was high, and above us the washing hung out to dry cast alternating rectangles of light and shade on to the ground.

'She wasn't your business alone when you were in the dungeons of the Inquisition or when we boarded the *Niklaas-bergen*.' The Captain was speaking softly, as if thinking aloud rather than talking to me. 'Nor was she only your business in the cloisters at Minillas or in El Escorial. She implicated friends of ours. People died.'

'She wasn't the problem. She was used.'

He turned slowly to face me and then glanced at the letter in my hand. I looked away, embarrassed. Then I folded up the letter and put it in my pocket. Some of the sealing wax had stuck to my nails, like dried blood.

'I love her,' I said.

'I heard you say that once in Breda, when you'd received just such a letter from her.'

'Now I love her more.'

He said nothing for some time. I leaned one shoulder against the wall. We were watching various people pass by: soldiers, women, kitchen hands, servants and errand boys.

The whole quarter, built by private individuals in the previous century at the instigation of the Viceroy Don Pedro de Toledo, housed most of the three thousand Spanish soldiers in the Naples regiment, for there was only room for a few in the barracks. The area was an unlovely, architectural mishmash of a place, but it served its purpose. There were no public edifices, only inns, hostels and tenements with rooms to let, in buildings of four or even five storeys. It was, in short, a vast military base populated by soldiers either just passing through or garrisoned there, and we all lived cheek by jowl. Some were married to Italian women, or to women who had come over from Spain and had children. We lived alongside the locals who rented us lodgings, fed us and, in short, made a living, and not a bad one, from what the military spent. On that day, as on every day, while the Captain and I were talking at the door to the inn, women called to one another from the windows above, old people leaned out to take the air, and loud voices, Spanish and Neapolitan, echoed from inside the houses. Some small ragged boys were shouting in both languages as they pursued a poor, tormented dog up the hill; they had tied a broken jug to its tail and were chasing it and calling it a Jew.

'There are some women ...' the Captain began, then stopped, frowning, as if he had forgotten the rest of the sentence.

For some unknown reason, I was irritated. Twelve years ago, in that same Spanish quarter, my former master – with too much wine in his belly and too much anger in his heart – had killed his best friend and marked the face of a woman with a dagger.

'I don't think you're in a position to give me lessons about women,' I said, raising my voice slightly. 'Especially not here, in Naples.'

Touché. His green eyes lit up with an ice-cold flash of lightning. Anyone else would have been afraid of that look; I wasn't. He himself had taught me not to be afraid of anything and anyone.

'Nor in Madrid,' I added, 'with poor Lebrijana crying her eyes out while María de Castro ...'

Now it was my turn to leave a sentence unfinished, uncertain how to continue, for the Captain had slowly got to his feet and was looking at me hard, from very close to, with eyes that were the same colour as the wintry water in the Flanders canals. I brazenly held his gaze, but swallowed hard when I saw him smooth his moustache.

'Hm,' he said, studying the sword and dagger on the stool beside him. 'I think Sebastián is right,' he went on after a moment. 'You've grown up too fast.'

He picked up his weapons and buckled them on. I had seen him do this a thousand times, but on this occasion, the clink of steel made my skin prickle. Finally, he donned his broad-brimmed hat, which cast a shadow over his face.

'You're quite the man now,' he added. 'Capable of raising your voice and, of course, of killing. But capable, too, of dying. Try to remember that when you talk to me about certain things.'

He continued to fix me with the same cold stare, as if he had just seen me for the first time. And then I did feel afraid.

The washing festooned along the narrow streets resembled shrouds floating in the darkness. Diego Alatriste left the broad, paved Via Toledo, with torches blazing at every corner, and made his way into the Spanish quarter, whose steep, straight streets rose up the gloomy San Elmo hill. You could just make out the castle above, still vaguely lit by the fading, reddish light from Vesuvius. Having stirred into life in recent days, the volcano was now falling asleep once more. A brief wisp of smoke hovered over the crater, its red glow reflected only faintly by the clouds and on the waters in the bay.

As soon as he felt safe among the shadows, Captain Alatriste allowed himself to vomit, grunting like a pig. He remained there for a while, leaning his head against the wall and holding his hat in one hand, until the world around him stopped spinning and a bitter clarity of mind replaced the vapours from the wine he had drunk – a lethal mixture of Greco, Mangiaguerra, Latino and Lacrima Christi. This was hardly surprising – he had spent all evening and part of the night alone, going from tavern to tavern, avoiding any comrades he met on that Via Crucis, and only opening his mouth to ask for more wine.

He looked behind him, towards the brightly lit Via Toledo, in case there should be any witnesses. He had sent the Moor Gurriato away with a flea in his ear, and he would probably now be sleeping in the modest barracks in Monte Calvario. There wasn't a soul in sight, so only the sound of his footsteps accompanied him when he put on his hat again and set off, orienting himself down the dark streets. He crossed Via Sperancella, making sure the hilt of his sword was easily accessible and keeping to the middle of the street to avoid any unfortunate encounters in porches or at corners, and then he continued on until he reached the arches where the street narrowed. Turning right, he walked as far as the small square and church of the Trinità dei Spagnuoli. That area of Naples brought him good memories and bad, but it was the latter that had been stirred into life again that afternoon. Despite the years that had passed, they were still there, fresh and vivid, like mosquitoes refusing to drown in a glass of wine.

It wasn't just that he had killed a man and scarred a woman's face. It wasn't a matter of remorse or of an ache that could be relieved by going into a church and kneeling down in front of a priest, in the unlikely event that Diego Alatriste would enter a church other than to seek refuge from the Law. He had killed many people during his forty-five years and knew that he would kill many more before the time came when he would have to pay for all his misdemeanours. No, the problem was of quite a different order, and the wine had helped him first to digest it and then to vomit it up. What dogged him was the chilling certainty that every step he took in life, every sword-thrust to left or right, every scrap of money he earned, every drop of blood that spattered his clothes, all formed a kind of damp mist, a smell that clung to his skin like the scent of a fire or a war. The smell of life, of the passing years with no turning back, of the uncertain, hesitant, or resolute steps he took, each one of which determined the steps that would follow. It was the smell of resignation and impotence before an irrevocable destiny. Some men tried to disguise that smell with fantastical perfumes or to ignore it by averting their gaze, while others steadfastly breathed it in, facing it head on, aware that every game, even life and death, had its rules.

Before he reached the church of San Matteo, Diego Alatriste took the first street on the left. The inn of Ana de Osorio was only a few steps away and was always lit at night by the candles that burned in the three or four wall niches dedicated to the Virgin and to various saints. When he reached the door, he looked up from beneath the brim of his hat at the dark sky between the houses and the lines of washing hung out to dry. Time changes some places and leaves others untouched, he thought, but it always changes your heart. Then he muttered an oath and went slowly up the unlit stairs that creaked beneath his boots. He opened the door to his room, fumbled around for flint and steel, and lit an oil lamp hanging from a beam. He unbuckled his belt, threw his weapons on the floor, not caring who he might wake up, then went in search of the demijohn of wine he kept in a corner and quietly cursed again when he found it empty.

The serenity he had felt at being back in Naples had vanished that afternoon with a brief conversation in the street below and with the realisation, once again, that nobody goes through life unscathed, and that with just a few rash words, a lad of seventeen could become a mirror in which one saw one's own reflection, along with the scars and disquieting memories that can only be avoided by those who have not lived enough. Someone had written that travelling and books led to wisdom. This was true, perhaps, for some men, but in the case of Diego Alatriste they led to a table in a tavern.

A couple of days later, I found myself involved in a curious incident. I will describe it to you now just to show that, despite the grand airs I put on and everything I had experienced during those years, I was still very much a babe newly weaned.

I was returning in the small hours from guard duty next to what we called the Alcalá tower, near Uovo Castle. Apart from the vague reddish glow in the sky above the volcano and its reflection in the waters of the bay, it was a dark night. As I walked up Santa Lucia, past the church, near the fountains and next to the little chapel there, which was adorned with ex-votos depicting babies, legs and eyes made from wax and brass, as well as bunches of withered flowers, medallions and almost anything else you care to name, I made out the figure of a woman on her own, her cloak wrapped about her. Being in that place at that hour, I thought, meant that she was either very devout or was craftily setting her nets. Anyway, on the premise that, to a young falcon, all flesh is good flesh, I slowed my pace, trying to get a look at her in the dim light of the oil-lamps burning on the altar. She seemed quite a handsome woman, and as I approached, I perceived the rustle of silk and the smell of amber. This, I thought, meant that she was no mere prostitute, and so I showed more interest, trying to catch a glimpse of her face, which was almost hidden by her mantilla. The parts of her I could see were very pleasing.

'*Svergognato anda il bello galante,*' she said charmingly.

'I'm not forward at all,' I responded calmly, 'but no man could remain indifferent before such beauty.'

I was encouraged by her voice, which was young and clear and Italian, not like the voices of so many of our proud compatriots, whether Andalusian or not, who worked in Italy and made out that they were of the highest nobility, yet always addressed potential clients in plain Castilian. I was standing in front of her now but still could not see her face, although her figure, which pleased me greatly, was silhouetted against the glow from the altar. Her mantilla seemed to be made of the finest silk, and from the little I could see of her, I was tempted to buy the whole bale.

'*Tan sicura crede Lei tener la sua caccia?*' she asked slyly.

I may have been young, but I was not entirely a fool. When I heard those words, I was sure: she was a lady of the night, albeit dressed as a lady of quality. She was not at all like the ordinary whores, trulls, drabs and stales who hung about on street corners, the kind who swore they would faint at the sight of a mouse, but didn't turn a hair when they saw half a company of harquebusiers arrive for business.

'I'm not on the hunt,' I said simply. 'I've just come off duty, and I feel more like sleeping than anything else.'

She studied me in the dim light, weighing me up. I assume

my youth was evident in my face and my voice. I could almost hear her thinking.

'*Spagnuolo e soldato bisogno*,' she concluded scornfully. '*Più fanfaronata che argento.*'

There she touched a nerve. '*Bisogno*' was the nickname given to the new Spanish soldiers who arrived in Naples as innocent as Carib tribesmen, unable to speak the language, apart from the word '*bisogno*' – 'I need'. And, as I say, I was very young. Anyway, somewhat piqued, I patted my purse, which contained three silver carlins, one piece of eight and a few smaller coins. I was forgetting, of course, Don Francisco de Quevedo's sage advice: 'When it comes to women, choose the cheapest.'

'*Mi piace il discorso*,' said the lady pirate with great aplomb.

And without more ado, she took my hand and tugged at me gently. Her hand was small and warm and young. That assuaged my fear that she might simply be putting on a youthful voice and that, beneath the disguise, I would find a haggard old whore trying to pass herself off as a sweet virgin. I still hadn't seen her face though. Then I decided to clarify the situation, saying that I had no intention of going as far as she was offering to go. However, fearing – fool that I was – that I might offend her with a brusque negative, I remained somewhat ambiguous. And so, when I told her that I was going back to my inn, she bemoaned my lack of manners in allowing her to return to her house unaccompanied; besides, her house was close by, in Pizzofalcone, at the top of those steps. A woman alone and at night, she said, must avoid any unfortunate encounters. As a final flourish, she allowed her mantilla to slip a little, as if by accident, revealing a firm mouth, very white skin and the kind of dark eyes that pierce and kill in a trice.

There was nothing more to be said, and we walked along,

arm in arm, with me breathing in her amber perfume, listening to the rustle of silk and thinking, with every step, and despite all my experience to date, that I was merely accompanying a woman through the streets of Naples and that nothing bad could possibly come of it. I even doubted, in my innocence, that she really was a strumpet. It occurred to me that she was perhaps merely a capricious young girl, a strange miracle of the night, out on a youthful adventure. You can see how very stupid I was.

'*Vieni qua, galantuomo.*'

These words, spoken in a whisper, were accompanied by a caress to my cheek, which did not displease me. We reached her house, or what I took to be her house, and the sweet girl removed a key from under her cloak and opened the door. I may have been losing what little sense I had, but I noticed at once how sordid the place was, which put me on the alert. I tried to say goodbye, but she again took my hand. We had walked up the steps that go from Santa Lucia to the first houses in Pizzofalcone – the large barracks I lived in years later had not yet been built – and once through the door, we entered a deep, dark, musty hallway. She clapped her hands, and an old serving-woman arrived bearing a light. She led us up more stairs to a room furnished only with a mat, two chairs, a table and a straw mattress. That room dispelled all my fantasies: this was clearly not a private house, but a place where flesh was bought and sold, one of those places that abound in fake mothers, shopkeepers selling their own nieces and very distant cousins. As the poet says:

The comely widow dressed in black
Swears to everyone, it's said,
That fearing to see her husband's ghost
She much prefers to share her bed.

Anyway, the woman removed her mantilla and revealed a reasonably attractive face, although rather more heavily made up and less youthful than it had seemed to me in the dark. She started telling me a long unlikely tale about a jewel a female friend of hers had pawned, and about a cousin or brother of one or the other, and some money that she needed desperately in order to save the honour of both ladies, and I don't know what else, but all very pertinent no doubt. I, meanwhile, hadn't even sat down and was still standing there, with my hat in my hand and my sword in my belt, waiting for her to finish speaking. My idea was to deposit a few coins on the table, in payment for wasting her time, then leave. However, before I could put that plan into action, the door opened again and, just as if we were in a farce by Quiñones de Benavente, the villain of the piece made his entrance.

'Gadzooks!' quoth the villain.

He was Spanish, dressed as a soldier, and bore himself very proudly, although clearly there was nothing of the military about him, and the closest he had ever got to a Lutheran or a Turk had been in the theatre. Otherwise, he was like a character straight out of a book, all bluster and bravado, swearing by Christ's wounds and affecting a false Andalusian accent as if he had just come hotfoot from Seville. He had the inevitable waxed moustache proper to all swashbucklers, and, having stalked into the room, he immediately struck a pose, legs astride, one fist on his waist and the other on the hilt of a sword seven spans long. He pronounced his 'g's as 'h's and his 'h's as 'j's – a sure sign of unassailable bravery. In short, he was the very image of the kind of pimp who takes young girls and lives off the fruits of their hard labour whilst he boasts of having killed no end of men, of regularly handing out beatings before he's even had breakfast, roughing up whores in the presence of their bully-boys, making mincemeat of catchpoles, holding his tongue on the rack, enjoying the admiration, respect and affection of his fellow ruffians, and Lord knows what else.

'God's teeth!' he spluttered, frowning furiously, 'I've told you before, Señora, that for the sake of my honour, you must never bring another man into this house!'

He continued in the same vein for some time, declaiming as if from a pulpit, thundering against the treachery and scandal brought on him by his dam. He declared that, even captive in Algiers, he would not have suffered such humiliation, and warned that his sword was very sharp, by God. Because when the rage took him and his bile was up, by all that's holy, he could as lief kill two as two hundred. He was within an ace of marking that trollop's face with the sign of the cross so that she would learn once and for all that Cannibals and Gorillas like him (he meant, of course, to say Hannibals and Attilas) would not put up with such excesses, and if anyone should abuse his good faith and try to put horns on his head, his wrath would be terrible to see. And woe betide the Turk in question if he, too, wasn't man enough to dispatch seven men and put them well beyond the help of any surgeon. By the Eternal Father and the mother who bore him, et cetera, et cetera.

While this jewel of the scoundrelry babbled on, I stayed where I was, my back to the wall, hat in hand and sword in sheath, saying nothing, but waiting to see when he would finally get to the point. And so I had the leisure to observe the poor sinner, who took her role very seriously, like someone who knows both words and music, and was looking troubled and contrite and fearful, wringing her hands in great sorrow, and occasionally interposing excuses and pleas. Her better half, without ceasing his deluge of words, would now and then raise his hand from his hip as if to slap her, only to hold back at the last moment. And he did all this without once looking at me.

'So,' said the pimp, coming at last to the nub of the matter, 'we'll have to reach some arrangement; otherwise, I can't be answerable for my actions.'

I stood where I was, silently studying him, while I pondered what Captain Alatriste would do in my shoes. However, as soon as I heard the words 'arrangement' and 'actions', I moved away from the wall and lunged at the villain so quickly that I had put my hand to my dagger, unsheathed it and slashed his face before he could cry 'God save me'. I didn't see much else apart from the braggart collapsing with a gash above his ear, his whore rushing to his aid with a yelp of horror, and then, fleetingly, the steps in the house and then those of Santa Lucia, which I took four at a time and in the dark, risking a fall, as I fled as fast as my young legs would carry me. For as the saying goes – and quite right too – it's every man for himself and the Devil take the hindmost.

8. THE CHORRILLO INN

Captain Alonso de Contreras was drinking from a fountain, cupping the water in his hands. Then, drying his bristly moustache on the sleeve of his doublet, he looked across at Vesuvius, whose plume of smoke melted into the low clouds on the far side of the bay. He took a deep, satisfied breath of the cool breeze blowing along the dock, where his frigate, ready to set sail, was moored alongside a square-rigged French vessel and two galleys belonging to the Pope. Beside him, Diego Alatriste also took a drink from the fountain, and then they both continued their walk towards the imposing black towers of Castel Nuovo.

It was midday, and beneath their feet the sun and the breeze were gradually drying the rivulets of blood left by eight Morisco corsairs who had been beaten to death in the early hours of that morning, almost as soon as they stepped off the galleys that had captured them off Cape Colonna five days earlier.

'I hate leaving Naples,' Contreras said. 'Lampedusa is so small and in Sicily I have the Viceroy on my back. Here, I feel free again, I even feel younger. I swear to God, this place could rejuvenate anyone, don't you agree?'

'I suppose so, although I think it might take rather more than that to rejuvenate us.'

'You're right. It's as if time were travelling post-haste. Speaking of post, I've just come from Don Francisco's, and someone said there was a letter for you. I've had a letter myself from Lope de Vega. Our protégé Lopito will be coming to Naples at the end of the summer. Poor lad, eh? And poor Laura – dead from a fever after only six months of marriage. God, how time flies! That trick we played on her uncle seems like only yesterday, and yet it's a whole year ago.'

Alatriste said nothing, his thoughts elsewhere. He was still staring at the dark stains that ran from the quay to the Customs house. The men from whose bodies the blood had flowed had been part of a group of twenty-seven corsairs from Algiers – all of them Moriscos – captured on board a brigantine that had plundered a number of ships along the coasts of Calabria and Sicily, among them a Neapolitan vessel on which every single member of the crew – from captain to cabin boy – had been put to death for flying the Spanish flag. As the prisoners were being taken off the vessel, those recently widowed and orphaned stood on the quay alongside the crowd that usually gathered for the arrival of galleys. Such was the public anger that, after a brief consultation with the bishops, the Viceroy agreed that those who were prepared to die as Christians would be hanged in three days' time without suffering any further torture, but those who refused to accept the one true faith would be handed over to the people, who were clamouring for a more immediate form of justice. Eight of the Moriscos, all of them *tagarinos* – Spanish Muslims from the same Aragonese village, Villefeliche – spurned the priests waiting for them on the quayside and affirmed their faith in Islam. It therefore fell to some Neapolitan boys, the urchins of street and port, to beat them to death with sticks and stones.

The bodies had been displayed beneath the lantern on the quay and on the tower of San Vicente; now what was left of them was being burned, amid much celebration, on the other side of the smaller harbour in La Marinella.

'By the way,' Contreras said, adopting a confidential tone,

'there's going to be another raid on the Levant. I've been asked to lend them Gorgos, my pilot, and they've spent days consulting my *Universal Map*, which details almost every inch of these coasts. And while I'm honoured that they should do so, I'm angry, too. I haven't seen my *magnum opus* since Prince Filiberto asked to borrow it in order to have a copy made. And whenever I demand it back, those bloodsucking cockroaches in black fob me off with excuses, devil take 'em!'

'Galleys or sailing ships?' Alatriste asked.

With a sigh, Contreras put thoughts of his map to one side.

'Galleys. Ours and those belonging to the Knights, I understand. The *Mulata* is one of them. So you have a campaign to look forward to.'

'A long one?'

'Fairly. They're saying one month or two, beyond the Mayna channel, possibly even as far east as the Dardanelles, where, as I recall, you wouldn't need a guide.'

Alatriste pulled a wry face in response to his friend's broad smile. They left the harbour and proceeded along the esplanade between the Customs house and the imposing moat surrounding Castel Nuovo. The last time Alatriste had seen the Dardanelles was in 1613, when the galley he was sailing in was captured by the Turks near Cape Troya. Many died and the lateen yard bristled with arrows. Gravely wounded in one leg, Alatriste had been liberated along with other survivors when the Turkish ship was, in turn, captured within sight of the fortresses overlooking the strait.

'Do you know who else is going?' he asked, raising one hand to the brim of his hat, to greet a few acquaintances — three harquebusiers and a musketeer on guard at the postern by the ramp leading up to the castle. Contreras did the same.

'According to Machín de Gorostiola, there will be three of our own galleys and two belonging to the Knights. Machín is embarking with his Basques, which is how he knows about the plan.'

They reached the esplanade, where carriages and cavalry and an animated crowd were heading towards the palace square and Trinità dei Spagnuoli, on their way back from the burning of the Moriscos. A dozen or so young lads marched alongside them. They were carrying on a broom handle the tattered, bloody tunic of a corsair.

'The *Mulata* will be carrying extra troops,' Contreras went on. 'I believe Fernando Labajos will be on board along with twenty experienced harquebusiers, all from your company.'

Alatriste nodded, pleased. He got on well with Lieutenant Labajos, a tough, efficient veteran who was accustomed to life on the galleys. As for Captain Machín de Gorostiola, he commanded a company made up entirely of Basques from Vizcaya; sturdy, long-suffering men who were both cruel and unrelenting in combat. It was set to be a serious expedition.

'That's fine by me,' he said.

'Will you take the boy?'

'I suppose so.'

A downcast Contreras twirled his moustache.

'I'd give anything to come with you. I do miss the good old days, my friend. Do you remember how the Turks used to call us the Catholic king's corsairs? And how we would fill our hats to the brim with silver coins? Ah, all those famous battles and beautiful whores! Dear God, I'd give Lampedusa, my Knights Hospitaller's habit and even the play Lope wrote about me, just to be thirty again. What times, eh, those of the great Duke of Osuna!'

They grew serious at the mention of the unfortunate Duke's name, and said nothing more until they reached Via dei Macellai, opposite the gardens belonging to the Viceroy's palace.

The great Duke of Osuna was the same Don Pedro Téllez Girón under whom Alatriste had fought in Flanders, during the siege of Ostend. Later made Viceroy of Naples and then of Sicily, he and the Spanish galleys had sown terror throughout the seas of Italy and the Levant during the reign of Philip III, gaining the respect of Turks, Berbers and Venetians alike. His private life may have been outlandish and scandalous, but the Duke was an efficient statesman and had met with great success as a soldier, always eager for glory and for booty, which he later squandered. He surrounded himself with the best soldiers and sailors and had made many men at Court, including the King, very rich indeed. However, the dazzling rise of his star had inevitably aroused a great deal of resentment and, after the King's death, his life ended in ruin and imprisonment. Subjected to a trial that never reached a conclusion, and refusing to defend himself because, he maintained, his exploits spoke for themselves, the great Duke of Osuna had died a miserable death in prison, to the applause and joy of the enemies of Spain, in particular Turkey, Venice and Savoy, whom he had held at bay during the period when the black flags bearing his ducal coat of arms victoriously ravaged the Mediterranean. His last words were: 'If I have served God as well as I have served my King, then I have been a good Christian.'

Don Francisco de Quevedo had been a close friend – indeed, his friendship with Diego Alatriste dated from that same period in Naples – and he was one of the few who had remained faithful to the Duke, even in misfortune. He wrote some of his finest sonnets by way of an epitaph. These lines, for example:

Although his country has denied him praise,
His deeds will always be his best defence;

Imprison'd by Spain, he died — poor recompense
For one who conquer'd Fortune all his days.

And this other poem, which reflects, better than any history book, the reward that our wretched Spain all too often gave its best sons:

Though he annulled the marriage of the sea and Venice
And crushed the waves beneath the keels of Spain,
Making shake both Cyprus Isle and Greece,
This conqueror was conquered by the Law's thin cane!

'Speaking of your young companion,' Contreras said suddenly, 'I have news of him.'

'Of Íñigo?'

'The very same. But I doubt very much that this news will please you.'

And having said that, Contreras brought Diego Alatriste up to date. In one of those coincidences so common in Naples, a certain acquaintance of his, a chief constable, had been interrogating a ne'er-do-well who frequented the Chorrillo Inn. At the first turn of the screw, the man in question, who was not made of the sternest of stuff, had blabbered everything he knew about man and God. Among other things, he mentioned that a certain Florentine gambler, a regular customer at such places and more astute than brave, was recruiting villains in order to recover — through blood and an ambush — a gaming debt incurred in Piazza dell'Olmo by two young soldiers, one of whom was lodged at Ana de Osorio's inn, in the Spanish quarter.

'Are you sure he was referring to Íñigo?'

''Od's blood! The only thing I'm sure about is that one day I'll have to meet my Maker, but the description and the fact that he's lodging at the inn fit like a glove.'

Alatriste smoothed his moustache and instinctively placed his left hand on the hilt of his sword.

'This happened at the Chorrillo, you say?'

'The very place. Apparently, the Florentine frequents the taverns in that area.'

'And did the snitch give the Florentine's name?'

'Yes, Giacomo Colapietra – a rogue and a rascal, by all accounts.'

They walked on in silence, Alatriste frowning beneath his hat, which cast a shadow over his cold, green eyes. When they had gone only a short distance, Contreras gave a chuckle.

'By my troth, my friend, I'm sorry to be leaving tonight. I would swear that the Chorrillo is about to become a very interesting place indeed!'

As it turned out, it was our room at the inn that was about to become a very interesting place, for shortly before the Angelus, just as I was about to go out for the evening, Captain Alatriste came in with a loaf of bread under one arm and a bottle of wine under the other. I was accustomed to divining his thoughts and his mood, and as soon as I saw the way he threw his hat down on the bed and unbuckled his sword, I knew that something was troubling him.

'Are you going out?' he asked, seeing that I was dressed in my street clothes.

I was, it must be said, rather smartly turned out in a shirt with a Walloon collar, a green velvet waistcoat and a fine cloth doublet – the latter bought at the sale of Ensign Muelas' effects after his death in Lampedusa – breeches, stockings and silver-buckled shoes. On my hat, I had a new green silk ribbon. I said that, yes, I was going out; that Jaime Correas was waiting for me at an inn in Via Sperancella, although I spared the Captain the details of our planned expedition, which included a visit to an elegant gaming den in Via Mardones. This would be followed by a supper of roast capon and cherry tart accompanied by a little wine at the house of the *Portuguesa*, a place near the fountain of the Incoronata, where there was music and you could dance the canario and the pavanne.

'And what's in the purse?' he asked, seeing me close it and put it in my pocket.

'Money,' I said curtly.

'It looks like a lot of money for one night.'

'How much I take with me is my business.'

He stood looking at me thoughtfully, one hand on his hip, while he digested my insolent riposte. It was true that our savings were shrinking. His savings, which he had placed with a goldsmith in Via Sant'Anna, would be just enough to pay for our lodgings and to help out the Moor Gurriato, whose sole wealth lay in the silver earrings he wore. The Moor had not yet received his first pay and, as a new soldier, he only had the right to stay in the barracks and eat whatever the troops ate. As for my money, about which the Captain never asked, there had been a number of drains on my purse of late, so much so that I needed a fair wind at the gaming table if I was not to end up without a penny.

'And I suppose getting knifed to death on a street corner is your business too?'

My hand, which had reached out to pick up my sword and my dagger, stopped halfway. I had spent many years by his side, and I knew that tone of voice.

'Are you referring to a possibility, Captain, or to one knife thrust in particular?'

He did not reply at once. He had opened the bottle of wine and poured himself a mugful. He drank a little and peered at the wine, assessing the quality of what the inn-keeper had sold him. Apparently satisfied, he took another sip.

'There are many reasons for getting yourself killed, but getting yourself killed over a gaming debt is simply shameful.'

He was speaking calmly, still gazing at the wine in his mug. I was about to protest, but he raised his hand to stop me.

'It is,' he concluded, 'unworthy of a true man and of a soldier.'

I scowled, for while the truth may hurt a Basque, it never breaks him.

'I have no debts.'

'That's not what I've heard.'

'Whoever told you that,' I retorted, 'is a lying Judas.'

'What's the problem, then?'

'What problem are you referring to?'

'Explain to me why someone would want to kill you.'

My surprise, which must have been written all over my face, was entirely genuine.

'Kill me? Who?'

'A certain Giacomo Colapietra, a Florentine gamester, and a regular at the Chorrillo and the Piazza dell'Olmo. He's currently hiring some ruffians with sharp knives to finish you off.'

I took a few steps about the room, stunned. I wasn't expecting such news and a wave of embarrassment swept through my body.

'It isn't a debt,' I said. 'I've never had any debts.'

'Tell me what happened.'

I explained as briefly as I could how Jaime Correas and I had been halfway through a card game with the Florentine when he had tried to cheat us by using marked cards, and how we had left without giving him the money he claimed we owed him.

'I'm not a child, Captain,' I said.

He looked me up and down. My account did not seem to have improved his view of the affair. While it was true that the Captain was often quite happy to drink everything that was put in front of him, it was equally true that he had never been seen with a deck of cards in his hand. He despised those who risked money which, in his profession, could pay either for a life or for the sword that took that life away.

'Nor yet a man, it seems.'

That roused my anger. 'No one has the right to say that to me,' I retorted, my pride injured, 'I won't allow it.'

'*I* have the right to say it.'

His eyes were as cold as the ice that had crunched beneath our boots in Flanders.

'And you,' he added after a heavy silence, 'will give me that right.'

This wasn't a statement; it was an order. Struggling to find a response that would not prove too humiliating, I glanced at my sword and my dagger, as if appealing to them for help. Like the Captain's weapons, they both bore scratches and dents on the blades and guards. And I had scars on my body, too, although not as many as him.

'I've killed ...'

Several men, I wanted to say, but I held back, out of shame. It sounded like an empty tavern boast spoken by a ruffian.

'Who hasn't?'

He was regarding me ironically, scornfully, in a way that made my gorge rise.

'I'm a soldier,' I protested.

'Even a deserter can say he's a soldier. The gaming dens and taverns and whorehouses are full of them.'

This comment enraged me still further, almost to the point

of tears. It was unfair, a dreadful thing to say, especially since the man saying it had seen me by his side at the Gate of Lost Souls, at the Ruyter Mill, in the barracks at Terheyden, on board the *Niklaasbergen*, on corsair galleys and in many other places.

'You know I'm no deserter,' I stammered.

He looked down at the floor, as if aware that he had gone too far. Then he took another sip of wine.

'Those reluctant to accept another's advice are often prone to err,' he said, barely raising his lips from his mug. 'You are not yet the man you think you are, nor the man you should be.'

That was the final straw. Almost mad with rage, I turned my back, buckled on my sword and dagger, picked up my hat and headed for the door.

'Not, at least, the man *I* would like you to be,' he added. 'Or the man your father would have liked you to be.'

I paused on the threshold. Suddenly, for some strange reason, I felt above him, above everything.

'My father ...' I began, then pointed to the bottle of wine on the table. 'At least he died before I saw him so drunk he couldn't tell a fox from a rabbit.'

He took a step towards me, just one, a murderous glint in his eye. I stood firm, holding his gaze, but he stayed where he was, looking at me hard. Then slowly I closed the door behind me and left the inn.

The following morning, while the Captain was on guard at Castel Nuovo, I took my trunk and moved into the barracks in Via Monte Calvario.

From Don Francisco de Quevedo
to Don Diego Alatriste y Tenorio
Company of Captain Armenta de Medrano
Naples Regiment

My dear Captain,

Here I am, still at Court, loved by the great and spoiled by the ladies, enjoying the good favour of everyone who counts, although time marches on and I find myself ever more unsteady on my legs and unable to walk now at more than an amble. The one cloud on the horizon is the appointment of Cardinal Zapata to the post of Inquisitor General. My old enemy Father Pineda keeps pestering him to include my works on the Index of Prohibited Books. However, God will provide.

The King is as kind as ever and continues to perfect himself in the art of hunting (of all kinds), as is only natural in a man in the full flower of youth. The Count-Duke, meanwhile, rises a little higher with each shot fired by our second Theodosius, so everyone is happy. However, the sun shines on both kings and commoners: my ancient Aunt Margarita is about to pass on to a better life, and I have reason to believe that her last will and testament will contain something that will raise me a little higher too. Otherwise, there is not much to tell after January's bankruptcy, except to say that the Treasury is surrounded by the usual folk, that is to say, everyone, and a few more besides, not counting the Genoans and those Portuguese Jews of whom the Count-Duke is so fond; for it is always far more galling to see a banker thrive than a Turk. As long as the galleons from the Indies continue to arrive, carrying in their holds large quantities of silver and that other sweet blond metal, everything will continue as usual in Spain: bring me some wine, roast me some pork, for as long as I can eat and drink, the maggots must fast.

Of the mudhole that is Flanders I will say nothing, because in Naples, among others of the same profession,

*I am sure you receive more than enough information.
Suffice it to say that the Catalans continue to deny the
King the money he needs for the war and barricade
themselves in behind their privileges and their laws.
Many predict a bad outcome for such obstinacy.
Regarding a new war, which, with Richelieu in the
Palais du Louvre, seems inevitable sooner or later, any
domestic troubles here would suit France perfectly, for
as they say, the Devil looks after his own. With respect
to your adventures on the wine-dark sea, whenever some
brief report is published here about what our galleys have
been up to, I imagine that you were involved in every
escapade, putting Turks to the sword, and that pleases
me. May the Ottoman bite the dust, may you win both
laurels and booty, and may I see and savour it all, and
drink to your health.*

*Now, because books are always a source of consolation,
I am sending with this letter a copy of my* Dreams *to
distract you when you are not at war. The ink is still
fresh, for Sapera the printer has only just sent it to me
from Barcelona. Give it to our young Patroclus, who,
I know, will find it an edifying read, since, according to
the censor Father Tomás Roca, it contains nothing that
offends against the Catholic faith or against good
manners, and you, I am sure, will be as pleased about
that as I am. I trust that Íñigo remains in good health
by your side, prudently accepts your counsel and bows to
your authority. Send him my warm regards and tell him
that my negotiations at Court on his behalf are progressing
well and with a favourable wind behind them, so if all
goes to plan, his entry into the ranks of royal couriers
will be as good as guaranteed as soon as he returns to
Madrid a fully accredited Miles Gloriosus. Tell him that,*

as well as adorning his mind with my words, he must not neglect those of Tacitus, Homer and Virgil; for even were he to don the armour of Mars himself, in the tumult of this world, the pen is still mightier than the sword, and of considerably more comfort.

There are more matters in hand about which I cannot tell you in a letter, but all will be well, and God will shed his light on us and bring us good fortune. Suffice it to say that I have been questioned lately about my Italian experiences under the great and much-missed Osuna. However, it is a delicate business the telling of which requires great tact, and the time for that is not yet ripe. By the way, there is a rumour going around that an old and dangerous friend of yours, whom you left in the hands of the Law, was not executed secretly as was first thought. Rather (and this is between you and me and has yet to be confirmed) he bought his life by providing valuable information about certain affairs of State. I do not know what stage these negotiations have reached, but it might be a good idea to glance over your shoulder now and then if you hear someone whistle.

I have more things to tell you, but I will leave them until my next letter. I end this one with regards from La Lebrijana, whose tavern I occasionally visit to honour your absence with one of those dishes she prepares so well and a pitcher of San Martín de Valdeiglesias. She remains a handsome woman, with a fine figure and a still finer face, and is as devoted to you as ever. Other habitués also send their regards: Father Pérez, Master Calzas, the apothecary Fadrique and Juan Vicuña, who has just become a grandfather. Martín Saldaña appears to have recovered at last, after spending almost a year hovering on the frontier between this life and the next –

*thanks to that cut you dealt him in the Rastro — and is
once again to be seen in the streets with his staff of office,
as if he had never left. I meet Guadalmedina at the
Palace occasionally, but he always avoids any mention
of your name. There is much talk lately of him being
sent to England or to France as ambassador.*

*Take great care of yourself, dear Captain. And look
after the boy so that he may enjoy many long and happy
years.*

A warm embrace from your friend
Francisco de Quevedo

It was late afternoon, and, as usual, the Chorrillo was beginning to get lively. Diego Alatriste sauntered round the small
crescent-shaped piazza, observing the people sitting outside
the taverns, of which there were many, all gathered around
the establishment that gave the square its name — a famous
inn that brought a flurry of old memories. The name Chorrillo
was a Spanish version of the Italian Cerriglio, which was the
real name of the inn situated near the Santa Maria Novella
church. Its reputation for good wine, food and pleasure dated
from the previous century. Almost since the legendary days
of Pavia and the Sack of Rome, the place had been frequented
by soldiers and by men hoping to enlist, or so they said, and
many rogues, ruffians and hired blades were to be found
amongst that rabble. Indeed, the term *chorrillero* or *chur-
rullero* was commonly used in Naples and in Spain to refer
to the kind of Spanish soldier, pretend or real, who spent more
time throwing dice and emptying wineskins than sticking a
sword in a Turk or knifing the odd Lutheran. The type, in
short, who would sigh 'Ah, what battles we've seen, comrade,
and what wine we've drunk!' when only the bit about the
wine was true.

Alatriste greeted a few acquaintances, but did not stop. Despite the warm weather, he was wearing a short grey cape over his doublet in order to conceal the pistol he had stuck in his belt at the back. At that hour and given his intentions, it was an understandable precaution, although the presence of the pistol was not directly related to the villainous faces dotted about the place. There were still a couple of hours of daylight left, a time of day when all kinds of idlers would arrange to meet: braggarts and bully-boys, regular inmates of the Vicaria prison or the military prison of Santiago, who would spend their mornings on the steps of Santa Maria Novella, watching the women going in to mass, and their evenings and nights in the various taverns, discussing the conditions of such and such an enlistment or – revealing the field marshal inside every Spaniard – mulling over stratagems and tactics and declaring how a certain battle should have been won. Almost all were Spanish and had been drawn to Naples either by the army or by a need to earn some money; and all were so proud and fierce that, even if they had been mere cobblers back home, here they boasted of high lineage. It was the same with the Spanish whores, who arrived by the cartload, calling themselves Mendoza or Guzmán, so that even their Italian colleagues ended up demanding to be treated as a *Signora*. This gave rise to the Italian word *spagnolata*, used to describe any kind of pomposity or boastfulness.

In Córdoba and fair Seville,
I've property a-plenty.
My parents, born into the gentry,
Are lords of all Castile.

There was no shortage of natives of the region either, as well as Sicilians, Sardinians and people from other parts of

Italy; a whole panoply of cutpurses, counterfeiters, gamesters, cape-thieves, deserters, ruffians and scum, gathered together to exchange blasphemies, perjuries and other such nonsense. Indeed the Chorrillo in Naples could have been cited alongside such illustrious locations as the steps in Seville, the Potro in Córdoba, La Sapienza in Rome or the Rialto in Venice.

Leaving the inn behind him, Alatriste strode across this noble venue and went up an alleyway known as the steps of the Piazzetta, which were so narrow there was barely room for two men wearing swords to pass. The smell of wine from the drinking-dens, from which floated the buzz of conversation and the tuneless singing of drunkards, mingled with the stench of urine and filth. And when the Captain stepped aside to avoid treading in some of that filth, he inadvertently got in the way of two soldiers who were descending. They were dressed in the Spanish style, albeit unostentatiously: hats, swords and boots.

'Why don't you damn well go and get in someone else's way?' one of them muttered angrily in Castilian, and made as if to continue down the steps.

Alatriste slowly smoothed his moustache. Both were military men in their late thirties. The man who had spoken was short and stocky and had a Galician accent. He was wearing expensive gloves, and his clothes, although of a sober cut, were made of good cloth. The other man was tall and thin and had a melancholy air about him. Both had moustaches and plumed hats.

'I would be delighted to do so,' he replied simply, 'and in your company too, if you have no other engagements.'

The two men had stopped.

'In our company? Whatever for?' asked the shorter man brusquely.

Alatriste shrugged, as if the answer were obvious. Indeed,

he thought, there was no other possible response. There was always one's wretched reputation to consider.

'To discuss a few of the finer points of fencing. You know the kind of thing: length of step, keeping the blade in line, feint and riposte ...'

'Upon my oath,' murmured the short man.

He did not say 'upon my oath as a gentleman', as was usual among those who were far from being one. Alatriste saw that both men were studying him carefully and that they had noticed the scars on his face as well as the sword at his waist. His left hand rested almost casually on the hilt of his dagger and they couldn't see the pistol hidden beneath his cape, but it was there. Alatriste sighed. This was not part of his plan, but if that was how things were, then so be it. As for the pistol, he hoped not to be obliged to use it. He had brought it along more as a threat than as a precaution, and had another purpose in mind for it.

'My friend is not in the best of moods,' said the taller of the soldiers in a conciliatory tone. 'He has just met with a problem.'

'What I have met with is my affair,' said the other man gruffly.

'Well, I'm sorry to say this,' replied Alatriste coolly, 'but if he doesn't mend his manners, he'll soon have another problem to deal with.'

'Be careful what you say,' said the taller man, 'and don't be deceived by my companion's appearance. You would be very surprised to learn his name.'

Alatriste had not taken his eyes off the shorter man. 'Well then, to avoid confusion, he should either dress in accordance with his name or choose a name in accordance with his dress.'

The two companions looked at each other, uncertain what to do, and Alatriste moved his hand away from the hilt of his dagger. They had the manners of decent people and did not appear to be men who would knife you in the street or in the back. And they were certainly not the kind to queue up on pay day at the arsenal to collect their four *escudos*. Beneath their soldiers' clothes one could sense that they were refined, clean and serious, employed by some noble or general, or else the venturesome sons of good family who were spending time in the army to add lustre to their reputation. Flanders and Italy were full of such men. He wondered what had thrown the shorter, stockier man into such a rage. A woman perhaps. Or some bad luck at the card table. Whatever the motive, he didn't care: everyone had their own problems.

'Anyway,' he said, offering an honourable way out, 'I have an urgent matter to attend to.'

The taller man seemed relieved to hear this. 'We ourselves are on duty in two hours' time,' he remarked.

He, too, had a Spanish accent, but somewhat harsher, from the north, Asturian perhaps. And the tone in which he said these words seemed genuine and dignified. The matter could have ended there had his conciliatory mood been shared by his stocky companion, who was looking at Alatriste with the dark tenacity of a hound who, furious at having lost a fox, is intent on attacking a wolf.

'There's plenty of time.'

Alatriste again stroked his moustache. He sensed that this was not a good situation to be in. Exchanging sword-thrusts with one of these men, or with both, could get him into trouble. He would like to have left things as they stood, but this was not easy. Wounded honour on both sides complicated matters. And he was beginning to find the shorter man's obstinacy irritating.

'Let's not waste words,' he said resolutely.

'Bear in mind,' said the tall man in the same reasonable

tone, 'that I couldn't possibly leave my companion alone. You would have to fight me as well. And then, of course, should there be—'

'Enough talk,' the other man interrupted. He turned to Alatriste. 'Where shall we go? To Piedegruta?'

Alatriste gave him a hard look, as if taking the measure of him. Now he really did feel like sticking a foot of steel into this importunate, conceited little cockerel. Damn it. It would be over in a trice. And he would finish off his companion as well, two for the price of one. That way, at least, he would make them pay for the trouble they had caused him.

'The Porta Reale is nearer,' he suggested. 'There's a discreet little meadow just crying out for someone to fall down dead in it.'

The taller man gave a resigned sigh. 'This gentleman will require a witness,' he said to his companion. 'We don't want people saying that we murdered him between us.'

A distracted smile flickered across Alatriste's lips. That was very reasonable, and considerate too. Duels were forbidden in Naples by royal ordinance, and any transgressor would go straight to prison, or to the gallows if there was no one to speak up for him. It was, therefore, best to keep to the rules, especially if people of quality were involved. It would, Alatriste concluded, be a matter of killing one – the shorter man – and leaving the other more or less unscathed, so that he could report that the fight had been fair and square. Although, if there were no witnesses at all, he could simply kill them both and vanish.

'We can sort that out on the way there, if you would be so kind as to wait for me for a moment.' He pointed up the steps, where the alleyway turned to the right. 'I have some business to see to.'

After exchanging a somewhat bemused glance, the two

men nodded. Then, calmly turning his back on them – life had taught him on whom it was safe to turn his back and on whom it was not – Alatriste went up the last few steps. He could hear the Spaniards following behind; they seemed to be in no hurry, he noticed, and he was pleased to be dealing with such reasonable people. He went round the corner and through an archway that was as narrow as the rest of the street, and there he found a tavern. Having first checked that he was in the right place and giving no further thought to his startled companions, he adjusted his hat and made sure that his sword and dagger were in position. Then he fastened the buff coat he was wearing under his cape, felt for his pistol and went inside.

It was one of the seamier places in Naples: a courtyard with an arcade along which tables were placed. Chickens pecked about on the floor and there were about twenty or so rough-looking customers – Italians, to judge by their appearance. At some of the tables, cards were being played, watched by the occasional onlooker, who might simply have been enjoying the game or else was spying on the cards of their accomplice's opponent – a trick know as 'Claramonte's mirror'.

Alatriste discreetly went over to the inn-keeper, greased his palm with a silver coin and asked which player was Giacomo Colapietra. A moment later, he was standing by a table where a very thin individual, all skin and bone, wearing a wig and sporting a waxed moustache, was drinking and shuffling cards. He was accompanied by a couple of nasty-looking toughs, the kind who carry sword and shield and whose collars are frayed and stiff with grease.

'Could we have a private word?'

The Florentine, who was busy separating the kings from the jacks, peered up at him inquisitively. Then he curled his lip.

'*Nascondo niente a mis amichis*,' he said, indicating his companions.

His breath stank of cheap, watered-down wine. Alatriste glanced at the aforementioned *amichis*. Obviously Italian. A bold front, but pure pasteboard inside; he needn't worry too much about them, even if they were carrying swords. The Florentine was the only one without a sword, although a dagger a span and a half long hung from his belt.

'I understand you're hiring men who know how to handle a knife, Signor Giacomo.'

'*Non bisogno nessuno piu.*'

The expression on Alatriste's face was like a sliver of glass.

'Perhaps I'm not making myself clear. Those men are being hired to kill a friend of mine.'

Colapietra stopped shuffling the cards and glanced at his comrades. Then he took a more careful look at Alatriste. A smug smile appeared beneath his waxed moustache.

'I've been told,' Alatriste went on impassively, 'that you have paid for a nasty surprise to be sprung on a certain young Spaniard very close to my heart.'

When he heard this, Colapietra burst into scornful laughter.

'*Cazzo*,' he said.

Then, with a sly look on his face, he made as if to get up, along with his companions, but was stopped in his tracks. Alatriste had whipped out the pistol from beneath his cape.

'Sit down, all three of you,' he said calmly when he saw that they had grasped the idea. 'Or I'll shit on your whorish mothers. *Capisci?*'

Silence had fallen all around. Alatriste kept his eyes fixed on the three ruffians, who had turned as pale as wax.

'Keep your hands on the table and away from your swords.'

Still not looking behind him, so as not to reveal any lack of confidence, Alatriste put the pistol in his left hand and rested his right hand on the hilt of his sword, just in case he needed to unsheathe it in order to make his way to the door. He had already worked out an exit strategy, including his retreat back down the steps. Should things get out of hand, he had only to get as far as the Chorrillo, where there would be no shortage of helping hands. He could, of course, have taken someone with him, Copons or the Moor Gurriato – who was longing to render him just such a service – or some other comrade. However, the theatrical effect would not have been the same. Therein lay the art.

'Now listen, you bastard.'

Pressing the barrel of his pistol to the ashen face of the gambler – who had dropped his cards on the floor – Alatriste brought his own face up close and then quietly, precisely and unequivocally detailed just what he would do to Colapietra, to his innards and to those who had engendered him, if any friend of his should come to harm. A fall in the street or a stumble would be enough for him to settle accounts with the Florentine, whom he would hold responsible for anything from a case of diarrhoea to a fever. And he, Diego Alatriste, resident in the Spanish quarter at the inn of Ana de Osorio, would have no need to hire anyone else to wield the knife, because people usually hired *him* to do such dirty work. *Capisci?*

'So, listen well. I'll always be here, or on some dark corner, waiting to slit you open. Do you understand?'

Shaken, Colapietra nodded, the futile dagger at his waist only accentuating his pathetic air. Alatriste's cold, pale eyes seemed to rob him of speech. His wig had shifted to one side and you could smell his fear. The Captain decided against tormenting him further – one could never foresee what would tip a man over the edge.

'Is that clear?'

As clear as day, said Colapietra's silent nod. Moving away a little, the Captain shot a sideways glance at the Florentine's consorts. They were as still as statues and, with angelic innocence, had kept their hands on the table, as if – apart from stealing from their mothers, murdering their fathers and prostituting their sisters – they had never done anything wrong in their whole sinful lives. Then, without lowering the pistol or removing his hand from the hilt of his sword, Alatriste left the table.

Without entirely turning his back on them and keeping a close eye on the other customers, who sat frozen and dumb, he made his way to the door. There he bumped into the two Spaniards, who had followed him and witnessed the whole episode. He was surprised to see them there, for so concentrated had he been on his own affairs, he had quite forgotten them.

'Right, to business,' he said, ignoring the expression of amazement on their faces.

The three went out into the street together, the other two men still speechless, while Alatriste lowered the hammer on his pistol and put it back in his belt, under his cape. Then he spat on the ground, looking angry and dangerous. The cold fury that had been building up in him since his encounter with these two men, plus the tension of the scene in the tavern, required some outlet. His fingers itched impatiently as he touched the guard of his sword. Christ's blood, he thought, imagining the coming fight. Maybe there was no need to go to Porta Reale to resolve the matter. At the first surly word or gesture, he decided, he would take out his dagger – the street was too narrow for a sword-fight – and stick them like pigs right there, even if it did bring down upon him the Law and the Viceroy himself.

'By my oath,' said the taller man.

He was staring at Diego Alatriste, as if seeing him for the first time, and his companion was doing the same. The latter was no longer frowning, but seemed pensive, even curious.

'Do you want to go ahead with this?' the taller man asked his comrade.

Without answering, the latter kept his eyes fixed on Alatriste. The Captain held his gaze, meanwhile making an impatient gesture as if inviting him to set off to some place where they could resolve their argument. The other man did not stir. Instead, after a moment, he removed his right glove and held out his hand – frank and bare – to Alatriste.

'I'd rather be basted like a runaway slave,' he said, 'than fight a man like this one.'

9. THE CATHOLIC KING'S CORSAIRS

The Turk ran up the flag of peace and took in his sails without a fight. The vessel was a black karamuzal with a long hull and a high stern: a two-masted merchant ship that our five galleys had prevented from making full use of her sails by cutting her off from both land and sea. It was our third capture since we had been keeping watch over the channel between the islands of Tinos and Mykonos, a much-frequented route on the way to Constantinople, Chios and Smyrna.

From the moment we came alongside to send a group of infantrymen on board, we could see that this was a very good catch indeed. Crewed by Greeks and Turks, the boat was carrying oil and wine from Candia; soap; leather from Cairo, and other valuable cargo. As passengers, it was carrying some Jews from Salonica – the sort who wear yellow turbans – and they came replete with silver coins. That day we used our fingers more than our swords, for we spent half an hour plundering the ship, and everything we touched stuck to our fingertips. Indeed when one soldier from another galley either fell or threw himself into the water to avoid the officers who were trying to impose order, he preferred to drown rather than give up his ill-gotten gains.

The karamuzal was a Turkish vessel, a worthy prize, so we sent it off to Malta with a Greek crew and a few of our soldiers. The two renegades (whom we hoped the Inquisition would deal with later), eight Turks, three Albanians and five Jews on board were shared out among the five galleys and set to the oars. The

Hebrew race not being built for rowing, one of the Jews died two days later, either because he was ill or because he could not bear to see himself a miserable slave. The others were then ransomed for less than a thousand *sequins* by the monks of Patmos, who later released them, as they usually did, charging them interest – for although the monks of Patmos spoke Greek, they counted money in Genoese.

The two renegades were allocated to the *Mulata*. One was Spanish, from Ciudad Real, and in an attempt to improve his lot, he gave us some interesting information of which I will tell you more in due course. First, though, I should say that our campaign was proving highly profitable. Back on board, our hair once again slick with tar, our skin with salt and our clothes with brine, we had set off from Naples with three galleys – the *Mulata*, the *Caridad Negra* and the *Virgen del Rosario*. Each was newly careened and well stocked with enough supplies and soldiers for a voyage of two months through the Aegean and along the Anatolian coast, whose islands were inhabited by Greeks dominated by the Turks. Once we had left Capri behind us, we met up with two Maltese galleys off Fossa de San Giovanni – the *Cruz de Rodas* and the *San Juan Bautista* – and sailed with them in convoy as far as the small islands near Corfu. From there, having taken on salt meat and fresh water, we followed the Morea coast past Kefalonia and Zante – which belonged to the Venetians – and then skirted round the island of Sapienza. We took on more water at the mills of Coron, where the Turkish artillery fired on us from the town, but missed. After that, we headed east along the Mayna channel and past Cap Sant Angelo, where we entered the limpid waters of the archipelago, blue in the gulf and crystalline green near the shores, in order to do as Vélez de Guevara proclaimed in *The Terror of the Turks*:

I sailed on the sea of Levant
In search of the arrogant Turk,
The one who, defying our Spain,
Must die, or be punished with work.

I was particularly moved when we sailed past the gulf of Lepanto, for here Spanish sailors and soldiers traditionally lined up on the landward side of the ship to say a prayer in memory of the many Spaniards who had died there, fighting like furies, when the fleet of the Holy League destroyed the Turkish fleet in the battle of 1571. I was also moved, although in a different way, when we passed the island of Sapienza and the town of Modon, which still belonged to the Turks, for I remembered reading the name of Modon in the Captive's tale in the first part of *Don Quixote*, never imagining that I would one day set to sea, just as Cervantes did, and witness the very lands and seas where he fought in his youth – when he was not much older than I was at the time. He had found himself in Lepanto, and on board the galley *Marquesa*, on 'the most memorable occasion that the centuries, past and present, have ever seen, or that future centuries can hope to see'.

But I promised to tell you about the information vouchsafed by the Spanish renegade captured on the karamuzal. We did not know it then, but what he told us would dramatically affect our future and cost the lives of many valiant men. In order perhaps to ameliorate his fate at the hands of the Inquisition and to improve his situation on the galley – for he had been given one of the worst places on the rowing benches – the renegade asked to speak to Captain Urdemalas, saying that he had something of great import to tell him. Having given an account of his life – full of the usual lies – he revealed something that our captain found quite unbelievable: a great Turkish vessel was preparing to set sail from Rhodes to Constantinople, carrying rich merchandise and people of quality, among them a woman who was either a relative or a wife of the Great Turk himself, or was being sent to him to become his wife – the renegade was unsure on this point. As we soon found out – for there are no secrets on a galley – the Spanish renegade advised Captain Urdemalas that if he wanted further information, he simply had to turn the screws on the master of the karamuzal, who was also a renegade and had been assigned the same rowing position. The master of the karamuzal was originally from Marseilles but, on being circumcised, had changed his name to Ali Masilia. As it became clear, the Spaniard had a few scores to settle with him, and this was the perfect way to do so.

Given the potential importance of this information, Ali Masilia was duly put to torture. He was full of bravado at first, declaring that he knew nothing and that, besides, there wasn't a Christian alive who could make him talk. However, the first turn of the screw by the galley overseer, who threatened to make the renegade's eyes pop out of their sockets, was enough to persuade him to change his tune. Indeed, he proved so loquacious and eager to cooperate that Captain Urdemalas, fearing that his shouts would be heard by everyone, took him below to the food store. The Captain emerged shortly afterwards, stroking his beard and smiling from ear to ear.

That afternoon, taking advantage of the windless conditions and the calm sea, we hove to about half a league to the north of Mykonos. There, the skiffs were lowered into the water and the various officers met under the awning of the *Caridad Negra*, which was our flagship, captained by Don Agustín Pimentel, great-nephew of the old Count of Benavente, and to whom the Viceroy of Naples and the Grand Master of

Malta had entrusted the expedition. In attendance were his galley captain, Machín de Gorostiola – who was also captain of the infantry on board; the chaplain, Father Francisco Nistal, and the chief pilot, Gorgos, a native of Ragusa, who had sailed with Captain Alonso de Contreras and who knew those waters like the back of his hand. Representing the other galleys were our own Captain Urdemalas and the captain of the *Virgen del Rosario*, a pleasant, talkative Valencian called Alfonso Cervera. The Maltese galleys sent their respective officers too, a gentleman from Mallorca called Brother Fulco Muntaner from the larger of the galleys, the *Cruz de Rodas*, and a Frenchman, Brother Vivan Brodemont, from the *San Juan Bautista*.

When the meeting ended, and before they had even returned to their respective galleys, the joyful rumour was already doing the rounds that there was a richly laden Turkish vessel travelling from Rhodes to Constantinople, and that we were in a good position to board it before it entered the Dardanelles. This made us howl with pleasure, and it did one good to see and hear all the soldiers and sailors on every galley cheering and wishing each other good luck.

That same evening, before prayers were said, orders were issued to give the galleymen some Candian wine, salt cheese from Sicily and a few ounces of bacon, after which the whips cracked from prow to stern and the five galleys set off into the night with the slaves rowing as hard as they could, a pack of wolves scenting prey.

Dawn found me, as usual, in the embrasure on the starboard side towards the stern, watching the light gradually fill the horizon and observing the pilot as he performed the first rituals of his day. It was still very early, and the oarsmen were sleeping on their benches or in between them because we were now under full sail. The canvas and the rigging creaked gently as we were pushed along by a reasonable north-easter which, with the galley keeping close to the wind, was carrying us along on our desired course. Almost all the soldiers and sailors were asleep as well, while the cabin boys on watch, high up on masts and yards, scanned the horizon for sails or land, keeping a particularly close eye on the spot where the sun would come up – the dazzle could conceal an enemy presence. I had my blanket over my shoulders, for I slept with it wrapped about me, and if I had put it down on the deck, it would have walked away on its own, so full was it of bedbugs and lice. I was leaning on some netting, which was damp from the night air, admiring the pinks and oranges of the sky and wondering if one of the many sayings I had learned on board would hold true: red sky at night, sailors' delight; red sky in the morning, sailors take warning.

I glanced along the side of the galley. Captain Alatriste was already awake, and from afar I saw him shake out his blanket and fold it up. Then he leaned over the side and, using a bucket attached to a rope, scooped up some sea-water and washed his face with it – drinking-water being far too precious a commodity to use for washing – before rubbing his skin briskly with a rag so that the salt didn't stick to his skin. He took some hard-tack from his pouch, dipped it in a little of the wine he shared with Sebastián Copons – they never drank it all at once – and began eating, staring out to sea. When Copons, who was sleeping beside him, began to stir and raised his head, the Captain broke the hard-tack in two and gave him half. Copons chewed in silence, holding the biscuit in one hand and rubbing the sleep from his eyes with the other. When the Captain noticed that I was observing him from the stern, he looked away.

We had spoken little since Naples. The bitterness of our

last conversation still rankled, and during our final days on shore, we had scarcely seen each other because I was staying at the military barracks in Monte Calvario, along with the Moor Gurriato, and I avoided the inns and taverns where the Captain might go to eat and drink. This, however, allowed me to get to know the Moor better. He was back on board the *Mulata*, not, this time, as an unpaid oarsman, but with a wage of four *escudos* a month. We shared the same food and billet, and had already had occasion to fight alongside each other, albeit briefly, during the capture of a samequin crewed by Albanians and Turks, which we came across within sight of the island of Milos. Since we were in the Argentera passage and therefore at risk of hitting a sandbank, we had boarded using a skiff. Not that the escapade had brought us much profit, for the ship was carrying only untanned hides; however, we returned with twelve men to put to the oars and with no losses on our side. Aware that Captain Alatriste was watching from a distance, I had been one of the first to jump aboard the samequin, followed by the Moor Gurriato, and I tried hard to distinguish myself in the eyes of everyone else, being the one to cut the sheets so that no one would tally them aft, and then fighting my way over to where the ship's master was standing, surrounded by the members of his crew, all of them wielding pikes and scimitars – although not with much enthusiasm, it must be said, for they had flagged visibly when they saw us boarding. When I reached the master, I dealt him such a blow to the chest that he almost died on the spot, just as he was about to open his mouth and ask for quarter, or so it seemed to me. I thus returned to the galley having earned the good opinion of my comrades, feeling prouder than a peacock and glancing round to see if Captain Alatriste was watching.

'I think you should speak to him,' said the Moor Gurriato.

He had just woken up and was lying next to me, his beard unkempt and his skin greasy from sleep and the damp morning air.

'Why? To ask his forgiveness?'

'No,' he said, yawning. 'I just mean that you should speak to him.'

I gave an impudent laugh. 'If he has something to say, let him say it.'

The Moor Gurriato was meticulously cleaning between his toes.

'He's older than you and wiser. That is why you need him. He knows things that you and I don't. On my soul, it is true.'

I laughed again, as proud as a cockerel at five in the morning.

'That's where you're wrong. It's not like it was before.'

'What was it like then?'

'Like looking at God.'

He eyed me with his usual curiosity. This was one of his most appealing characteristics, the way he gave absolute attention even to the tiniest and apparently most insignificant of details. He appeared to find everything interesting, from the composition of a speck of dust to the complex workings of the human heart. He would ask a question, listen to the reply and then give an opinion, if required, seriously and frankly, and without any pretence at discretion, wit or bravery. He faced the good sense, stupidity or ignorance of other people with equanimity and possessed the infinite patience of someone determined to learn from everything and everyone. Life is written in each thing and each word, he said once, and the wise man tries to read and listen in silence. This was a strange philosophy to find in a man like him, who could neither read nor write, despite knowing Castilian, Turkish and the Arabic of the Moors, as well as the Mediterranean lingua franca. In fact, a few weeks in Naples had been enough for him to gain a reasonable grasp of Italian.

'And he no longer resembles God?'

The Moor was observing me with the same close attention. I made a vague gesture towards the sea. The first rays of sun touched our faces.

'I've discovered aspects of his character that I didn't see before, and there are others that I can no longer see.'

He shook his head almost sadly. He came and went between Captain Alatriste and me, acting as our one link on board, apart from our military duties. That rough, brusque Aragonese, Copons, lacked the necessary subtlety to ease the tension between us; his clumsy attempts at conciliation always hitting the wall of my youthful obstinacy. The Moor Gurriato was just as uneducated as Copons, but he was more perspicacious. He had taken my measure, and was patient. He moved between us discreetly, as if providing this contact was a way of repaying the strange debt that he believed he owed the Captain, the man he had met on that cavalcade on Uad Berruch. And he believed this all his life – until Nördlingen, that is.

'A man like him deserves respect,' he commented, as if concluding a long internal train of thought.

'So do I.'

'*Elkhadar*,' he said, with a shrug of the shoulders. 'Time will tell.'

I thumped the netting with my fist.

'I wasn't born yesterday, you know. I'm just as much a man and a gentleman as he is.'

He ran one hand over his smooth head, which he shaved each day with a razor and sea-water.

'Ah, of course ... a gentleman,' he murmured.

He was smiling. His dark, gentle, almost feminine eyes glittered.

'God blinds those who want to lose,' he added.

'The Devil take God and all the rest.'

'Sometimes we give to the Devil what he already has.'

And having said this, the Moor Gurriato got to his feet, picked up a handful of oakum and walked along the gangway to the ship's head, next to the ram, instead of doing as so many other men did and crouching between the timber knees at the sides of the ship. Because another of the Moor Gurriato's peculiarities was that he was as modest as the mother who bore him.

'We may be in luck,' Captain Urdemalas said. 'They say that the ship was still in Rhodes three days ago.'

Diego Alatriste took another sip of the wine that Captain Urdemalas had ordered to be served beneath the faded red-and-white striped awning at the stern. The wine was good – a white Malvasia rather like a San Martín de Valdeiglesias. Given Urdemalas' proverbial meanness – he was about as likely to spend a *maravedí* as the Pope was to give up his piscatory ring – this augured well. Between sips of wine, Alatriste discreetly observed the other men. Besides the pilot, a Greek named Braco, and the galley-master, there were Ensign Labajos and the three soldiers placed in charge of the eighty-seven infantrymen on board: Sergeant Quemado, Corporal Conesa and Alatriste himself. Also present was the master gunner who had replaced the man injured in Lampedusa. He was a German who swore in Castilian and drank in Basque, but was as adept at handling moyens, sakers, culverins and swivel-guns as a cook was his pots.

'Apparently it's a large ship – a square-rigged mahone with no oars, but some artillery. The escort is a lantern galley manned by janizaries.'

'That will be a hard nut to crack,' said the galleymaster when he heard the word 'janizary'.

Captain Urdemalas scowled at him. He was in a bad mood because he had been suffering from appalling toothache all week and didn't dare place himself in the hands of the barber, or indeed in anyone else's.

'We've cracked harder nuts than that,' he snapped.

Ensign Labajos, who had already drunk his wine, wiped his moustache with the back of his hand. He was a young, thin, swarthy man from Malaga, and was good at his job.

'They're sure to put up a fight, and they'll battle like demons if they think they're about to lose their prize passenger.'

Sergeant Quemado burst out laughing. 'Is the woman really the Great Turk's wife? I thought he never let them out of the seraglio.'

'She's the favourite wife of the Pasha of Cyprus,' Urdemalas explained. 'His term there ends in a month's time, and he's sending her ahead with some of his money, servants, slaves and clothes.'

Quemado mimed applause. He was a tall, lanky man, whose real name was Sandino. The nickname Quemado – Burned – dated from a highly profitable attack on the island of Longos, which had involved sacking the town, setting fire to the Jewish quarter and acquiring a booty of almost two hundred slaves. A petard had scorched his face while he was trying to blow in the door to the castle, but despite his unfortunate appearance, or perhaps because of it, he was always the joker. He was also rather short-sighted, although he never wore glasses in public. 'When did you ever see Mars wearing spectacles?' he would quip.

'She's a tasty morsel then,' he said.

'If we can capture her, yes,' said Urdemalas, 'tasty enough to justify the whole campaign.'

'Where are they now?' asked Ensign Labajos.

'They had to stop off in Rhodes, but now they've set sail again, or are about to.'

'What's the plan?'

Urdemalas gestured to Braco the pilot, who unrolled a sea chart on the large plank that served as a table. The map showed the Aegean Islands, Anatolia and the coasts of Europe. It went as far up as the strait of Constantinople and as far down as Candia. Urdemalas ran his finger along the easternmost coast.

'Don Agustín Pimentel wants to capture them before they pass the strait of Chios, so as not to cause any trouble for the monks and the other Christian folk who live there. According to the chief pilot, Gorgos, the best place is between Nicalia and Samos. That's the most obvious route from Rhodes.'

'Those are treacherous waters,' said Braco. 'There are shallows and rocks.'

'Yes, but the chief pilot knows them well. He says that if the mahone is being sailed by people who know where the sandbanks are, then the natural route to follow would be between the chain of islands and the mainland. It's protected from the winds and safer.'

'Yes, that would be logical,' Braco agreed.

Diego Alatriste and Corporal Conesa — a plump, stocky fellow from Murcia — were studying the map with great interest. They didn't usually get a chance to see such documents, and as subalterns, they knew how unusual it was to be invited to such meetings. Alatriste was an old dog, though, and he could read between the lines. The ship they were planning to attack would be a major prize and Captain Urdemalas needed everyone to know that. This way, he could be sure that the troops would find out the facts and be eager to put their all into the enterprise. Being in the right place at the right time and capturing the mahone would require them all to pull together, and soldiers and sailors who were aware of what was at stake would be more likely to obey.

'Do you think we can get there in time?' Ensign Labajos asked.

He showed his empty glass, in the hope that Urdemalas would summon his page to pour him some more wine.

Urdemalas pretended not to notice. 'The wind is in our favour,' he said, 'and, besides, we have the oarsmen. The Turkish mahone is a heavy sailing ship and will be travelling against the wind, and in calm weather the galley will have to tow her. The weather will turn cooler this evening, but we'll still have the wind in our favour. The chief pilot thinks we can catch up with them off Patmos or the Fournoi islands, and the other pilots and captains agree. Isn't that so, Braco?'

The Greek nodded as he rolled up the chart. Quemado wanted to know what the Knights of Malta thought about the matter.

'Those bastards don't give a damn,' said Captain Urdemalas, 'whether it's one mahone and one galley or fifty, whether they're carrying the Pasha of Cyprus's wife on board or the wife of Suleiman himself. The merest whiff of booty is enough to set their mouths watering. The more Turks, the bigger the profit.'

'What about the other captains?' Quemado asked.

'I don't know anything about the French captain. He's got knights who are on their first expedition with him, as well as soldiers from France, Italy, Spain and Germany. Brave men, as always. But I do know the captain of the *Cruz de Rodas*.'

'Brother Fulco Muntaner,' said the galleymaster.

'The one who was at the battle of Cimbalo and at Syracuse?'

'The same.'

Some of those present raised their eyebrows, while others nodded. Even Alatriste had heard, through Alonso de Contreras, of this Spanish Knight of St John. At Cimbalo, after losing three of the Maltese galleys in a storm, Muntaner had dug himself in on an island along with his shipwrecked men, all defending themselves like tigers against the Moors of Bizerta who had disembarked en masse to capture them. Not that there was anything surprising about that, for not even the most optimistic Knight expected mercy from the Mohammedans. This partly explains why it was that, at the battle of Lepanto, when the Maltese flagship was finally recaptured — it had been attacked and boarded by a swarm of Turkish sailors — only three Knights were found alive, badly wounded, but surrounded by the corpses of three hundred of the enemy. Almost the same thing happened again in 1620, off Syracuse in Sicily, when the same Muntaner, by then in his sixtieth year, was one of only eighteen survivors on the Maltese flagship, after the bloody battle fought between four Maltese and six Berber galleys. The Knights of Malta, feared and hated by their enemies, were tough professional corsairs, and Brother Fulco Muntaner was among the very toughest. Since the five galleys had met in Fossa de San Giovanni, Alatriste had often seen him at the stern of the flagship, *Cruz de Rodas*, with his bald head, long grey beard and face disfigured by cuts and scars, and had heard him haranguing the men in thunderous tones in his own Mallorcan tongue.

The proverb proved to be correct: that evening there was rain and, that night, there were occasional gusts of the promised north-easterly wind and more rain. The sea was so rough that, despite the lanterns lit on the stern of each ship, all five galleys lost sight of each other. However, despite the weather, we soon covered the forty miles separating us from the island of Nicalia. The sailors had to keep a constant eye on the sails, while everyone else, oarsmen included, crouched on the deck, numb with cold, sheltering as best we could from the spray.

We proceeded thus until the wind turned to the south-east, and the following morning, which dawned peacefully, with the heavy rain moving off over the island's steep, rocky peaks, we found ourselves opposite Pope Point, where two of the ships in our convoy were waiting for us. The other two arrived safely a short time later.

Nicalia, which some call Ikaria — the island where Icarus fell into the sea — is a rugged place, and while many torrents rush down its rocks, there is no harbour. However, since both weather and sea were calm, we were able to go in close to land and happily fill casks, barrels and kegs with water — given the number of people on board a galley, it is in constant need of fresh supplies.

According to our reckonings, the mahone would be sailing into the north wind and, we thought, would still be somewhere en route from Rhodes. To confirm this, Agustín Pimentel ordered four galleys to cover the strait between Nicalia and Samos, while the fifth went south to garner more information. One Spanish ship would attract less attention than five galleys gathered together like birds of prey. Moreover, the Greeks who lived on those islands seemed no better than the Ottomans, for, having no schools, they were the most barbarous people in the world, cowed by the cruelty of the Mohammedans and quite capable of selling us to the Turks simply to gain favour with them.

The *Mulata* was chosen to be the scout, and so we set sail that night and by the dawn watch had reached the deep, sheltered harbour of Patmos, the best of the three or four good ports on the island, at the foot of the fortified Christian monastery that dominates the harbour from above. We spent the morning there, but the only people allowed ashore were Captain Urdemalas and the pilot Braco. As well as finding out further information, they negotiated with the monks the ransom of the Jews we had taken on board as oarsmen – at least that was the pretext for the visit – although, for some reason or other, an agreement was reached not to free them until later, when we would leave them on Nicalia.

And so I did not have a chance to set foot on the legendary island to which St John the Evangelist was exiled by the emperor Domitian and where he dictated the *Apocalypse* to his disciple Procoros. And speaking of books, I remember that Captain Alatriste spent the day sitting in one of the crossbow embrasures, reading the copy of *Dreams* sent to him by Don Francisco de Quevedo. It was a small octavo volume, which he usually carried in his pocket. That same day, when he left it lying on his pack in order to go to deal with some matter at the prow, I picked up the book and, glancing through it, found this passage marked:

Truth and Justice came down to Earth: the first, being naked, found it most uncomfortable, as did the second, being rigorous. They wandered about for a long time, until Truth, out of necessity, fell silent. Justice, at a loss what to do, roamed the earth, pleading with everyone; but seeing that no one took any notice of her and that everywhere her name was used to support tyrannies, she determined to flee back to Heaven ...

We soldiers and sailors spent part of that day resting, delousing each other and eating a meal of boiled chickpeas and a little salt cod – for it was a Friday – while the oarsmen, beneath the awning that protected the rowing benches, were given their usual ration of hard-tack. The sun was very strong, and the heat so intense that tar was dripping down from the rigging.

Gone midday, Captain Urdemalas and the pilot returned, looking very cheerful, having dined well with the monks and imbibed wine made from honey and orange blossom – God curse them. Anyway, the Turkish mahone, they were told, had not yet passed through the strait, but had been seen, still with its galley escort, sailing towards the isle of Longos, struggling against the contrary wind, for it was a large and heavy vessel. And so, in less time than it takes to say 'knife', we had dismantled the awning, weighed anchor and set off, rowing hard to rejoin the other galleys.

For two days and nights, sailing with lanterns extinguished and eyes alert, we almost chewed our fingernails to the quick. The sea was leaden, with no wind to bring us that wretched mahone. Finally, a south-westerly breeze ruffled the surface of the water, and our patience was rewarded, for the order came to clear the decks and prepare ourselves for battle. The five galleys were skilfully deployed, being positioned almost, but not quite, out of sight of each other, and covering an area of more than twenty miles. A signal had been agreed to indicate when the prize was spotted. Behind us lay the island of Fournoi, on whose southernmost peak, from which one could see for leagues around, we had posted four men with orders to send up a smoke signal as soon as they spotted a sail. The island had a long corsair tradition, for its name, which means 'oven' or 'furnace', dated from the days when the Turk Cigala had the hard-tack for his galleys baked there. To the south, we had also posted a caique – manned by our people, but rowed by Greeks who had been pressed into service – as a reconnaissance vessel that would not arouse suspicion that the wolf was in the sheep pen. The unusual thing about the ambush was that, in order to get as close to the enemy as possible, and to avoid the mahone firing on us from a distance, we had made our ships look like Turkish galleys. We had shortened the mainmast, made the lateen yard seem stubbier and heavier, and lowered the topmast. Miguel de Cervantes, who knew a thing or two about corsairs and galleys, had written about this too:

In war there are a thousand ploys
Full of tricks and lying noise:
The thunder grumbles distantly,
Yet lightning strikes us instantly.

This disguise was completed with the Turkish flags and pennants we carried for such occasions – as other ships would carry ours – and men wearing Ottoman clothes were placed in the most visible parts of each ship. Such tricks were part of the dangerous game that all nations played along those ancient shores, the theatre for this vast exercise in corsair chess and chance. For when there are eight or even ten cannon pointing at you, gaining time is of no small importance, even more so when they start firing and all you can do is row hard and grit your teeth until you're close enough to board and pay them back for it. Had England's encounter with the Armada in the English Channel been a frank confrontation between two infantries, as at Lepanto, that day would now be remembered quite differently.

Anyway, whoever happened to be in the appropriate place donned a Turkish costume and was much mocked for it. I, thank God, escaped, but others – the Moor Gurriato was one, condemned by his appearance – had to put on baggy trousers, the long tunics or robes that the Turks call dolmans, as well as fancy bonnets, taffetas and turbans. They formed a blue, white and red rainbow; and their skins were now so tanned by the sun that they needed only to start bowing to Mecca at the appropriate times to be taken for real Turks. One even made fun of his own disguise, kneeling down and shamelessly invoking Allah, but when some of the Muslim slaves protested, angered by such blasphemy, Captain Urdemalas sternly reprimanded the wretch, threatening him with a public whipping if he upset the oarsmen again. It was one thing, he said, to force them to row, but there was no need to insult them.

'Row hard, my lads! Harder, or they'll escape us!'

When Captain Urdemalas addressed the slaves as 'my lads' this was a sign that more than one of them was likely to row himself to death and be whipped for his pains. And so it was. Keeping up the hellish rhythm set by the galleymaster's whistle and the merciless crack of his whip on their bare backs, the oarsmen alternately stood up and fell back, again and again, breathing so hard it seemed their lungs would burst.

'The dogs are ours! Keep it up and we'll have 'em!'

The long, slender hull of the *Mulata* seemed to fly over the rippling waves. We were to the south of Samos, leaving behind its bare, rocky coast on the port side. It was a luminous blue morning, marred only by a faint trace of mist on the strip of land to the east. The five galleys were in full pursuit, with sails and oars working; two lay ahead of us, nearer to Samos, and another two behind, forming a line that gradually shrank as we converged on the galley and the mahone. They, in turn, were trying desperately to escape along the strait between the island and terra firma or else find some beach on which to take shelter.

The day, however, was ours, and even the most inexperienced soldier on board realised it. The north-west wind wasn't blowing hard enough to drive the heavy mahone along, and its galley escort, of course, had to remain by its side. Meanwhile, our galleys, spaced out about a mile apart, were visibly gaining on them. We had begun our approach when, almost simultaneously, the men on the caique and a tiny puff of smoke from the isle of Fournoi told us that the enemy ship's sails had been spotted. At first, the Turkish uniforms and the general appearance of our ships had confused the new arrivals – later, we learned that they had mistaken us for galleys from Mytilene sent to escort them – and so they had kept their course, unsuspecting. However, the scales had soon fallen from their eyes when they saw the way we were rowing and manoeuvring the galley. And so the Turks tried to set course for the north-east, with the mahone to leeward of the galley, the latter trying to interpose itself and cover the larger ship's flight.

Now the chase was as good as over. The Maltese flagship was already near the coast of Samos and would reach the strait first; the *Caridad Negra* had its ram pointing at the Turkish galley; and the *Mulata*, along with the *Virgen del Rosario* and the *San Juan Bautista*, slightly to starboard of us, was heading straight for the mahone, whose three masts – trinquet, cross and lateen – had now all filled with sail.

'Fetch your weapons and to your posts!' Ensign Labajos shouted. 'We're going to board her!'

At the stern, the drumroll beat out the rallying call and the bugle sounded the attack. The corridors seethed with people preparing for battle. The master gunner and his assistants were readying the cannon in the central gangway as well as the *pedreros* mounted on the sides of the ship. The rest of us had padded the pavisades with shields, palliasses, blankets and packs to protect us from Turkish fire, and we were now making our way to the chests and baskets from which we would take our heavy weapons. The galley-men were still rowing, drenched in sweat, their eyes popping from their heads, chains clanking, and to that sound, from prow to stern, was added the clank of metal armour and weapons being strapped on by the soldiers and the sailors who had been designated either to defend the galley or to board the other ship. All of this equipment was vital in close combat: breastplates, morions, shields, swords, harquebuses, muskets, pikes and half-pikes with the end of the shaft greased so that the enemy could not grab hold of it. Smoke was rising from the harquebusiers' match-cords and the linstocks ready in their bowls of sand. The skiff and the other small boat were in the water, being towed along at the stern. The cook had put out the oven and any other fire on board, and the pages and cabin boys had washed down the deck with sea-water so that neither bare feet nor espadrilles would slip.

At the stern, under the awning, along with the pilot and the helmsman, the Captain was barking out orders: "Row, my lads, row, a quarter to port, damn it, now to starboard, row, you buggers, row, slacken that rope, tighten that halyard, row hard, the dogs are ours now, row or I'll have the skin off your backs, you wretches, yes, by God's teeth and the holy host, we're gaining on the bastards." Luther could not have put it better, for no one blasphemes like a Spaniard in a storm or in combat.

The fighting on the mahone was hard. We arrived first, just as the *Caridad Negra*, which was slightly closer to the island than we were, rammed the Turkish galley; and we heard the distant sound of firing and the shouts of Machín de Gorostiola and his Basques as they rushed on board. Meanwhile, every eye on the *Mulata* was fixed on the black portholes open along the sides of the mahone. There were six cannon on each side, and when the mahone saw that she could not avoid us, she turned two or three quarters to port and unleashed a volley which, even though it struck us only a glancing blow, took down our trinquet sail along with the four sailors who were, at that moment, hauling it in to secure it. Their guts were left hanging grotesquely from the rigging. Another such volley would have done much greater damage, because galleys have very fragile frames. The experienced Captain Urdemalas, however, foresaw this: when the helmsman hesitated, the Captain pushed him out of the way – indeed, he very nearly stuck him with his sword – and flung the tiller to one side so that we were heading instead for the stern of the mahone. This, as I said, was as high as that of galleons and carracks, but had no cannon, therefore allowing us to get close without too much risk. The *Virgen del Rosario* bore the brunt of the second volley, which came from the other side, and that, it seemed to us, was the lesser of two evils. After all, these things must be shared out, and Jesus Christ may have told us all to be brothers, but not to be arrant fools.

'Prepare to board!' Ensign Labajos roared.

We were almost within harquebus range, and if the oarsmen did their job well, the Turkish gunners would not have time to recharge the cannon. I slung a small shield over my shoulder, and with my steel breastplate on and my helmet, with my sword in its sheath, I joined a group of soldiers and sailors with grappling-irons at the ready. At the prow, the sail on the broken yard had been taken in and stowed, and the mainsail was furled and at half-mast. The embrasures were packed with men bristling with metal. Another large group, gathered around the felled trinquet sail and near the fighting platform atop the bow, were waiting for our artillery at the prow to fire so that they could occupy the foredeck and the ram. Among them I could see Captain Alatriste, who was blowing on the match-cord of his harquebus, and Sebastián Copons, who was, as usual, tying an Aragonese scarf about his head. I too was wearing such a scarf, on top of which I wore my helmet, which was very heavy and hellishly hot, but since we would be climbing upwards to board the ship, it seemed advisable to protect one's belltower from storks. As we drew close to the mahone, my former master saw me there, as I had seen him, and before looking away, I noticed that he nodded to the Moor Gurriato, who was by my side. The Moor nodded back.

I don't need either of you, I thought; but that was all I had time for, because at that very moment, the cannon in the gangway and the moyens on the prow fired off some chain shot to shatter the enemy ship's rigging and leave it without sails. *Pedreros*, harquebuses and muskets blasted them, too, the last filling the galley deck with smoke, which, in turn, was filled with Turkish arrows and lead and stone pellets that penetrated planks and flesh alike. We had no option but to grit our teeth and wait, which is what I did, crouched and afraid that a few of the many things falling on us would fall on me. Then the galley hit something solid, which made the whole vessel shudder and creak. The galley-slaves let go of the oars and, screaming, sought shelter among the benches. When I looked up, I saw above our heads, in among the clouds of smoke, the enormous stern of the mahone, which seemed to me as tall as a castle.

'Forward for Spain! Attack! Attack!'

Men were yelling furiously as they crowded onto the prow. No one was there simply because he had to be, apart from the oarsmen, of course; we knew that here was a prize that could make us all rich. The grappling-irons were thrown, and the lateen yard of the mainmast was lowered so that it rested on the side of the enemy ship for our men to climb along it.

With the galley heeled slightly to starboard, the troops – and I was among the first – shinned up the ropes on the mahone as if they were a flight of steps.

Lope Balboa, that soldier of our King, slain in Flanders with great pride and honour, would not have been ashamed of his son that day, watching me scale the high side of that Turkish mahone with all the youthful agility of my seventeen years, up to that place where your only friend is your sword, and where living or dying depends on chance, God or the Devil.

As I said, the fighting was fierce and lasted more than half an hour. There were about fifty janizaries on board, who all fought valiantly and, grouped together at the prow, killed quite a number of our men. The janizaries, Christians by birth, had been taken as children by way of a tax or tithe and had then been brought up in the Islamic faith to show unthinking loyalty to the Great Turk. It was a point of honour among them to fight to the bitter end, and they fought with extraordinary ferocity. We had to fire on them several times at point-blank range with our harquebuses – which we did gladly, for they had done the same to us through the portholes, hatchways and grilles as we were climbing up. Then we had to go in with shield and sword to finish them off and seize the mainmast, which they defended like rabid dogs.

I fought hard, although without letting myself get too carried away, protecting myself with my shield and lunging forward, always looking around me, as the Captain had taught me to do, only taking a step when I knew it was the right moment, and never retreating, not even when I felt Corporal Conesa's brains – blown out by a harquebus shot – splatter onto the back of my neck. The Moor Gurriato was beside me, scything his way through the crowd, and our comrades were not far behind. And so, step by step, sword thrust by sword thrust, we pressed the janizaries hard, driving them back as far as the trinquet sail and the prow itself.

'*Sentabajo, cane!*' we screamed at them in lingua franca, calling on them to surrender. By then, the men from the *Virgen del Rosario* and the *San Juan Bautista* were coming at them from behind, boarding at the prow, with the Spaniards shouting out the name of Santiago − St James − and the Maltese Knights that of St John. Once the three galleys came together, the sentence had been read. The last of the wounded and exhausted janizaries, who had, until then, been hurling insults at us − *guidi imansiz*, which, in Turkish, means 'infidel cuckolds' or *bir mum*, 'sons of bitches' − suddenly changed their tune and started addressing us as *efendi* and *sagdic*, 'sirs' and 'skippers', begging us to spare their lives, *Ala'iche*, 'for the love of God'. Once they had finally thrown down their arms, a large part of our squad began scouring every corner of the ship and tossing bundles of booty onto the decks of our galleys below.

By God, we had a good day, stealing right, left and centre. For a while, permission was given to plunder freely, and we took our captains at their word, for the mahone was more than seven hundred tons and was carrying all kinds of merchandise: spices, silks, damasks, bales of fine cloth, Turkish and Persian carpets, gemstones, seed pearls, silverware, and fifty thousand gold coins, not to mention several barrels of arrack − a Turkish liquor − to which we all paid lavish homage. Smiling like Democritus himself, I stole along with the best of them, without waiting for the general share-out, and by God I deserved it, for I was one of the men who had made the Turks work hardest, and had been the first to stick my dagger in the mainmast as proof that I was there, for this brought both honour and the right to a larger share of the booty. Testament to how hard I had fought were the seventeen Spaniards who had died boarding the mahone, as well as the various dents in my helmet and breastplate, and the bucket of water that was needed to wash the blood off me – other men's blood, fortunately.

Captain Alatriste and Copons had boarded at the stern, fighting first with harquebuses and then with axes and swords, breaking down doors and pavises behind which the Turkish officers and some of the janizaries had barricaded themselves. I later found out that when Captain Alatriste asked the Moor Gurriato how things had gone on my part, the Moor had summed up the situation elegantly, saying that he would have had a hard time keeping me alive if I hadn't roundly despatched everyone trying to stop him doing just that.

The men on the *Caridad Negra* and the *Cruz de Rodas* did their fair share of killing too. First one and then the other had boarded the Turkish galley, and the ensuing battle was fierce and without quarter, for it happened that, as the *Caridad Negra* rammed the enemy vessel, taking with it all the oars on that side, a stone had killed Sergeant Zugastieta, a jolly Basque, valiant trencherman and an even braver drinker, who was very popular among the other soldiers. They were all, as I explained, from the same part of Spain, and while the Basque people – and I speak as someone from Guipúzcoa – might sometimes be short on brains, we are always long on generosity and courage. The Basques therefore leapt onto the Turkish galley, yelling '*Koartelik ez!*' and '*Akatu gustiak!*', and other such things, which, in our language meant that no mercy would be shown, not even to the Captain's cat. And so everyone down to the last cabin boy was put to the knife and no attempt was made to distinguish between those trying to surrender and those who were not.

The only men left alive were the galley-slaves who had survived the attack, of whom ninety-six were Christians, half of them Spaniards. You can imagine their joy at being liberated. Among them was one fellow from Trujillo who had spent twenty-two years as a slave since his capture in 1615 at the taking of Mahomet, and who, miraculously, was still alive, despite all his time at the oars. How the poor man wept and embraced us all!

For our part, we liberated fifteen young slaves from the hold of the mahone: nine boys and six girls, still virgins, the oldest being fifteen or sixteen. They were all fine-looking youths, Christians captured by corsairs on the Spanish and Italian coasts, who were being taken to be sold in Constantinople, where an all too foreseeable future awaited them, given the licentious nature of the people there.

However, the most notable prize was the Pasha of Cyprus's favourite wife, who turned out to be a Russian renegade of about thirty. She had blue eyes and was tall and voluptuous, the most beautiful woman I have ever seen. Agustín Pimentel placed her in a cabin along with Chaplain Nistal and a four-man escort, threatening with death anyone who bothered her. We queued up at the door to admire her, for she was lavishly dressed and accompanied by two handsome Croat slave-girls, and it was very strange to have such a woman among coarse men like us, when the blood was still not dry on the deck. We did not even touch the booty she brought with her, for two days later she was sent to Naples in the mahone, with the liberated captives and the *Virgen del Rosario* as escort, the Turkish galley having been holed and sunk. She was ransomed there some time later in exchange for three hundred thousand gold coins of which we never caught so much as a glimpse, despite all the dangers we had faced. We learned that the Pasha grew quite mad with rage when he was told what had happened and that he swore revenge. Our poor pilot Braco paid the price in full when, a year and a half later, he was captured on board one of our ships on the sandbanks off Lemnos. He was identified as one of the men involved in the capture of the Cypriot mahone, and the Turks flayed him alive, slowly, and then stuffed his skin with straw, hung it from the topsail of a galley and paraded it from island to island.

That is what the Mediterranean was like. Between its narrow shores, everyone knew everyone else and there was always unfinished business. And such, too, was piracy and war: as you sow, so shall you reap. On that day, off the island of Fournoi, the people doing the reaping were the one hundred and fifty dead and wounded Turks, give or take a few, whom we threw into the sea, for they all duly sank to the bottom. Then the overseers chained fifty or so of the uninjured Turks to the benches, despite the protests of the Basques from the *Caridad Negra*, who wanted to cut off their heads for good measure. In the end, the Basques were so up in arms about it, refusing even to obey their captain, that Don Agustín Pimentel had to allow them to cut off the ears and noses of the five or six renegades found among the captured Turks.

As for private booty, by the time the order came to stop the plundering, I had filled my pockets with a few handfuls of silver, five good strands of pearls and fistfuls of Turkish, Venetian and Hungarian gold coins. It is no exaggeration to say that what we felt as we fell upon all that wealth was sheer joy. It was quite something to watch grown men, bearded soldiers clothed in leather and metal, laughing like children over their full purses. After all, that is why we Spaniards had left the safety of our own country, left hearth and home, prepared to suffer vicissitudes, hard work and danger, rough weather, the fury of the seas and the devastation of war. As Bartolomé de Torres Naharro had written in the previous century:

We soldiers only prosper
If there's a war to fight;
Like the poor in darkest winter
Who long to see the light.

Better dead or rich, we thought, but at least gentlemen, than poor and wretched, bowing the knee to the latest bishop or marquis. This was a concept defended by Cervantes in the character of Don Quixote, who placed the honour of the sword above the glory of the pen. If poverty is good because Christ loved it, I say, may those who preach poverty enjoy it. Disapproving of a soldier stealing gold for which he has paid with his blood, be it in Tenochtitlán or from under the nose of the Great Turk, as we were doing, shows a complete ignorance of the harshness of a soldier's life, and of the suffering he must endure to win that booty in battle, where he is exposed to bullets and injury, to cold steel and to fire, and all to earn a reputation, a living, or both things at once, for it comes to the same thing:

Here we do not die in bed,
Sipping from a sweetened cup,
Cosseted before we're dead;
No – bullets or a thrusting sword
Will cut our life-blood's precious cord.

Anyone who quibbles over a soldier's booty is forgetting that rewards and honour are what drive us all: sailors set to sea in search of both, farmers plough the fields, monks pray and soldiers fight. But honour, even if won through danger and wounds, never lasts long if it does not come with the reward that sustains it. The fine image of the hero covered in wounds on a battlefield soon turns sour when people look away in horror at the sight of his mutilated limbs and face while he begs for alms outside a church. Besides, Spain has always been rather forgetful when it comes to handing out rewards. If you want to eat, they tell you, go and attack that castle. If you want to be paid, board that galley. And may God help you and reward you. Then they watch from behind the safety of a barricade and applaud your feats – because applause costs nothing – and rush to profit from them, bestowing on that booty far more perfumed names than we do and wrapping themselves in the colours of a flag torn to shreds by the same shards of metal that have torn our flesh. For in our unfortunate nation, there are few generals and still fewer kings like the general, Caius Marius, who was so grateful for the help given by Barbarian mercenaries during the wars with Gaul that he made them citizens of Rome, in contravention of the local laws. When he was criticised for this, he replied: 'The law speaks in too quiet a voice to be heard above the clash of war.' Not to mention Christ himself, who honoured and, above all, fed his twelve soldiers.

10. THE ESCANDERLU CHANNEL

In the previous chapter, I used the expression: 'as you sow, so shall you reap', and it is very true. It's also true, as the Moor Gurriato said, that God blinds those who want to lose, to which I would add, don't count your chickens. Five days after capturing the mahone, we fell into a trap. Or perhaps it would be truer to say that we entered a trap of our own accord by pushing our luck too far.

Emboldened by that large prize, Don Agustín Pimentel decided to travel north, following the coast, to sack a small town inhabited by Ottomans: Foyavequia, which is in Anatolia, on the narrow Escanderlu channel. And so, after burying our dead – Sergeant Zugastieta, Corporal Conesa and other good comrades – in Turkish soil on the island of Fournoi, we sailed north, past Chios, and from there to the east of Cap Nero and the entrance to Smyrna. We entered the aforementioned channel, where we hove to far from the coast, waiting for night to fall. We did so confidently, despite one disquieting sign: having sent the Maltese galley, the *San Juan Bautista* ahead as scout, we had heard no more from her; indeed, no one has seen or heard of her since. We will never know if she sank or was captured, if there were survivors or not, because not even the Turks gave an explanation. Like so many mysteries that sleep beneath the waves, the galley was swallowed up by the sea and by history, along with the three hundred and forty men on board – knights, soldiers, sailors and oarsmen.

*

Misfortunes rarely come singly. Even though the *San Juan Bautista* had not rejoined us as planned, Don Agustín Pimentel was confident that she had simply been delayed and would join us later, and that, besides, three galleys were quite sufficient to attack the rather insignificant fortress of Foyavequia, which had already been sacked by the Maltese Knights in 1616. Darkness fell. We weren't allowed to light a fire, so we filled our stomachs with cold boiled beans, a handful of olives and one onion between four.

Then, at the angelus hour, with an overcast sky and not a breath of wind, and with our lanterns extinguished, the galleys began to row across the sea towards land. It was a dark night, and we were about a mile from the town, the three vessels close together, when the lookout thought he saw something behind us, out to sea: the shapes of ships and sails, he said, although he couldn't be sure because there were no lights to betray their presence. We stopped rowing. The galleys moved even closer together and a meeting took place around the flagship. It might be that the shapes were low clouds lit by the last light of evening, or some vessel far out to sea; but they could also be enemy ships – one or several – in which case, having our escape route cut off by them was very worrying indeed, as was the possibility of our galleys being attacked while anchored off the beach and our men fighting on shore. Greatly put out, our General despatched the skiff to reconnoitre, while we waited anxiously. The reconnaissance party returned at the start of the middle watch and reported that there were five or more shadows, galleys to judge by their shape, which apparently dared not approach for fear of being discovered or captured. This disturbing information persuaded Don Agustín Pimentel not to proceed. They might be Turks from Chios or Mytilene, merchants travelling in convoy, or perhaps a flotilla of corsairs preparing to travel west.

We discussed each possibility and wondered if we could simply disappear off into the dark, but it was unlikely that we could do so without being seen or heard, and dangerous too, given that we did not yet know who we were dealing with. And so, holding firm to the order not to light fires on board and with the guard doubled to warn us of any attack, we were told to take it in turns to rest, but to be ready for action. Thus, with our weapons beside us, with one eye open and unease in our hearts, we waited for the light of day to decide our fate.

'We're in for a rough time, gentlemen,' Captain Urdemalas said.

He had just climbed from the skiff up the ladder at the stern, after a meeting in the captain's cabin on board the *Caridad Negra*. The three galleys were all facing out to sea, their oars motionless in the leaden water.

'It's quite simple: tonight, we'll either be dining with Christ or in Constantinople.'

Diego Alatriste turned towards the Turkish galleys, studying them for the hundredth time since the dawn had first begun to define their shape against the dark horizon, where a distant storm was threatening. There were seven ordinary galleys with one lantern apiece and a larger one with three, possibly their flagship. There must have been a thousand or so soldiers on board, not including the crew. Twenty-four pieces of artillery adorned the eight prows, as well as swivel-guns and sakers on the sides. There was no way of knowing whether they had sought us out or just happened to be sailing those waters at the right moment. Whatever the truth of the matter, they were now less than a mile away, formed up in battle order, and astutely covering any escape route to the open sea. They had waited patiently all night, knowing that their prey was trapped. Whoever was in charge knew what they were doing.

'The Maltese galley will go first,' Urdemalas told us. 'Muntaner insisted. He said that the statutes of his Order oblige him to do so.'

'Well, rather them than us,' said the galleymaster, relieved.

'It makes no difference. None of us will get off lightly.'

The officers and subalterns on the *Mulata* exchanged glances. No one needed to say a word; their thoughts were written on their faces. Captain Urdemalas had merely confirmed what Diego Alatriste and the others already knew: there were two enemy galleys for every Christian galley, and two more besides, and there was no point in taking refuge on land, because we were in Turkish territory. There was nothing for it but to risk life and liberty. We were certain to end up either dead or captive, unless a miracle occurred – and it was up to us to make that miracle happen.

'We'll have to be under oars at all times,' Urdemalas went on, 'unless those black clouds to the west bring us some wind, in which case, we'll have more of a chance. But we can't count on that.'

'What's the plan, then?' Ensign Labajos asked.

'Very simple. There is no other option. The Maltese galley will go first, the *Caridad Negra* second, and we'll bring up the rear.'

'I don't like the idea of being last,' said Labajos.

'It amounts to the same thing. I doubt any of us will get through because as soon as they see us move, the bastards will close in. Anyway, Muntaner is going first, which gives us some space to try our luck. We'll make as if we're heading straight at the enemy, then try to cut away and escape along their left flank, which seems to be their weaker point.'

'Are we to help each other?' Sergeant Quemado asked.

Urdemalas shook his head and, as he did so, raised a hand to his cheek, quietly cursing God and all the saints because his toothache was still tormenting him and had only been made worse by too many hours without sleep. Diego Alatriste knew what he was thinking. For Urdemalas, and for all of them, it had been a very long night, but a good one in comparison with what might lie ahead: either at the bottom of the sea or at the oars of some Turkish galley. Soon, that toothache would be the least of Captain Urdemalas' problems.

'No one is to help anyone else,' Urdemalas replied. 'It's every man for himself, and the Devil take the hindmost.'

'Unfortunately, we're the hindmost,' Sergeant Quemado remarked.

Urdemalas shot him a scathing glance. 'It was just a figure of speech, damn it. If we don't help each other and row hard, there's a small chance that one of our ships might escape.'

'Then the Maltese galley is done for,' Labajos commented coldly. 'If they're the first in line, the Turks will fall on them immediately.'

Urdemalas pulled a face.

'That's why they call themselves Knights and take their vows, and when they die, they go to Heaven. Things are less cut and dried for the rest of us, so we must tread carefully.'

'That's what it says in the Gospels, sir,' Quemado said. 'I once saw a Flemish painting of hell, very life-like it was, too, and I swear on the King of Spades that I, for one, am in no hurry to weigh anchor.'

This was the usual banter, thought Alatriste, what was expected of them. Everything was happening according to the rules, including that light, nonchalant air, even at the mouth of Hell itself. Any fears you had, you kept to yourself. Eight centuries of war against the Moors and one hundred and fifty years of making the rest of the world tremble had refined both language and manners: a Spanish soldier, like it or not, could not allow himself to be killed just anyhow, but in accordance with the expectations of both enemies and friends. Those gathered at the stern of the *Mulata* knew this, as did the other men. This was what they were paid to do, even if they never received that pay, and it was with these thoughts in mind that Alatriste was studying his fellow soldiers. At that moment, any one of them would have preferred to be in bed with a fever rather than fit and healthy on board that ship. Standing in groups, in the embrasures, in the corridors and in the central gangway, soldiers and sailors were watching their officers in silence, knowing how the cards would fall. Among the oarsmen, though, some were afraid and others joyful, imagining themselves already free, because for the captive chained to the bench by the enemy religion, every sail on the horizon meant hope.

'How are we going to deploy the men?' Labajos asked.

Urdemalas made a sawing motion with the edge of one hand on the palm of the other.

'Our aim is to cut through their lines and repel all would-be boarders. And if we get through, I'll need two falconets, the two-pounders, at the stern. The chase might be a long one.'

'Shall we give the men some food, just in case?'

'Yes, but I want no ovens lit. Give them some raw garlic and wine to warm their stomachs.'

'The galley-men will need something too,' said the galley-master.

Urdemalas leaned back against the stern, underneath the lantern. There were dark circles under his eyes, and he looked grimy and exhausted. A combination of toothache and

uncertainty had drained the colour from his face. Alatriste
didn't even bother to wonder if he too looked like that; even
without the toothache, he knew that he did.

'Check the shackles on all the forced men, and the manacles
on the Turks and Moors. Give them a little of that arrack we
got from the mahone, a measure per bench. That's the best
encouragement we can give them today. But no concessions,
eh? If anyone's caught slacking, we cut off his head, even if
I'm the one who has to pay the King. Do I make myself
clear, galleymaster?'

'As clear as day. I'll tell the overseer.'

'If you're giving the forced men drink,' commented Sergeant
Quemado, with a grin on his face, 'they're either fucked or
about to be.'

Unusually, no one laughed. Urdemalas fixed the sergeant
with a mirthless stare. 'As for the other men,' he said curtly,
'give them a sip of arrack as well as the garlic and wine.
Then keep some wine to hand, but make it weak, mind.' At
this point, he turned to the German gunner. 'As for you, sir,
you will fire using langridge-shot and tinplate, from close to
and at my orders. Otherwise, Ensign Labajos will be at the
prow, Sergeant Quemado on the starboard side and Señor
Alatriste on the port side.'

'It would be a good idea to give the oarsmen as much
protection as possible,' Alatriste said.

Urdemalas gave him a surly look and held it for just a
moment longer than necessary.

'You're right,' he said at last. 'Pad the pavisades with
whatever we have, sails included. If they kill a lot of our
oarsmen, we're done for. Pilot, make sure the compass and
all the instruments are well secured in the binnacle. And I'll
need the two best helmsmen, the pilot and eight good
musketeers by my side. Any questions?'

'None, sir,' said Labajos, after a silence.

'Needless to say, there's to be no attempt to board their ships. We'll concentrate on bombarding them with langridge, stone shot and harquebus and musket fire. And that's that. If we hang around, we're lost. And if we get through, then we'll have to row like madmen.'

There were a few tense smiles.

'God willing,' someone murmured.

Urdemalas shrugged. 'And if He's not willing, then at least He'll know where to find us come Judgement Day.'

'Let's just hope He puts the right pieces back together,' added Sergeant Quemado.

'Amen,' muttered the galleymaster, crossing himself.

And glancing at each other, everyone followed suit, including Alatriste.

Anyone who claims never to have experienced fear is a liar, because you never know what might happen. And on that morning, facing the eight Turkish galleys blocking our exit to the open sea, in the prelude to a confrontation that is now described in reports and history books as the naval battle of Escanderlu or Cap Nero, I recognised the feeling. I had known it on other occasions: my stomach tightening to the point of nausea, creating an unpleasant tingling in the groin. I had grown up a lot since my first experiences at Captain Alatriste's side, and for all my smugness and youthful arrogance, the two years that had passed since the Ruyter Mill, Breda and Terheyden had made me more sensible and more conscious of danger. What was about to happen was not an adventure to be undertaken with the flippancy of a boy; it was a grave event whose outcome was unknown, and which could end in death – not, after all, the worst of endings – but also in captivity or mutilation. I was sufficiently mature to understand that in a few hours' time I might find myself chained to the oars of a Turkish galley for the rest of my life – no one in Constantinople would be prepared to ransom a poor soldier from Oñate – or else biting into a piece of leather as they amputated an arm or a leg. It was the idea of being mutilated that frightened me most, for there is nothing worse than having an eye missing or a wooden leg and finding oneself transformed into some kind of waxen image, condemned to endure others' pity and to begging for alms, especially when one is still in the full flower of youth. This, among other things, would not be the image Angélica de Alquézar would want to encounter if we were ever to see each other again. And I have to say that the prospect of such a meeting made my legs quake.

These were my rather grim thoughts as, along with my comrades, I finished preparing the pavisade along the sides and prow of the *Mulata* with rolled-up sailcloth, palliasses, blankets, packs, rigging and whatever else we could put between us and the Turkish bullets and arrows that would soon fall on us like hail. Every man was thinking his private thoughts, but the truth is that we all put on a brave face. There were, at most, depending on the individual, a few tremulous hands, incoherent words, distracted stares, mumbled prayers or macabre jokes that met with uneasy laughter.

Our three galleys were almost oar to oar, our prows facing the Turks, who were now about a cannon shot away, although no one fired a cannon to check this, for they and we knew that there would be ample opportunity to fire – and to better purpose – when we were nearer. When the moment came, everyone would try to be the first to fire, but only when we were as close as possible to the enemy. The silence on the enemy galleys was absolute, as it was on ours. The sea was as smooth as a sheet of lead, reflecting the black storm clouds that moved southwards over the coast of Anatolia, which lay behind and to each side. We were armed and ready, the match-cords lit, and all that was missing was the order to row towards our fate. I had been assigned to the port side of the boat where, duly provided with half-pikes, spears and pikes, we would have to repel any attempt by the Turks to board.

The Moor Gurriato was beside me – I suspect on Captain Alatriste's orders. He seemed utterly calm, apparently oblivious to everything that was happening. Although he was as prepared to fight and die as everyone else, it was as if he were merely passing through, an indifferent witness to his own fate, despite the fact that, as a Moor, this would be a far from enviable one if he fell into Turkish hands. It would not be long before he was betrayed by some galley-slave or even by his own comrades; for the energy that makes men throw themselves into battle can turn to something quite contemptible when it's a matter of survival. Even more so in captivity, where so many strong spirits wavered, reneged or submitted in exchange for liberty, life or even a miserable piece of bread. We are, after all, only human, and not everyone is capable of facing difficulties with the same courage.

'We will fight together,' the Moor Gurriato said to me. 'All the time.'

That consoled me a little, although I knew perfectly well that, when you are fighting on the threshold of the next life, each man is fighting for himself, and there is no greater solitude than that. But he had said the right thing, and I was grateful for the friendly look that accompanied his words.

'You're very far from your country,' I said.

He smiled and shrugged. He was dressed in Spanish fashion, in breeches and espadrilles, but his chest was bare; he carried a curved dagger tucked in his belt, a half-sword at his waist and a boarding axe in his hand. He had never seemed so serene, or so fierce.

'You and the Captain are my country,' he said.

His words touched me, but I disguised my feelings as best I could, and said the first thing that came into my head: 'Still, there are better places to die.'

He bowed his head, as if thinking.

'There are as many deaths as there are people,' he replied. 'No one ever really expects his own death, although he may think he does. He merely accompanies it and remains at its disposal.'

He stood for a moment, staring at the tar-smeared deck, then looked at me again. 'Your death is always with you, and mine is always with me. We each carry our own death on our backs.'

I looked around for Captain Alatriste and finally spotted him at the prow end of the corridor, giving orders to the harquebusiers on the fighting platform. He had been put in command of the port side of the galley and had appointed Sebastián Copons as his adjutant. He seemed as cool and calm as ever, his hat down over his eyes, his thumbs hooked in the belt from which hung sword and dagger. He was wearing his old buff coat, which bore the marks of former battles, and was clearly ready once more to confront whatever fate might bring him, with no fuss, no bravado, but with the aplomb one would expect of such a man or of the man he was trying to be. There are as many deaths as there are people, the Moor Gurriato had said. I envied the Captain's death, when it came.

I heard the Moor's soft voice beside me: 'One day, you might regret not having said goodbye to him.'

I turned and came face to face with his intense, dark eyes.

'God,' he continued, 'gives us a very brief light in between two long dark nights.'

I studied the Moor for an instant: his shaven head, the silver earrings, the pointed beard, the cross tattooed on one cheekbone. I did so for as long as his smile lasted. Then, giving in to the impulse his words had placed in my heart, I walked down the corridor, avoiding the many comrades crowding it, and went over to the Captain. I said not a word, because I didn't know what I could say; I merely leaned against the fighting platform, looking across at the Turkish galleys. I was thinking about Angélica de Alquézar, about my mother and my little sisters sewing by the fire. I was thinking, too, about myself, when I first arrived in Madrid, sitting at the door of Caridad la Lebrijana's inn one sunny winter's morning. I was thinking of the many men I could become, and who would perhaps remain there for ever, cut short, nothing but food for the fishes.

Then I felt Captain Alatriste's hand on my shoulder.

'Don't let them take you alive, son.'

'I won't, I swear it,' I answered.

I felt like crying, but not out of sorrow or fear. I was overwhelmed, rather, by a strange sense of melancholy. Far off, above the silence and stillness of the sea, a flash of lightning flared, so distant that we couldn't even hear the accompanying thunder. Then, as if that zigzag of light had been a signal, the drum sounded. At the stern of the *Caridad Negra*, next to the lantern and with a crucifix held up high, Brother Francisco Nistal raised his other hand and blessed us all. We bared our heads, knelt down and prayed. The chaplain's words came to us in short bursts: *In nomine ... et filii ... Amen.* As we knelt, the royal pennant was raised on the stern of the flagship, while on the galley of the Knights of Malta, the silver eight-pointed cross appeared, and on ours the white flag bearing the St Andrew's cross. Each flag was greeted with a blast on the bugle.

'Shirts off!' the galleymaster ordered.

Then we took our places and the galley began to row towards the Turks.

The silent storm continued to rage in the distance. The glow of the lightning flashed across the grey horizon, illuminating the still waters. The galley was equally silent, apart from the sound of the oars in the sea – the rhythm as yet quite relaxed. The oarsmen were taking it in turns to row, slowly, so as to conserve their energy for the final stretch, and even the galleymaster refrained from using his whistle. We were quiet, too, our eyes fixed on the Turkish ships that bristled with weapons, ready for battle. Halfway there, while we veered slightly off to the left, the Maltese galley began to overtake us on our right. We watched her forge ahead, sails furled, muskets, harquebuses and pikes sticking up above the pavisade, oars keeping to a precise rhythm. At the stern, where the awning had been taken down, stood its captain, Brother Fulco Muntaner, clearly visible with his long grey beard, white corslet, red over-tunic and white cross. Bareheaded and sword in hand, he was surrounded by his trusted comrades: Brother Juan de Mañas from Aragon, son of the Count of Bolea; Brother Luciano Cánfora from Italy, and the novice Knight Ghislain Barrois from Provence. As they passed us, almost brushing our oars with theirs, Captain Urdemalas took off his hat to them. 'Good luck!' he cried.

Muntaner, as calmly as if he were sailing into port, made a dismissive gesture in the direction of the eight Turkish galleys and said in his strong Mallorcan accent, 'Small fry.'

When the *Cruz de Rodas* had passed us, the *Caridad Negra* followed at the same easy pace, the flag bearing the royal arms fluttering feebly at the stern, for the only breeze was that created by the movement of the galley. Thus we watched the Basques preceding us in the attack, and we waved to them with hands, hats and helmets. There went Captain Machín de Gorostiola and his surly men, the match-cords of their muskets and harquebuses burning from prow to stern. There was Don Agustín Pimentel with his page holding his helmet. He stood very erect and elegant in his expensive Milanese armour, one hand on the hilt of his sword, showing all the aplomb befitting his rank, his country, his King and the God in whose name we were about to be hacked to pieces.

'May Our Lady help them,' someone murmured.

'May she help us all,' said another.

The three galleys were now rowing in single file, keeping very close together, nose to tail, while the silent lightning continued to flicker over the sea. I was at my post, between the Moor Gurriato and the man in charge of one of the *pedreros*, who was holding a smoking linstock in one hand and fingering a rosary with the other as he murmured a prayer. I wanted to swallow, but my mouth and throat were dry from the sip of arrack and watery wine I had drunk.

'Row harder!' Captain Urdemalas shouted.

The order, the galleymaster's whistle and the crack of the whip all came at once. Trying to conceal my shaking fingers, I tied my scarf around my head and put on my steel helmet, securing it with a chinstrap. I checked that I could easily unfasten the chains on my breastplate if I were to fall into the sea. My espadrilles with their rope soles were tied on tightly at the ankles; in my hands I held the shaft of a half-pike with a razor-sharp blade and the upper third of the shaft carefully greased. At my waist were my sword and dagger. I took several deep breaths. I had all I needed, but there was a hollow in my stomach. I unfastened my breeches and urinated into the scupper – even though I didn't much feel like it – in between the rhythmically moving oars; no one paid any attention, indeed most of my fellows were doing the same. We were all battle-hardened men.

'Everyone to the oars! Now – row hard!'

We heard the sound of cannon shot at the prow and stood on tiptoe to get a better view. The Turkish galleys, which we were fast approaching and which, until then, had not stirred, were beginning to move. The decks swarmed with turbans, red hats, the tall toques worn by janizaries, jelabs, Moorish cloaks and colourful haiks. A puff of white smoke appeared at the prow of the Turkish galley nearest to us. The silence following the explosion was broken by a shrill clamour of whistles, flutes and trumpets, and from the Ottoman ships came the usual battle cries. The *Cruz de Rodas* responded with three short blasts on the bugle, followed by a roll on the drums and cries of: 'St John! St John!' and, 'Remember St Elmo!'

'That's the Maltese galley,' said an old soldier.

A series of explosions and arrows burst from the Turkish galleys; cannon and moyens began to fire on the *Cruz de Rodas*, with some loose bullets reaching us and whistling over our heads. The galleymaster, his assistant and the overseer raced up and down the gangway, lashing the backs of the slaves.

'Full ahead now!' howled Captain Urdemalas. 'Row for your lives, my boys!'

The smoke was growing denser by the minute, and the harquebus fire increased along with the Turkish arrows scudding through the air in all directions. The enemy ships were closing on our lead galley, now that it was clear she was making a rash attempt to escape. We saw the *Cruz de Rodas* plunge into the smoke, in between the two nearest galleys, so determinedly that we heard the crunch of planking and oars as they broke. Our flagship followed, heading off to the

left. We could hear Machín de Gorostiola and his fellow
Basques shouting: 'Santiago! *Ekin! Ekin!* Spain and Santiago!'
The *Mulata* went behind, into the roar of combat and the
cries of men fighting for their lives.

The galleymaster's whistle shrilled in our ears as the galley
flew over the waves; for that fast, intermittent whistling
marked the space that separated us from death or captivity.
Still unable to believe our momentary good luck, we were
looking back at the galleys now pursuing us. We had crossed
the Turkish lines, although the distance between us and our
pursuers was minimal. The sea was as smooth as oil, and the
silent flashes of lightning lingered in the west. There would
be no saving wind. The *Caridad Negra*, which had gone
ahead of us, was to the right of the *Mulata* now, rowing
desperately in a bid to escape the five Turkish galleys at our
rear. Behind us, still only a cannon-shot away, the Maltese
ship, surrounded by three enemy vessels, was fighting furiously, swathed in smoke and flames. Amid the din of its
hopeless struggle we could still hear cries of, 'St John! St
John!'

It had been a miracle, albeit of limited scope. Once the
Cruz de Rodas had penetrated the Turkish line, where it
immediately came under attack, the *Caridad Negra* had taken
advantage of the space left by that manoeuvre to pass through,
not without attracting enough cannon fire to smash her
trinquet mast and not without breaking some of her oars as
she slipped between the Maltese galley and the nearest enemy
ship. This gave us an advantage, fast behind her as we were,
because we reached them just as the enemy cannon had been
fired and before they had a chance to reload; thus we met
only with harquebus fire and a rain of arrows. Our starboard
oars touched those of the *Cruz de Rodas*, which, caught

helplessly among the Turkish galleys, with more approaching at full speed, was boarded from three sides simultaneously, twice on one side and once at the prow.

With all our senses focused on avoiding a Turkish galley approaching from the left, we were too preoccupied to appreciate her sacrifice at the time – although we saw Captain Muntaner and his Knights fighting for their lives at the stern. There ensued a pandemonium of shouts and curses; arrows flew past, impaling themselves in the pavisade, in masts and in flesh. Our helmsman, with Captain Urdemalas screaming orders into his ear – like one of those devils you get in plays put on at Corpus Christi – flung the tiller to one side in order not to collide with the *Caridad Negra*, which, with its felled mast dragging through the water, was lurching off course. As he did this, the enemy galley rammed us in the stern. Three or four oars splintered and broke, there came a babble of Turkish voices, and the battle cries of those of us who rushed to repel the boarders. The contact lasted only an instant, but it was enough for a group of vociferous janizaries to leap across. Our half-pikes, harquebuses, muskets and *pedreros* soon dealt with them, while from the topmasts, the cabin boys emptied firepots and bottles of tar onto the enemy, drenching their foredeck and forcing them to retreat, while we continued on our way.

'Come on, lads!' Captain Urdemalas roared. 'We're nearly there! Come on!'

Our Captain was, perhaps, optimistic, but then, given the circumstances, he had a duty to be, urging on the frantically rowing slaves, whose backs were now raw and bleeding.

'Overseer! Give them another drink of arrack! Now row, damn it! Row!'

But not even the strong Turkish liquor could work miracles. The oarsmen, almost mad with exhaustion, their backs covered in sweat, bruises and blood, were almost at their limit. The galley was flying along, as I said, but so were the five Turkish galleys in hot pursuit. Occasionally their cannonballs scored a hit – with a subsequent crunch of broken planks and cries of pain – or else cut through the air and fell into the sea, sending up a column of spray at our prow.

'The *Caridad* is getting left behind!'

We all rushed to the starboard side to see what was happening, and a woeful clamour filled the ship. Badly battered as she crossed the Turkish line, with many oars broken and too many oarsmen dead, wounded or exhausted, our flagship was losing momentum and we were gradually overtaking her. In a matter of moments, she had gone from being a pistol shot away from our prow to almost abeam. We could see Don Agustín Pimentel, Machín de Gorostiola and the other officers looking anxiously behind at the Turkish galleys that were fast catching them up. The *Caridad*'s oars were out of rhythm, sometimes clashing with each other, and several were utterly still, dragging through the water. We also noticed that a few dead galley-slaves had been thrown into the sea.

'That's them done for,' said one soldier.

'Better them than us,' commented another.

'There'll be plenty more of that to go around.'

The *Caridad Negra* was slipping further and further behind. Some of us shouted encouraging words, but it was no use. Crowded along the edges of the boat, leaning over the pavisades, we saw that she was hopelessly lost, her oars all awry, with the Turks almost upon her, her crew powerless to do anything but watch as we moved away. Some Basques called out to us from the fighting platforms, but we could no longer hear what they said. Then they raised their hands in farewell and rushed to the stern, harquebuses and muskets smoking and at the ready. At least the Turks would pay a high price for their booty.

'Officers to the stern!' came the cry, as the order was passed down the ship.

A deathly silence filled the galley. As the saying goes, shepherds only gather when a sheep has died. We saw Sergeant Quemado, Ensign Labajos and the galleymaster heading, grave-faced, towards the back of the ship, while the other men made way for them. Captain Alatriste joined the group. He passed by without seeing me, or so it seemed. His eyes were expressionless, as if they were contemplating something beyond the sea, beyond everything. I knew that look. That was when I realised: the Basques on the other galley were only preceding us into disaster.

'The oarsmen can't go on,' said Captain Urdemalas.

Diego Alatriste glanced at the rowers. They were clearly exhausted, indifferent now to the lashes of the assistant galleymaster and the overseer, and incapable of keeping up the necessary rhythm. Like the *Caridad Negra*, the *Mulata* was flagging, and the Turks were gaining fast.

'They'll be on us in no time.'

'Perhaps the soldiers, or at least some of them, could row,' said the galleymaster.

Ensign Labajos retorted indignantly that this was out of the question. He had discussed the matter with some of the men, and no one was prepared to take up the oars, not even in the present situation. God will provide, they said. Since it looked like they were going to end their lives here, no one wanted to die a galley-slave.

'Besides, it would be a waste of time with five ships on our tail. My men are soldiers, and they need all their energy to do their job, which is fighting, not rowing.'

'If they catch us, many of us will end up rowing in chains anyway,' said the galleymaster grimly.

'Well, that's for each man to decide.'

Diego Alatriste studied the men crowding the corridors and the fighting platforms. Labajos was right. As they waited for a sentence to be handed down against which there could be no appeal, and despite their anxiety, those men still looked as fierce and formidable as ever. They were the best infantry in the world, and Alatriste knew why. Soldiers like them – or *señores soldados* as they demanded to be called – had been soldiering for almost a century and a half and would continue to do so until the word 'reputation' was erased from their limited military vocabulary. They might suffer misfortune and exposure to fire and steel, they might find themselves mutilated or dead, unpaid and inglorious, but they would never cease to fight as long as there was a comrade living before whom they must maintain faith and decorum. Of course they wouldn't row, not even to save themselves. They would, of course, as individuals, be prepared to row for their lives and liberty, but only if they could be sure that no one would ever hear about it. Alatriste himself was capable, if it came to it, of taking his seat at a bench and placing his hands on an oar. Indeed, he would be the first, but neither he nor the biggest rogue on board would do such a thing if he lost stature in the eyes of the world, for this was what Spain was like. The one thing that neither kings nor favourites, priests nor enemies, not even illness or death, could take from him was the image he had forged of himself, the chimera of someone who proclaimed himself to be a gentleman rather than a slave. For a Spanish soldier, his profession was his honour. All this went entirely against the words spoken by a Berber corsair in a play Diego Alatriste had seen, words that came unbidden to his lips:

The Christian takes his stubborn honour
To such absurd extremes,
That even to touch the end of an oar
Is a great dishonour, it seems.
And while their foolish, childish ways
Cause them to preen and smirk,
Our ships come home stuffed full of these jays,
But for us it's simply work.

He said nothing, however. This was not the moment for poetry, nor was it in his nature to quote lines of verse. He merely concluded to himself that this attitude would doubtless seal the fate of the *Mulata*, just as it would, in time, bring about the ruin of Spain, although, by then, it would no longer be any business of his. At least, in men like him, such desperate arrogance offered a certain degree of consolation. There was no other rule to cling to once you knew of what stuff flags were made.

'Bloody honour,' Sergeant Quemado said.

They all looked at each other solemnly, as if there were nothing more to be said. They would have given anything to be able to find alternative words, but there were none. They were professional soldiers, rough men-at-arms, and rhetoric was not their strong point. They could allow themselves few luxuries, but choosing where and how to end their lives was one of them. And that was what they were doing.

'We have to turn round and fight,' Ensign Labajos said. 'Better that than running away like cowards.'

'As the Captain said,' Sergeant Quemado put in, 'it's a choice between dining with Christ or in Constantinople.'

'With Christ it is then,' Labajos said sternly.

Everyone turned to Captain Urdemalas, who was still stroking his sore cheek. He shrugged, as if leaving the decision

to them. Then he glanced over the stern. In the distance, far
behind, the Maltese ship was still embroiled with the three
Turkish galleys, battling away amid smoke and harquebus
fire. Between them and the *Mulata* lay the *Caridad Negra*,
about to be caught by her pursuers, the enemy ships seething
with people ready to board. He turned back to face his men,
resigned to the inevitable.

'There are five galleys,' the pilot Braco reminded them
glumly, 'plus the others who will arrive once they've finished
off the Maltese crew.'

Labajos removed his hat and threw it down on the deck.
'There could be fifty of them for all I care!'

Captain Urdemalas was studying Diego Alatriste, who was
clearly keeping his opinions to himself, for he was the only
one who had not yet spoken. Alatriste nodded soberly. Words
were not what was expected of him.

'Right,' Urdemalas said, 'let's go to the aid of those Basques.
They'll be glad to know they're not going to die alone.'

11. THE LAST GALLEY

What Lepanto was like I do not know, but I will never forget the battle of Escanderlu: the deck shifting beneath our feet, the sea always ready to swallow us up if we fell, the shouts of men killing or dying, the blood pouring down the sides of the galleys, the air thick with smoke and fire. There was still no wind and the water remained as smooth as a sheet of tin, while, in the distance, the strange silent storm continued to unleash its lightning, a remote imitation of what men are capable of doing with their will alone.

Once the officers had reached a decision, and we men had screwed up our courage for what lay ahead, the helmsman turned the galley round so that we could go to the aid of the *Caridad Negra*. She was now locked in battle with the first of the Turkish galleys, its deck filled with furiously fighting men, with shouts, screams and the sound of shots being fired. On the basis that it would be better to fight together rather than separately, Captain Urdemalas performed a brilliant manoeuvre. With the help of some skilful rowing elicited from the exhausted oarsmen by more lashes, he placed our prow right at the stern of the flagship, so that the galleys were virtually touching, allowing us to pass from one to the other if necessary. You can imagine the relief and the shouts – '*Ekin! Ekin!*' – that greeted our arrival, because by the time our prow touched their stern, Captain Machín de Gorostiola and his men, although still stoutly fending off the boarding parties from the two enemy galleys, had basically given up any hope of winning. Another two galleys were heading towards us; the fifth was approaching from the rear, hoping to batter us with its artillery before attempting to board. We had tied ropes and hawsers around the masts to keep the two Spanish vessels together, forming a kind of fortress besieged on all sides, the difference being that we were in the middle of the sea, and the only 'walls' we had to protect us from the enemy assault were the pavisades that were becoming ever more tattered and holed by the hail of bullets and arrows and by our own fire, pikes and swords.

'*Bir mum kafir! … Baxá kes! … Alautalah!*'

The janizaries were extraordinarily valiant. They came on board in waves, urging themselves in the name of God and the Great Turk to cut off the heads of these infidel dogs. And such was their scorn for death, one would have thought the houris of Mohammed's paradise were right at our backs. They clambered along the rams of their galleys, even running along the yards of their own ships or across the oars, which they leaned against the sides of our galley. Their battle cries and guttural shouts were terrifying, as was their appearance – brilliant caftans, shaven heads, tall hats and large moustaches – and their scimitars, which they wielded with deadly precision.

God and King were nevertheless well served, for the Spanish infantry, in the face of the enemy's valour and scorn for death, still had a few cards up its sleeve. Each wave of Turks crashed into the wall of our harquebuses and muskets, which unleashed volley upon volley. It was remarkable how, in the midst of all that madness, our old soldiers remained as serene as ever, calmly firing, reloading and firing, occasionally asking pages and cabin boys to fetch them more ammunition. And us younger folk, lithe and more agile, attacked in good order, first with pikes and half-pikes and then, in close combat, with swords, daggers and axes. This combination of lead, steel and sheer courage more or less kept the enemy at bay, biting and nipping at them like a dog with fleas; and the fragile redoubt of the *Caridad Negra* and the *Mulata* continued to spit fire at the five Turkish galleys surrounding them. Some drew nearer while others retreated so that their crew could rest, attack with more artillery fire and then try to board again, and after a long period of intense fighting, it became clear to the enemy that victory was going to cost a great deal of their blood and ours.

'Forward for Spain and Santiago! Attack! Attack!'

The show, as they say, had only just begun, and we were already hoarse with shouting and sick of the smell of smoke and blood. Others, less constrained, hurled insults at the Turks in whatever language came most naturally – Castilian, Basque, Greek, Turkish or Frankish – calling them dogs and sons of whores, and *bardağ*, which, in Arabic, means 'sodomite', not forgetting the pig that impregnated some Muslim mother and other such pleasantries. The Ottomans responded with imaginative variants in their own tongue – the Mediterranean has always been particularly fertile in insults – on the debatable virginity of Our Lady or the dubious manhood of Jesus Christ, as well as acerbic comments on the chastity of the mothers who bore us. It was, in short, all very much in accord with the place and the situation.

Bravado apart, we all knew that for the Turks it was merely a question of patience and keeping up the attack. They had at least three times as many men and could cope with any losses, withdrawing now and then to rest and regroup without ever giving us a moment's respite. Moreover, whenever we managed to fight off one of the enemy galleys, it would take advantage of the greater distance to fire on us to devastating effect. As well as the cannon-ball itself, there were the splinters and fragments that flew in all directions, demolishing the pavisades that were our only protection.

Bodies were blown to pieces, and there were guts, blood and debris everywhere. In the water, between the ships, floated dozens of corpses, either men who had fallen in while boarding or dead men who had been thrown in to clear the decks. Many galley-slaves — ours and theirs — had been killed or wounded. Still in their chains, unable to seek protection, they clung together among the benches and beneath their broken oars, shrieking in terror at the furious attacks from both sides and begging for mercy.

'Alautalah! Alautalah!'

We must have been fighting for at least two long hours when one of the Turkish galleys, in a skilful manoeuvre, managed to position its ram right by the prow of the *Mulata*, and another great horde of janizaries and Turkish soldiers poured on board, determined to overwhelm us.

Our men fought like tigers, defending every inch of deck with remarkable courage, but the Turks were stronger than we were, and gradually we had to relinquish control over the benches and the fighting platforms at that end of the ship. I knew that Captain Alatriste and Sebastián Copons were there somewhere, but in the smoke and confusion I couldn't see them. An order came to cover the breach, and as many of us as were able rushed to do just that, filling the gangway and the corridors on both sides. I was among the first, for I was not prepared to stand by while they made mincemeat of Captain Alatriste.

We closed on the Turks just beyond the mainmast, the yard of which lay on the deck. I jumped over it as best I could, shield and sword before me, trampling over the wretched oarsmen who were crouched between the benches and the shattered oars. One, in his agony, even grabbed my leg. He looked like a Turk, so I dealt him a blow with my sword that almost severed his manacled hand. In situations of such pressing danger, reason has no place.

'Forward for Spain and Santiago! Attack!'

Finally, we fell upon the enemy, and again I was among the first, caring little for my own safety, so caught up was I in the fury of the fighting. A swarthy Turk came at me, as hairy as a wild boar. He was wearing a leather helmet, shield and sword. Before he even had time to make a move, I closed on him, shield to shield, and grabbing him round the neck – my fingers slipping on his sweat-slick skin – I managed to unbalance him and deal him a couple of thrusts with my sword before we both fell to the deck. I tried to get his sword from him, but it was tied to his wrist. Then he grabbed the edge of my helmet, intending to push my head back so that he could slit my throat, meanwhile uttering the most fearful of screams. Silently I felt behind me, took out my dagger and stuck it in him two or three times, inflicting only minor wounds, which seemed to hurt him nonetheless, because his screams took on another quality. He stopped screaming altogether when a hand pulled back his head and a curved dagger sliced open his throat. I scrambled to my feet, feeling bruised and wiping the blood from my eyes, but before I could thank him the Moor Gurriato was already furiously stabbing another Turk. And so I put away my dagger, picked up my sword and my shield and returned to the fight.

'*Sentabajo, cane!*' yelled the Turks, as they attacked. '*Alautalah! Alautalah!*'

That was when I saw Sergeant Quemado die. In the ebb and flow of combat, I had ended up at his side. He was gathering a group of men to attack the janizaries on the fighting platforms. We leapt onto the galley benches – there was scarcely an oarsman left alive – and fought our way along the corridors, gradually retaking what they had taken from us, until we reached our trinquet mast and the ram of their galley. It was then that Sergeant Quemado, who had been urging on any laggards, was hit by an arrow that pierced his cheeks from side to side. While he struggled to remove it, he was killed stone-dead by a shot from a harquebus. This caused some of our men to hesitate, and we nearly lost what we had gained, but then we raised our faces to heaven – although not to pray exactly – and attacked like wild beasts, determined to avenge Quemado or to die there on the ram of that Turkish galley.

What happened subsequently beggars description, and I will not say here what I did – only God and I know that. Suffice it to say that we regained the prow of the *Mulata*, and that when the battered Turkish galley turned and retreated, not one of the Turks who had boarded our ship went with it.

And so we spent the rest of the day, as stubborn as any Aragonese, withstanding volleys of artillery and repelling successive boarding parties from not just five galleys now, but seven. The three-lanterned flagship and the other Turkish galley had joined the fight in the afternoon, bearing the heads of Brother Fulco Muntaner and his Knights impaled on their yard-arms. And by way of a trophy, for it would bring them little in the way of booty, the Turks were also towing the shattered *Cruz de Rodas*, which was now as flat as a pontoon. It had been no small feat to take it either, for the Knights had fought so ferociously that, as we learned later, not one was taken alive. Luckily for us, neither the Ottoman flagship nor its escort was in any state to fight again that day, merely approaching now and then to relieve the others or to fire on us from a distance. The third Turkish galley, badly damaged in the battle, had sunk without trace.

*

By late that evening, both the Ottomans and we Spaniards were utterly exhausted, but while we were comforted that we had been able to resist so great a number, they were enraged because they had been unable to break our spirit. The sky was still stormy and the sea still the colour of lead, which only accentuated the grim nature of the scene. As the light faded, a slight westerly breeze got up; but being a shoreward wind, it was of no use to us. Not that even a favourable wind would have changed the situation, for our ships were in a terrible state. The rigging was peppered with bullets, the yards had been toppled and the sails reduced to tatters; the *Caridad Negra* had lost its mainmast, which floated beside us along with corpses, ropes, planks and broken oars. The cries of the wounded and the stertorous breathing of the dying rose like a monotonous chorus from the two galleys, which remained tied to each other. The Turks had retreated a little towards land, until they were about a cannon-shot away; there they threw their dead overboard and repaired rigging and other damage, while their captains met in council. We Spaniards could do nothing but lick our wounds and wait.

We were a pathetic sight, lying, along with the galley-slaves, among the broken benches or in the gangway, in the corridors or on the fighting platforms, exhausted, broken or badly wounded. We were smeared with soot from the gunpowder, and our hair, clothes and weapons were caked with blood. To give us some cheer, Captain Urdemalas ordered what little remained of the arrack to be shared out, while to eat – the oven had been destroyed and the cook was dead – there was dried shark's meat, a little oil and some hard-tack. The same was done on the other galley, and men even came and went between the two ships, talking over the events of the day and enquiring about such and such a comrade, mourning those who had died and celebrating the living. This did cheer people a little, and some even began to think that the Turks would go away or that we could repel further attacks – there were sure to be more the following day, if the Turks didn't try to board us during the night. But we had seen that they, too, were in a bad way, and that gave us hope, for in a desperate plight, the doomed man clings to any illusion.

The fact is that our gallant defence had emboldened the most hopeful among us, and some even thought of a funny trick to play on the Turks. Two live chickens were kept in cages in the storeroom; their meat and eggs – although they did not lay much while on board – were used to prepare stews and broths for the sick. The jokers made a raft with a little sail on it, and after tying the two creatures onto it, they took advantage of the gentle breeze to send the creatures off towards the enemy galleys, amid much laughter and shouts of defiance. We all laughed, too, especially when the Turks, although stung by the insult, picked up the birds and took them on board. This raised our spirits, which was something we certainly needed, and some men even began to sing, loud enough that our enemies could hear, the old shanty that the sailors used when they hauled the yard. In the end, the men formed a large chorus of voices, broken but not beaten, as they stood facing the Turks:

Heave ho, the pagans,
Heave ho, the saracens,
Heave ho, Turks and Moors,
They all bow down to Abram's sons.

Soon we were all leaning over the sides, shouting at the top of our voices and telling the dogs to come closer, that we'd be delighted to have a couple more boarding parties to finish off before we went to bed, and that if they weren't man enough to do that, then they should go back to Constantinople to fetch their brothers and their fathers (if they knew them), and their whorish mothers and sisters, on whom, of course, we would bestow some very special treatment. Even the wounded, swathed in bloody bandages, raised themselves up on their elbows and joined us, howling out all the rage and fear we carried within us, and finding comfort in that boasting – so much so that not even Don Agustín Pimentel or the captains made any attempt to stop us. On the contrary, they urged us on and even joined in, aware that, condemned to death as we were, we needed something that would encourage us to put a still higher price on our heads. If the Turks wanted to hang *them* on their yard-arms too, they would first have to come and cut them off.

In a further act of defiance, our commanders ordered the lanterns on the poop rail to be lit, so that the Turks would know where to find us. We reinforced the ropes keeping the two galleys together and let go the anchors – we were in shallow water – so that no unforeseen wind would carry us towards the enemy. The men were also allowed to rest, albeit with their weapons at the ready and taking turns on watch, just in case the enemy should decide to attack in the dark. But the night passed calmly and without wind, the sky clearing slightly to reveal a few stars.

I was relieved from my watch just as I was about to fall asleep through sheer exhaustion. Feeling my way past the men lying on the deck – both galleys were filled with a chorus of moans worthy of a troupe of French beggars – I reached the embrasure where, in a kind of bastion made of torn blankets and remnants of rigging and sailcloth, Captain Alatriste, the Moor Gurriato and Sebastián Copons had taken shelter. The last was snoring loudly, as if he were putting his heart and soul into it. They, like me, had been lucky enough to escape unscathed from that terrible day, apart from the Moor Gurriato, who had suffered a slight scimitar wound to one side, which Captain Alatriste had bathed with wine and then sewn up – an old soldier's skill – with a thick needle and thread, leaving one stitch loose so that any bad humours could drain out.

I lay down without saying a word, too tired even to open my mouth, but I couldn't sleep, my body ached so. That encounter with the hairy Turk and with all the others who came after him had left me stiff in every limb. I was thinking – and I knew I was not the only one – about what the next day would bring. I couldn't imagine myself at the oars of a Turkish galley or in a prison on the shores of the Black Sea, and so, since victory on our part seemed improbable, my future looked set to be distinctly brief. I wondered what my head would look like hung from a yard-arm, and what Angélica de Alquézar would think if, possessed of some mysterious clairvoyant powers, she were to see it. You might imagine that such thoughts would have plunged me into despair, and there was something of that, but the horse does not think the same thoughts as its rider. Viewed from the warmth of a good fire and a well-stocked table, things look very different than when viewed from a trench or from the fragile deck of a galley, where placing life and liberty at risk is one's daily bread. We were certainly desperate, but we were like young bulls bred only to fight, so that lack of hope seemed natural. As Spaniards, our familiarity with death allowed us to stand and wait patiently for it; we had no alternative. Unlike other nations, we judged each other according to how we bore ourselves in the face of danger. That is why our character was such a curious blend of cruelty, honour and reputation. As Jorge Manrique said, centuries of fighting

Islam had made us free men, proud and certain of our rights and privileges.

They're earned by monks and pious nuns
Through prayers and supplications;
By valorous knights through waging wars
'gainst Spain's old enemies – the Moors.

And that is why, accustomed as we were to the vicissitudes of fortune, with Christ's name on our lips and our soul on a knife-edge, we accepted our fate on that sad day – if indeed it was to be our final day – as we had on so many similar days. We did so with the resignation of the peasant watching the hail flatten his crops, of the fisherman finding his nets empty, of the mother certain that her child will be born dead or will be carried off by a fever before it has even left the cradle. Only the pampered and the comfortable and the cowardly, who live with their backs turned to the realities of life, rebel against the inevitable price that sooner or later we all have to pay.

There was the sound of a harquebus shot and we all sat up, uneasy. Even the wounded stopped moaning. Then there was silence, and we relaxed.

'False alarm,' Copons muttered.

'Fate,' said the Moor Gurriato stoically.

I lay down again next to the Captain, with nothing to cover me but my steel breastplate and my tattered doublet. The night dew was already soaking us and the planks we were lying on. I felt cold and moved closer to the Captain in search of warmth. After the rigours of the day, he smelled, as ever, of leather and metal and sweat. I knew he would not mistake my shivering for fear. I sensed that he was awake, although he did not stir for a long time. Then, very carefully, he removed the scrap of torn sail from his own body and placed it over me. I was no longer a child, as I had been in Flanders, and that gesture did not so much warm my body as my heart.

At dawn, we shared more wine and hard-tack, and while we were eating that sparse breakfast, the order came to unchain any of the slaves who were prepared to fight. We looked at each other; we knew we must be in very bad straits if we had to resort to such extremes. Turks, Moors and natives of enemy countries, such as the English and the Dutch, were excluded, but for the others this offered a chance, if they fought well and survived, of having their sentence or part of it redeemed on the recommendation of our General. It was not a bad opportunity for the slaves from Spain and from other Catholic nations, for if they stayed at the oars, they were doomed to go down with the ship if it sank – no one would bother to unchain them in the event of shipwreck – or else remain as slaves, but rowing for the Turks, which they could avoid only if they renounced their religion. (In Spain, a slave baptised a Christian always remained a slave.) Some did choose that route to freedom, especially younger men, for reasons that are easy to understand. This, however, happened less often than you might think, for even among galley-slaves, religion is a serious, deep-rooted matter, and despite the misery of captivity, most Spaniards taken by the Berbers or the Turks remained true to the one faith, so that the words of Cervantes – a captive who never renounced his faith – would not be applied to them:

Perhaps they are simply cruelly bored
By the harshness of a captive's life,
And so, in the jaws of that bitter vice,

they embrace Mohammed's faith as lord:
A way that's easy, a way that's broad.

And so it was that we unshackled as many Spanish, Italian and Portuguese slaves as offered their services, and they were duly issued with spears and half-pikes. The two galleys, which had lost a third of their soldiers and sailors, thus found themselves with sixty or seventy new recruits who were determined to die fighting rather than be drowned or cut to pieces in the fury of battle. Among them was a rower at the stern called Joaquín Ronquillo, a gipsy and jewel of Malaga's ruffianry, as well as an acquaintance of ours; he was a very dangerous man and much feared on board, so much so that for some time we had kept our savings under his bench, where they were safer than in the house of a Genoese banker.

This Ronquillo fellow – shaven head, black doublet edged in red, a treacherous gleam in his eye – joined our group, bringing with him a small band of like-minded men, who looked about as honest as he did. Shortly afterwards, we were given orders by Ensign Labajos, who appointed Captain Alatriste as our commander – he and Labajos were the only officers of any rank left among the soldiers on the *Mulata* – to form a fighting squad to provide reinforcements wherever the Turks proved most of a threat, especially the area around the skiff and the ladders on either side of the stern, which would give the enemy access to the corridors leading to the fighting platforms. We were all urged to defend the galley plank by plank; Father Nistal blessed us again from the deck of the *Caridad Negra*; and we and Machín de Gorostiola's Basques – to whom we were still bound for good or ill – wished each other luck.

Just as we took up our positions, with the sun barely risen in a clear sky over the dead-calm sea, the seven Turkish galleys, with shouts and the noise of cymbals, flutes and trumpets, began to row towards us.

Ensign Labajos had died in the midst of the battle, overwhelmed by Turks, as he repelled yet another boarding party at the stern of the *Mulata*; Captain Urdemalas had also been wounded. Diego Alatriste was leaning against the awning supports, washing blood from his face and hands with sea water, which made the scratches and surface wounds sting. His whole body hurt. He was watching the men throw overboard any dead bodies that cluttered the deck, which was a chaos of broken planks and shattered rigging. The fighting had lasted four hours, and by the time the Turks had withdrawn to recover and to disentangle and replace the broken oars on their galleys, both masts on the *Mulata* had been brought down, the yards and torn sails lying either in the water or on top of the *Caridad Negra*, whose trinquet mast had been lost and its mainmast cut in two. Both galleys were still tied together and afloat, although the losses on both ships had been appalling. On the *Mulata* the galleymaster and his assistant were dead, and the German gunner had been killed when a cannon he was firing exploded, killing him and his helpers. As for Captain Urdemalas, Alatriste had just left him, or what remained of him, lying face down on the floor of his cabin at the stern, where the barber and the pilot were using their fingers to scoop out gobbets of blood from the huge gash – from kidney to kidney – inflicted by a Turkish scimitar.

'You're in command,' Urdemalas had managed to say between groans, cursing the man who had wounded him.

In command. There was a grim irony to those words, thought Alatriste as he surveyed the bloody, splintered mess that had once been the *Mulata*. All the storage compartments, including the one set aside for gunpowder, were full of wounded men, body piled on body, begging for a sip of water or something to cover their wounds. But neither water nor bandages were to be had. Above, in what had been the rowing chamber, and which was now a confusion of blood and debris, lay galley-slaves alive and dead, the survivors moaning amid what remained of their benches and the shattered fragments of mast, rigging and oars. And in the corridors and on the fighting platforms, beneath a searing sun that made the steel of breastplates and weapons burn, the remaining soldiers, sailors and freed slaves were tending their wounds or those of their comrades, handing round whetstones to repair the battered blades of swords and knives, and gathering together what they could find of gunpowder and bullets for the few muskets and harquebuses that still worked.

To drive all of this from his head for a few moments, Alatriste sat down with his back against the side of the ship, unfastened his buff coat and, with a mechanical gesture, took out his copy of Don Francisco de Quevedo's book, *Dreams*. He used to leaf through it in quiet moments, but now, however hard he tried, he couldn't read a single line; the words danced in front of his eyes, his ears still ringing with the recent sounds of battle.

'You've been called to a meeting on the flagship, sir.'

Alatriste looked at the young page delivering the order, not understanding at first. Then, reluctantly, he put the book back in his pocket and slowly got to his feet. He walked down the starboard corridor and, putting one leg over the side and then the other, he grabbed hold of a loose rope to swing himself across to the *Caridad Negra*. As he did so, he glanced over at the Ottoman galleys. They had retreated the same distance as on the previous night, while they prepared for their next assault. One of the vessels, badly damaged during the last attack, was sitting dangerously low in the water, almost sinking, and there was a lot of coming and going on deck. The flagship with the three lanterns had lost its trinquet mast. The Turks were also paying a high price.

The situation on board the *Caridad Negra* was not much better than on the *Mulata*. The galley-slaves had suffered terrible losses, and Captain Machín de Gorostiola's Basques, their eyes vacant and their faces black with gunpowder, were taking advantage of the breathing-space to rest and recover as best they could. No one broke the grim silence or looked up as Alatriste walked past on his way to the General's cabin, the floor of which was covered with trampled pieces of paper and dirty clothes.

Standing round a table, with a pitcher of wine that was being passed from man to man, were Don Agustín Pimentel, with a wound to his head and his arm in a sling; Captain Machín de Gorostiola; the *Caridad Negra*'s galleymaster, and a corporal named Zenarruzabeitia. The pilot Gorgos and Father Francisco Nistal had both died during the last assault. Gorgos had been slit open and the chaplain had been felled by a musket shot as he was walking up and down the gangway, oblivious to everything, brandishing crucifix and sword and promising eternal glory for all – a glory he would now be enjoying himself.

'How's Captain Urdemalas?' Pimentel asked.

Alatriste shrugged. He was no surgeon, but the fact that he was there alone made it clear that no one of higher rank on board the *Mulata* was still standing.

'The General thinks we should surrender,' Machín de Gorostiola said bluntly. Many thought he adopted this manner deliberately, to be like his men, who adored him.

Alatriste looked at Gorostiola rather than at Don Agustín Pimentel. He was a short man with a black beard, very white skin, a large nose, bushy eyebrows that met in the middle, and the rough hands of a soldier. He was a sturdy Basque, a peasant with little education but a great deal of courage; the very opposite of the elegant General who, pale from loss of blood, grew still paler when he heard the Basque's words.

'It's not that simple,' he protested.

This time, Alatriste did turn to look at the General. He suddenly felt tired, very tired.

'Simple or not,' said Gorostiola in a neutral tone, 'after the way we've fought, would it be honourable now to strike the flag?'

'Honourable ...' repeated Alatriste.

'Or whatever word you want to choose.'

'In the eyes of the Turks.'

'Yes.'

Alatriste shrugged. It wasn't his business to gauge whether or not it would be honourable to surrender after the sacrifice of so many lives. Gorostiola was observing him with great interest. They had never been friends, but they knew and respected one another. Then Alatriste looked at the galley-master and at the corporal. Their faces were set hard; in fact, they looked somewhat embarrassed.

'Are your men on the *Mulata* going to surrender?' Gorostiola asked, handing him the pitcher of wine.

Alatriste drank – he had the devil of a thirst on him – then wiped his moustache with his hand.

'I imagine they would agree to anything, whether it be surrendering or fighting on. They're beyond reason now.'

'They've already done more than could be expected of them,' said Pimentel.

Alatriste put the pitcher on the table and looked hard at the General. He had never seen the man from such close quarters. He reminded Alatriste slightly of the Count of

Guadalmedina, the same style: the fine figure beneath the splendid Milan steel breastplate, the trim moustache and goatee beard, the white hands, the gold chain around the neck, the sword with a ruby in the hilt. The General came from the same aristocratic caste, although this highly inelegant situation had tempered his arrogance – it's always best to talk to noblemen, Alatriste thought, when they've just been punched in the face. Nevertheless, the General retained his noble appearance, despite his pallor, the bandages, and the blood staining his clothes. Yes, he definitely reminded him of Guadalmedina, except that Álvaro de la Marca would never have considered surrendering to the Turks. Then again, the General had held up fairly well, far better than would many others of his class and character. But courage can be dented too, Alatriste knew this from experience, especially in a man who has been wounded and who bears a heavy burden of responsibility. The Captain decided that he was in no position to judge someone who had been fighting for two days, sword in hand, alongside everyone else. Every man has his limits.

'I see you have a book with you.'

Alatriste patted the book distractedly, then took it out of his pocket and handed it to the General, who leafed through its pages with curiosity.

'Hmm, Quevedo,' said the General, returning it to him. 'What's the point of a book like that on a galley?'

'It makes days like this seem slightly more bearable.'

He put the book back in his pocket. Gorostiola and the others were staring at him in bewilderment. They could understand having some kind of religious book, but not a book like that, although needless to say, none of them had even heard of Quevedo.

The General picked up the pitcher again and said, 'I'm sure I could obtain satisfactory conditions.'

Alatriste and Gorostiola exchanged glances. There was neither surprise nor scorn in those glances, only the weary impartiality of two veterans. Everyone knew what conditions the General was referring to: a reasonable ransom for himself, who would be well treated in Constantinople until the money arrived from Spain, and a ransom perhaps for another officer. The others, the soldiers and sailors, would remain on the galleys and in captivity for the rest of their lives, while Pimentel would return to Naples or to Madrid, where he would be admired by the ladies and congratulated by the gentlemen as he recounted the details of his Homeric battle. It would have made more sense, Alatriste thought, to have surrendered before the slaughter began. The dead would still be alive, and the maimed and wounded would not be piled up on the galleys, howling in agony.

Machín de Gorostiola interrupted his thoughts.

'We need to know your opinion, Señor Alatriste, as the only officer left on the *Mulata*.'

'I'm not an officer.'

'You're all we have, so let's not split hairs.'

Alatriste looked at the trampled papers and clothes beneath his tattered, blood-stained espadrilles. Having an opinion was one thing; being asked to give it another.

'My opinion . . .' he murmured.

He had known what his opinion was the moment he walked into the cabin and saw those faces. Everyone, apart from the General, knew as well.

'No,' he said.

'I beg your pardon?' said Pimentel.

Alatriste wasn't looking at him, but at Machín de Gorostiola. This wasn't a matter for the likes of Pimentel, it was a matter for soldiers.

'I said that the men on the *Mulata* do not agree to surrender.'

There was a long silence, during which the only sound came from behind the bulkhead, the moans of the wounded lying in the hold.

'Surely you need to ask them,' said Pimentel at last.

Alatriste shook his head. His cold eyes fixed on the General.

'You have just done so, Your Excellency.'

A faint smile flickered cross Gorostiola's bearded face, while the General grimaced, clearly displeased.

'What does that mean?' he asked curtly.

Alatriste continued to hold his gaze. 'The past few days were for killing; perhaps today is the day to die.'

Out of the corner of his eye, he saw that the galleymaster and the corporal were nodding approvingly. Machín de Gorostiola had turned to Pimentel. He seemed pleased, as if a heavy weight had been removed from his shoulders.

'As you can see, Your Excellency, we are all in agreement. We're Basques, devil take it.'

Pimentel raised the pitcher of wine with his good hand, but when it reached his lips, it trembled slightly. Finally, half-angry and half-resigned, he placed the pitcher on the table with a sour look on his face. No General, however respected at Court, could surrender without the agreement of his officers. That could cost you your reputation or, sometimes, your head.

'Half of our men are dead,' he said.

'Fine,' replied Alatriste, 'let's avenge them with the other half.'

The attack that afternoon was by far the fiercest. One of the Turkish galleys had sunk, but the other six came rowing towards us against the westerly breeze, their flagship first, intending to board us all at once. That would mean six or seven hundred men – more than a third of them janizaries – against just over one hundred Spaniards, those of us who could still fight. Battering us with their artillery as they approached, they ploughed straight into both galleys, crushing our already broken oars as they did so and trying to hole the sides with their rams, hoping to sink us if they could. We were able to repel some boarders with our swords and muskets, but other galleys attached themselves to us with grappling-irons. And such was the impetus of their attack that, whereas on the *Caridad Negra*, the Basques were so mixed up with the Turks that it was impossible to fire a musket with any certainty that you would hit one and not the other, on the *Mulata*, they managed to seize the port-side fighting platform and the trinquet mast and got as far as the mainmast and the skiff, taking over half the ship.

Somehow, though, we held firm and fought back, largely because of a piece of good luck. Leading the Turks on this attack was a janizary of massive build, a man who shouted and yelled and dealt fierce two-handed blows with his scimitar. We found out later that he was a famous captain, Uluch Cimarra by name, and highly esteemed by the Great Turk. Now it happened that, just as this mighty beast reached the skiff from which our men were retreating, he met the group of freed galley-slaves led by the gipsy Ronquillo, armed with spears, half-pikes, scimitars and swords taken from the dead. They fell on the giant janizary with such ferocity that Ronquillo managed to stick a spear through the giant's eye with his first blow. The janizary let out a howl, pressed his hands to his face and dropped to the deck, whereupon the other men, producing from somewhere or other yellow-handled slaughterer's knives, finished him off in a trice, like dogs to a boar. Astonished to see their paladin slain in this fashion, the Turks stopped in their tracks.

They were still standing there, hesitating, when Captain Alatriste decided to take advantage of the situation by rounding up all the men who were there, some twenty of us. We rushed forward, certain in the knowledge that we had either to fight hard or be killed. And since killing or dying were all one to us, we charged shoulder to shoulder, Captain Alatriste, Sebastián Copons, the Moor Gurriato and I, along with Ronquillo and his gang, as well as others who joined forces with us. And since there is nothing more consoling in a disaster than the sight of a group behaving in a disciplined manner, standing firm and attacking, all the other men who had become scattered or were fighting alone attached themselves to us as well, like men rushing to fall in with the last infantry squad on the parade ground. And so, growing in numbers as we went, we advanced down the galley, the Turks stopped killing, and even turned tail and ran, trampling on the galley-slaves lying between the shattered benches. Finally we reached the ram of the Turkish galley, still laying about the enemy with our swords and knives.

When many of them dived into the water, some of us ventured onto the galley itself, and you can imagine the brio with which our handful of men boarded the ship, shouting 'Spain and Santiago!' – all except me; I was shouting 'Angélica! Angélica!' Seeing us there, black with gunpowder and red with blood, as fierce and pitiless as Satan himself, the Turks started hurling themselves into the sea in even greater numbers or running to the captain's cabin at the stern to take refuge there. Thus we seized their trinquet mast with no effort at all and could have seized the mainmast, too, if we had dared.

Captain Alatriste had stayed behind on the *Mulata*, urging

people to attack the other ships surrounding us, but I, hothead that I was, boarded the Turkish vessel along with the boldest of our men. However, as I was fighting a group of Turks, one of them, dealing me a swingeing two-handed blow, broke the blade of my sword. With what remained of my blade I attacked the man nearest to me and wounded him badly in the neck. Another man struck me with his scimitar – fortunately with the flat of the sword – but he could not strike a second time because the Moor Gurriato sliced open his head with an axe. Another man, lying on the deck, tried to grab my legs. I fell on top of him and he stabbed at me with a dagger and would have killed me if he could. Three times he raised his arm and three times his strength failed him, so when I started knifing him in the face with my broken sword, he finally let go and leapt over the side into the sea.

It was quite some prize, a whole galley to ourselves, but more men are killed by over-confidence than by adversity, and so, dragging two of our wounded with us, we beat a cautious retreat, while the Turks in the cabin pelted us with arrows and musket-fire. Then, seeing the quantities of gunpowder and lit match-cords available at our end of the ship, someone had the idea of setting fire to it – which was imprudent to say the least, given that their ship was attached to ours and this action could have brought disaster on us all.

The Christian galley-slaves, many of them Spaniards, were still chained to the benches and they cried and pleaded with us, for with our arrival they had thought their freedom was assured. Now, though, seeing us about to set fire to the ship, they begged us desperately not to leave them there, but to unchain them, otherwise they would be burned alive. But we could not delay or do anything for those poor unfortunates and so, with heavy hearts, we ignored their pleas. As the flames grew, we returned to the *Mulata*, cut the boarding ropes that bound us to the Turkish galley and pushed it away as best we could with pikes and bits of broken oar, taking advantage of the favourable breeze. It moved off gradually, shrouded in black smoke and with flames devouring the trinquet mast. The screams of the galley-slaves as they were roasted alive were terrible to hear.

Halfway through the afternoon, the *Caridad Negra*, holed in one side and slowly sinking, suffered such a fierce attack from the Turks that the survivors, with the prow in Turkish control, along with most of the rowing chamber, had to seek refuge in the captain's cabin, even though we were helping them from our side. General Pimentel had been wounded again, this time by arrows, and he was carried – like a St Sebastian – onto the *Mulata* where he would be safer. Then it was the turn of Captain Machín de Gorostiola to be laid low by musket-fire, which blew off one hand, leaving only a limp remnant hanging from his wrist. He wanted to cut it off completely so that he could continue fighting, but his strength failed him and his knees buckled. He fell to the floor where he was finished off by the Turks before his soldiers could save him. This might have discouraged other men, but it had the opposite effect on the Basques, who, beside themselves with rage, bawled out their desire for revenge. Urging each other on in Basque and cursing in Castilian, they fought with unimaginable fury. Not only did they clear their decks of Turks, they boarded the enemy ship as well, and whether the galley had been so badly damaged or had been holed by cannon shot below the water, it began to list, still attached by grappling hooks to the *Caridad Negra*, which also continued to sink.

The Basques returned to their own ship, and seeing that it was about to go under and that nothing could be done, they started climbing onto the *Mulata*, bringing with them as many of their wounded as they could and, of course, their flag. Shortly afterwards, we had to cut the ropes and hawsers and leave the vessel to sink, which it did, along with the Turkish galley, which turned up its keel before going down. It was a terrible sight: the sea full of debris and struggling Turks, the galley-slaves screaming as they struggled in vain to remove their chains before they drowned. In the face of such a tragic scene, we stopped fighting, while the Turks went about rescuing their men from the water.

In the end, the five surviving Turkish galleys retreated to their usual distance; every one of them was badly damaged, with blood running into the scuppers and between the oars, many of which were broken or not moving at all because the oarsmen had died.

There were no more attacks that day. As the sun set, the *Mulata* lay motionless on the sea, surrounded by enemy galleys and corpses floating in the still water, with one hundred and thirty wounded men crammed together below decks and sixty-two uninjured men scanning the darkness. As a defiant act, the *Mulata* again lit her lantern. But there was no singing that night.

EPILOGUE

The following morning, at sunrise, the Turks were not there. The men on watch woke us at first light, pointing to the empty sea: all that remained was the debris of combat. The enemy galleys had slipped away in the dark, having decided that it wasn't worth capturing a miserable, ruined galley at such a high cost. Still incredulous, looking in all directions and seeing not a trace of the Ottomans, we embraced each other, weeping with happiness and giving thanks to heaven for such grace. We would have called it a miracle but for the suffering and blood it had taken to preserve life and liberty.

More than two hundred and fifty comrades, including the Knights of Malta, had lost their lives in combat, and of the four hundred galley-slaves of all races and religions who had made up the crews of the *Caridad Negra* and the *Mulata*, only about fifty remained. Of the captains and officers, the only survivors were Don Agustín Pimentel and Captain Urdemalas, who somehow managed to recover from his wound. Among the soldiers and sailors, the only subaltern officers who survived were Captain Alatriste, the pilot Braco and Corporal Zenarruzabeitia, who had taken refuge on our galley along with General Pimentel and twenty or so Basques. Another survivor was the galley-slave Joaquín Ronquillo, who, on the recommendation of our General — once informed of his action against the janizary — had his six remaining years at the oars reduced to one. As for me, I emerged in reasonably good health, apart from a wound inflicted in the latter stages of the battle by an arrow from a Turkish crossbow, which pierced my right thigh; it didn't do too much damage, but left me with a limp for two months.

The *Mulata* remained afloat, although in need of innumerable repairs. We spliced together bits of rope to make cables, and while some men worked at bailing out, we patched up the broken deck, and after improvising a mast and sail from what remnants we could find and recovering several oars, we managed to make it to dry land, partly under sail power and partly under oars. Then we set up a watchtower in case of any surprise attacks, but, fortunately, the place proved to be rocky and uninhabited, and in only two days we had made the galley seaworthy again. During that time, many of our wounded died. We put them with the other Spaniards who had died on board and those whose bodies we had rescued from the sea and from the beaches. And before weighing anchor again, we buried them all at Cap Nero – a melancholy business. Since we had no chaplain to provide a funeral service, and since both General Pimentel and Captain Urdemalas were incapacitated, it fell to Captain Alatriste to provide a graveside prayer. We gathered around, bare heads bowed, and said a paternoster together. Then the Captain, for lack of anything more appropriate to say, and after swallowing hard and scratching his head, recited a few short lines which, despite coming from a soldierly comedy or some such thing, struck everyone as perfectly suited to the occasion:

Free they are of all their guilt,
To eternal glory they have risen,
There to taste far greater joys
Than exist in this our earthly prison.

All these events happened in the month of September 1627, at Cap Nero, which is on the coast of Anatolia, facing onto the Escanderlu channel. And while Captain Alatriste pronounced that unusual prayer for the dead, the setting sun lit up our motionless figures as we stood around the graves of all those good comrades, each one with its own cross made of Turkish wood – a last defiant act in their memory. There they stayed, accompanied by the murmur of the waves and the cries of the seabirds, waiting for the resurrection of the flesh, when they will perhaps rise up from the earth fully armed, with the pride and glory that befits all faithful soldiers. And until that distant day, they will stay where they are, sleeping the long, honourable sleep enjoyed by all valiant men, next to the sea on which they sold their lives at such a high price, fighting for gold and booty, but fighting, too, for those things that are far from trifling – country, God and King.

EXTRACTS FROM A
FLORILEGIUM OF POEMS
BY VARIOUS SPANISH WITS

Printed in the seventeenth century with no place of pub-
lication or date and preserved in the 'Count of Guadalmedina'
section of the Archive and Library of the Dukes of Nuevo
Extremo in Seville.

BY DON MIGUEL
DE CERVANTES SAAVEDRA

TO THE MEMORY OF THE SPANISH
SOLDIERS WHO PERISHED WHEN
LA GOLETA WAS LOST

From this battered, sterile land,
From these clods of earth brought low
Three thousand soldiers' holy souls
Rose, still living, to a better home,
Having, first, expended all
The strength and effort of their arms,
Until, at last, so few, so weary,
T' the enemy's blade they gave their life.
This land has been eternally,
Down the centuries, till now,
Full of doleful memories.
Yet no better souls from that hard breast
Will ever rise to heaven's light,
Nor heaven receive such valiant hearts.

BY LICENCIATE
DON MIGUEL SERRANO

FROM SANTA FE DE BOGOTÁ, TO THE
YOUNG SOLDIER ÍÑIGO BALBOA

By destiny, a son of Flanders field,
And now the faithful shadow of your leader.
You're young – apprentice still – and keenest reader
Of the Don and Lope – no men to yield!

You're faithful, loyal and marked out by fate,
To suffer at the hands of treach'rous love
Put in your path by destiny above —
Revenge for that and Alquézar must wait.

A good companion in the darkest night,
With dagger drawn, you were the bravest soul
– I speak unvarnished truth, entire and whole.

And that is why my words ring true and right,
That though you were a boy, a love-sick foal,
Nor you nor Alatriste lost a fight.

BY THE SAME

TO CAPTAIN DON DIEGO ALATRISTE Y TENORIO, VETERAN OF FLANDERS, ITALY, BARBARY AND THE LEVANT

Through old Madrid, where once he used to live,
Wanders a ghost, the erstwhile valiant Captain.
Be careful what you call him – he'll not forgive;
Wound him, and the price could be your skin.

As vassal to his king, he used his sword
To save a sovereign and a favourite.
His footsteps pace the spot where once his lord
Ignored him quite and never gave him credit.

He finds no rest, when easeful rest is sought;
His sword is up for hire, but not his honour,
For, shorn of honour, life for man is naught.

He came from glory, to glory goes, ready
To face dread destiny – his bella donna —
And though his heart may tremble, sword stays steady.

BY DON FRANCISCO DE QUEVEDO

TO THE MEMORY OF THE DUKE OF OSUNA, VICEROY OF NAPLES, WHO DIED IN PRISON

Although his country has denied him praise,
His deeds will always be his best defence;
Imprison'd by Spain, he died — poor recompense
For one who conquer'd Fortune all his days.

They wept in envious mourning, one by one,
Those other grateful nations not his own,
His fitting epitaph, the blood-red moon,
His tomb, the Flanders battles that were won.

Vesuvius, at his funeral, made roar,
And Naples, Sicily and Etna shook;
His soldiers' flood of tears grew more and more.

I' the heaven of Mars, a favour'd place he took;
The Danube, Tagus, Meuse and Rhine forsook
Their calm, and moaned and murmured, weeping sore.

BY SISTER AMAYA ELEZCANO, ABBESS OF THE CONVENT OF THE BLESSED ADORATRICES

TO THE PERSON OF CAPTAIN DON DIEGO ALATRISTE

O my gallant and venturesome captain,
My gentleman, faithful and true,
You reap, with the blade of your sword,
Still more laurels to add to your fame,
Yet, woe to the man who finds fault
With the cut and the dash of your life,
For the man who knows how best to keep quiet
Is the same man who knows how to fight.

TRANSLATOR'S ACKNOWLEDGEMENTS

I would like to thank Arturo Pérez-Reverte, Annella Mc-Dermott and Palmira Sullivan for all their help and advice, and give a special thank you to my husband Ben Sherriff for his ever-willing assistance in translating the poetry.